HRAC

MAR 1 1 2021

NIGHTHAWK'S WING

Books by Charles Fergus

Fiction:

A Stranger Here Below: A Gideon Stoltz Mystery

Shadow Catcher

Nature and Nonfiction:

Swamp Screamer

Summer at Little Lava

The Wingless Crow (nature essays)

Thornapples (nature essays)

Trees of New England

Trees of Pennsylvania

Wildlife of Pennsylvania

Natural Pennsylvania

Bears Wild Guide

Turtles Wild Guide

Common Edible and Poisonous Mushrooms

Make a Home for Wildlife

Hunting:

A Rough-Shooting Dog

A Hunter's Book of Days

Gun Dog Breeds

The Upland Equation

NIGHTHAWK'S WING

A Gideon Stoltz Mystery

Charles Fergus

ARCADE
CrimeWise

First Arcade CrimeWise Edition

This is a work of fiction. Names, places, characters, and incidents are either the products of the author's imagination or are used fictitiously.

Arcade Publishing books may be purchased in bulk at special discounts for sales promotion, corporate gifts, fund-raising, or educational purposes. Special editions can also be created to specifications. For details, contact the Special Sales Department, Arcade Publishing, 307 West 36th Street, 11th Floor, New York, NY 10018 or arcade@skyhorsepublishing.com.

Arcade Publishing® and CrimeWise® are registered trademarks of Skyhorse Publishing, Inc.®, a Delaware corporation.

Visit our website at www.arcadepub.com.

10 9 8 7 6 5 4 3 2 1

Library of Congress Cataloging-in-Publication Data is available on file.

Cover design by Erin Seaward-Hiatt

Cover artwork: Night Hawk, from John James Audubon's *Birds of America*, 1827–1838. Image courtesy of John James Audubon Center at Mill Grove, Audubon, Pennsylvania, and the Montgomery County Audubon Collection. See https://www.audubon.org/birds-of-america.

ISBN: 978-1-951627-46-1

Ebook ISBN: 978-1-951627-50-8

Printed in the United States of America

To NMB

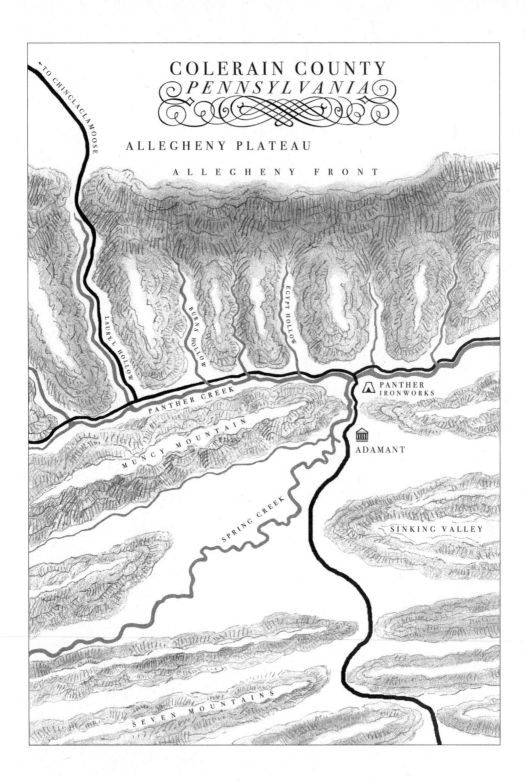

Cover my defenseless head
With the shadow of Thy wing

From the shape-note hymn "Martyn," 1834

Ich verbiete dir mein Haus und mein Hof, ich verbiete dir meine Pferde und Kühstall, ich verbiete dir meine Bettstatt, dass du nicht über mich tröste.

I forbid thee my house and premises, I forbid thee my horse and cow stable, I forbid thee my bedstead, that thou mayest not breathe upon me.

Incantation against witches from *Der Lang Verbogene Freund* (*The Long Lost Friend*), published in Reading, Pennsylvania, 1820

God of my life look gently down,
Behold the pains I feel

Chapter 1

———⟨∞⟩———

H E FLINCHED AND SHOT A GLANCE OVER HIS SHOULDER.
Nothing there but the empty street, hot and dusty and flooded with light.

Gideon Stoltz faced forward again. He was a tall, broad-shouldered man who normally stood up straight, but now his head hung and his shoulders slumped.

He squinted at the sky.

There it was again—the thing that had *shpooked* him. The strange blurry object hung in the upper right corner of his vision. Like an errant cloud, or a dirty cobweb. It had been there, he reckoned, since he had fallen off Maude and hurt his head.

He didn't remember falling off his mare. He didn't—couldn't—remember much of anything from that time.

He wiped the sweat from his face with his shirt sleeve. His head *schmatzed* him something fierce, and pain also throbbed in his neck.

He checked and made sure no one had been watching when he startled and looked behind himself. He didn't want to appear daft, or scared of his own shadow. He was the sheriff of Colerain County. A sheriff was supposed to be sensible. Brave.

The Dutch Sheriff, they called him. Said he was too young.

Well, he was undeniably *Pennsylfawnisch Deitsch*, Pennsylvania Dutch, unlike most of the other folk hereabouts. Maybe he *was* too young to have the responsibilities of a sheriff—although for the life of him he couldn't recall exactly what those responsibilities might be. Anyway, he wasn't *that* young. He was . . .

He frowned. Why couldn't he remember how old he was? It was

now 1836; August of 1836. He had been born on April 1, 1813. He tried to subtract: thirty-six take away thirteen. He let out an impatient huff of breath. Finally it came to him.

He was twenty-three years old.

Twenty-three and addlepated from a fall off his horse.

Was he daft? Maybe only a *verrickt* man would go out in the sun on a blistering day like this. But he needed to walk around town. Sheriff Payton, his predecessor, had said it was part of the job: to patrol the town and county, to travel about and be seen, keep an eye peeled for strangers and potential lawbreakers, nip any trouble in the bud.

The sun stood high in the sky. He blinked against its glare. He tried to get a look at the gray cobwebby thing, but it leaped sideways, his eyes chasing after it until the object darted off his field of view.

He looked forward again, and there it was, hovering on the upper right edge of his vision. Like it was watching him. Judging him.

He set off down the street, his boots sinking in the dust.

He passed brick and stone and log and wood-sided buildings, stores and shops and dwellings on both sides of the street, some of them separated by empty lots grown up with pokeweed and briars.

Clanging from a smithy beat against his ears, followed by the screech of red-hot iron quenched in a slack tub.

He smelled rotting garbage and cooking meat and wood smoke and burning charcoal.

He trudged three more blocks until a dizzy spell hit him. He found a patch of shade cast by a small barn and steadied himself with a hand pressed against its wall. His stomach felt queasy. Pain rippled through his shoulders, his neck, his head.

After his fall, True said he should go see the doctor. He had nixed that idea right away. Doc Beecham would bleed him or burn him or dose him with some vile potion that would make him gag and puke. No, he wanted True to nurse him. She was his wife; she ought to take care of him. Which she'd done—half-heartedly, it seemed, maybe even grudgingly. He set his jaw. He didn't like this unease that lay between them. He wished she would get over her grief and return to being a real wife to him. He needed her. Needed them to be together again.

He pushed off from the barn. The heat rose up around him. He went through an alley, intending to head back to the jail. Rounding the next corner, he ran into a wall of stench.

In the street lay a dead horse. Nearby a wagon listed to one side, its tongue in the dust.

He pinched his nose shut. What the devil happened here? Then he remembered. Yesterday, Old Man Greevey's horse bolted and crashed his wagon into the watering trough. The horse broke a leg. Greevey pitched into the street, breaking his own leg. Gideon's deputy, Alonzo Bell, shot the horse. They carried Greevey to the doctor, the old man moaning that they might as well shoot him, too.

Greevey's son said he'd get rid of the horse. Clearly he hadn't done it yet.

Gideon asked himself why he hadn't remembered the horse as soon as he smelled the stench. Or before he went out for his walk. Or maybe he *had* remembered it and had gone out from the jail to check on whether the horse had been removed, and then forgotten why he'd ventured out in the first place.

Why couldn't he remember such things?

Why couldn't he write a clear sentence, or sign his name with facility, or add up a column of numbers?

Why couldn't he remember anything about his own accident, getting thrown off Maude or otherwise falling off her, striking his head on the ground, and (so he'd been told) lying insensible on the road?

He worried about the gap in his memory. He didn't know how far back it went.

He edged around the dead horse until he was upwind of it. The horse lay on its side, belly bloated, legs jutting out save for the left front, whose hoof and part of the cannon bone hung down below the knee, the bone's jagged end sticking out through the hide. Flies swarmed over the carcass. Greenish fluid leaked from the horse's anus. A Christ-awful stench. Soon they'd be bombarded with complaints to get the thing off the street before contagion spread.

Greevey's son said he'd get rid of the horse. Clearly he hadn't done it yet.

Gideon realized it was the second time in less than a minute that his mind had registered the exact same thought.

He skirted the broken wheel with its splintered spokes and shattered felloes and twisted iron rim. He stopped at the stone watering trough. Water trickled into the trough through wooden pipes from a spring in one of the brushy hills that hemmed in Adamant. In the past, those hills had been forested; now they were studded with stumps, here and there a single tree standing like a confused and bereft survivor of what had once been a great tribe.

He took off his hat and set it on the wagon's seat. He bent over the trough, cupped water in his hands, and splashed it into his face. He ran his hands through his short sandy hair and wiped the back of his neck. He picked up his hat and put it back on his head.

Setting off down the street, he stared at round marks in the dust made by horses' hooves, straight lines unspooled by wagon wheels, irregular scuffings of human and animal feet.

He passed two hogs lying in the patchy shade of a box elder, their sides slowly rising and falling. He stopped for a cart piled with hay, pulled along by a swaybacked horse, the driver standing in the bed holding the reins in one hand and a sun-shielding umbrella in the other hand.

After the cart he found himself confronted by a dozen gray geese. They waddled along, panting, driven by a hatchet-faced woman carrying a stick. The geese seemed to have angry expressions on their faces, but then all geese looked that way. Beneath her sweat-stained bonnet the woman looked angry, too.

The geese gave Gideon a wide berth. He figured they were butcher-bound.

He passed the courthouse, three stories tall and easily the most elegant structure in Adamant. A portico held up by white columns shaded the courthouse's polished walnut doors. Twelve-over-twelve windows interrupted the gray limestone walls. Dazzle from the building's copper roof struck his face like a slap.

Climbing the hill to the jail, he felt sweat running down his sides beneath his shirt. He took his time ascending.

Inside, the jail was cool and dim. Alonzo sat behind the desk. He looked up from the newspaper lying open on the desktop.

"What are you reading?" Gideon asked his deputy.

"An account of the massacre at the Alamo."

Gideon drew a blank.

"The Alamo," Alonzo repeated. "In the Republic of Texas." He returned his attention to the paper.

"The battle happened back in March," he said. "Don't know why it took our so-called *new*spaper five whole months to print a story about it. Listen to this: 'The event, so lamentable, and yet so glorious to Texas, is of such deep interest and excites so much our feelings that we shall never cease to celebrate it.' Wait, it gets better. 'Who would not rather be one of the Alamo heroes, than the living merciless victors?' Well, that's up for debate, since all of them heroes got bayoneted or shot." Alonzo stuck his face closer to the paper. "'The Mexican force being six thousand strong, having bombarded the Alamo for two days without doing any execution, a tremendous effort was made to take it by force, which they succeeded in doing after a most sang . . . sang . . . *sangui-nary* engagement lasting nearly an hour.'" Alonzo looked up again and folded the paper shut. "Them Texians got wiped out. The Mexicans heaped their corpses in a pile and burned 'em."

Gideon vaguely recognized the words "Texians" and "Mexicans," but little else of what his deputy had read made any sense. "Corpses," however, jogged his memory.

He sat down on the couch. There was something he needed to tell Alonzo. Something about a corpse. Or was it a carcass? He gazed at his deputy, trying to recall. Alonzo was twenty years Gideon's senior. A bachelor, he lived in a boardinghouse but slept at the jail when they had a prisoner. Right now Gideon couldn't remember whether any prisoners were housed in the cells or not.

What was it that he needed to tell Alonzo? Gideon stared. Coarse black hairs bristled from his deputy's nostrils. Alonzo was bald as an egg, built dumpy, competent at most every task. Like cleaning a firearm, or tracking down someone to give them a summons, or putting a broken-legged horse out of its misery.

"There is a dead horse on . . ." Gideon paused.

"On Decatur," Alonzo said. "Bill Greevey said he'd borrow a team and drag it off. That horse still there?"

Gideon nodded.

"I'll get after him," Alonzo said.

Gideon blinked. "Can you tell me about my accident?"

"Again?" Alonzo scratched his pate, causing small flakes of dried skin to drift down onto the desk. "All right. 'Proximately 'bout two weeks ago a peddler found you laying in the middle of the road to Sinking Valley. Just before dawn. Said he didn't notice you till his horse stopped short of stepping on you. A Jew man, he was; must've been a Good Samaritan, because he got you up on his cart, which it weren't much more than a yellow-painted cupboard on wheels, tied your horse in back, and brought you here." Alonzo jutted his chin toward Gideon. "The Israelite even fetched your hat."

Gideon reached up and touched his hat's brim. He took his hat off and set it on the couch.

"We laid you down right where you're at. You had a big knot on your head and blood all over your face." Alonzo's bushy eyebrows bobbed. "You don't remember that?"

Gideon shook his head. No memory of a peddler or a cart, yellow or any other color. However, he did seem to recall lying on the couch. Aching all over, pain sheeting through his skull. When he opened his eyes, he saw double: two Alonzos hovered over him, not a pleasant sight.

After a while, a woman came in through the door. She was handsome and shapely, and even in his misery he found her agreeable to look at, though there were two of her as well. He stared up at the woman until the figures coalesced and he realized he was looking at his wife. Something was wrong with her. Her dark hair, usually clean and pinned back, hung drab and lank. Her cheekbones were sharp, as if she'd lost flesh. At about that time, he faded out again. Then he remembered sitting in a chair in the kitchen of their house while True cleaned the blood off his face. She wouldn't let him crawl into bed. She kept him sitting in the chair the rest of that day, a damp rag over his eyes. Now and then she removed the rag and made him drink tea that left a bitter taste in his mouth.

Suddenly he wanted to see her in the worst way. He picked up his hat and got up slowly, in stages, from the couch.

"I'm off home," he said.

As he stepped out of the jail, he saw a boy coming up the street on a mule. The animal's long upper lip stated that it grudged being ridden. No saddle. The boy sat on a girthed sheepskin with the fleece side down. He held a loop of rope tied to the bit rings on both sides of the mule's broad, disgruntled mouth. The boy was small, and his legs stuck out sideways from the mule's sweat-slick barrel—uncomfortable enough, Gideon thought, even for one so young.

The boy's bare feet were mottled with grime. He wore a broad-brimmed straw hat and a pale homespun shirt above breeches held up by a single leather suspender crossing his chest.

The boy hallooed the closed door of the jail, clearly not realizing that the man standing in front of him, his hat pulled low to block the sun, was the sheriff of Colerain County himself.

"Why don't you get down off that mule," Gideon said, tipping back his hat, "and tell me what it is that you want."

The boy looked at him.

"I haff for the sheriff a message," the boy said.

Instantly Gideon recognized the *Pennsylfawnisch Deitsch* speech pattern accompanied by an accent even thicker than his own.

"I am the sheriff," Gideon said.

The boy's face opened with recognition. "You came to our farm this spring. The Trautmann farm. In Sinking Valley." The last word came out as "walley."

Gideon groped down in his memory and vaguely recollected going to a farm in Sinking Valley, a place where many Dutch families had bought land. He'd gone there to sort something out, a dispute between neighbors.

". . . dead body," the boy was saying.

It woke Gideon up.

"In the *sinkloch*," the boy said.

The word meant "sinkhole." One of those strange depressions that pocked the land in areas underlain by limestone rock.

"A dead body?" Gideon asked.

The boy nodded.

"Whose body is it?"

The boy looked down at the mule's broad back and shrugged.

"A man or a woman?"

The boy raised his eyes. "A woman," he said. "*Meeglich*."

A woman. Probably?

"And you rode here to tell me."

"Father sent me. Jonas Trautmann." The boy pronounced his father's first name in the *Deitsch* manner: *Yonas*. "You talked with my *dawdy* this spring about the *bissel feld* down by the stream, the one the Rankins own, but they can't get to it because the bank is too steep there. We planted on it corn. You said to pay them for what we harvested."

This gushing of information was too much for Gideon to take in. "Why don't you get down off that mule and have a drink of water and tell me more about this dead body."

The boy shook his head. "I don't know more. They wouldn't let me look. *Dawdy* told me to ride to town and tell you and come straight back."

Gideon studied the boy's face. The Trautmann farm. In Sinking Valley. Likely he would remember how to get there. If not, Alonzo would know.

A dead body in a sinkhole. Probably a woman. Maybe an accident. Maybe something else.

He said to the boy, "Tell your father I will be there tomorrow."

The boy nodded. He pulled on one rein, bending the mule's thick neck. He tapped the mule with his calves. A john mule, Gideon noticed. The mule didn't move; clearly he did not want to go any farther on this hot day. The boy lifted his heels and kicked. The mule kept his big hooves planted in the dust. His eyes hardened, and he laid his ears back. The mule seemed to Gideon to be contemplating the unjustness and perversity of the human race, and weighing whether or not to buck this flea off his back. Then a resigned look slackened his features. The mule sighed, turned ponderously, and started off down the street, walking at first, then, as if exacting a sort of vengeance, commencing to trot, the boy trying to grip with his thighs while jouncing along on the mule's back.

That boy will be very sore tomorrow, Gideon thought.

He went back inside the jail and told Alonzo what the boy had said. He instructed his deputy to have a team and wagon ready first thing in the morning, and to come pick him up at his house. In case he forgot about it.

Do not turn away Thy face,
Mine's an urgent, pressing case

Chapter 2

———∞∞∞———

I T SEEMED A LONG WAY HOME, THOUGH IT WAS ONLY SIX BLOCKS. When Gideon's vision blurred, he stopped and held onto a hitching rail or a porch post. Once he slogged down an alley that dead-ended in a pile of broken boards, splintered lath, and chunks of horsehair plaster. He stared dumbly at the debris before turning and retracing his steps.

He passed a cobbler's shop, an apothecary, a dry goods. On the boardwalk in front of a tobacconist's two men sat beside a squatty Indian carved out of wood. The Indian, scarcely taller than the seated men, had a scowling heavy-featured face, painted red. One of the two men was missing both legs below the knees. The other chanted "Got damn, Got damn, Got damn." The legless man had been in some kind of an accident, logging or mining. The Got Damn Man, as he was known, was syphilitic. Gideon dug into his vest pocket, found two nickels, and put them in the jars in front of the men. The legless man thanked him profusely. The Got Damn Man squinted up his eyes and muttered "Got damn."

Gideon walked on. His mind felt like a whirlpool in a muddy creek: thoughts swirled about, were glimpsed momentarily at the surface, then were sucked down into murk again.

He considered the gap in his memory and wondered whether he might someday recall his accident—where he had been, how he had fallen off Maude. He hadn't come off a horse since he was a boy. He was a good rider. He loved the swift fluid motion of the animal coming up through his seat and into his body so that it seemed as if he had four legs himself and flew across the ground on them. He liked to gallop flat out—he'd won races on Maude back home in the Dutch country. But he hadn't been in a race since he'd come west to Colerain County—when? Two years ago? Three?

He wondered why he was having so much trouble getting over a little bump on the head. What if he woke some morning with his brain stuck in a rut like the Got Damn Man's?

And why was it taking True so long to get over her grief or melancholia or whatever you wanted to call the condition that had turned his gay young wife into a stumbling crone?

What if he was stuck with that crone for the rest of his life?

He came out of his reverie to find himself standing in front of their house. He noticed that the siding needed whitewashing. Weeds thrust up around the sills. He tried the door. It was latched.

He thumped on it with the meat of his hand. With each blow, pain blossomed in his skull.

After a while he heard footsteps. The latch lifted and the door slowly opened.

True stood there, her eyes cast down. She wore a rumpled dirty shift. Gideon went in, closed the door, and took her in his arms. He tried to kiss her, but she turned her face away.

That rejection kindled a fire in his mind. "You need to pull yourself together," he said sharply. "You need to get over this."

She raised her face. On it was a mulish resentful look that slowly dissolved into tears. He held her close, and she pressed against him.

His vexation drained away and was replaced by his love for her. "I miss him, too," he said. He rested his lips on her temple. He thought about all of the misery in the world. He thought about the two men in front of the tobacco shop, and what life had done to them. He thought about the influenza epidemic that had swept through the county last fall and carried off True's and his baby, David. He remembered back a long way, to a time when he was a boy, when thoughts of grief and suffering had no place in his mind. And then he'd stepped across the threshold into their kitchen, that place of fragrant smells and warmth and love, and discovered the evil thing that had taken place there—he clenched his jaw and forced that memory into the darkest corner of his mind.

He kissed True gently. He wanted to ease her heart and bring back the woman he had married. What could he say? He could remind her that they were not alone in their sorrow: at least a dozen other children had died of the flu last fall. And then there was the typhus and the bloody flux that struck during the hot time of the year, claiming other young lives. "We must remember," he murmured, "that children die all the time." He winced immediately, realizing what a clumsy, belittling thing he'd said.

She put her hands on his chest and pushed him away. Anger and pain etched her face.

He reached out and took her by the arms. "I'm sorry, I didn't mean it to sound like that." He had to get through to her. He had to comfort her. True was devout. And so he said, "David has gone home to God. He's in a better place—"

She cut him off. "Don't give me that tripe." She glared at Gideon. "Our little boy is dead. Dead and gone forever." Her shoulders began shaking. Her eyes filled again with tears. "I tried to save him. I dosed him and poulticed him. I prayed hard for him."

"I know you did."

"I begged God not to take my baby." The tears ran down her cheeks. "They say if we lack faith, God punishes us. Maybe he punished me by taking David."

Gideon had heard that sentiment before. Some people called disease "God's flail" and said the Almighty used it on those who had turned away from him.

"Many families lost children last fall," Gideon said. "God was not punishing them, and he wasn't punishing us."

"You almost died, too," she said.

"But I didn't. And you got the flu, and you didn't die, either." He caressed her cheek. "Honey, we are still here. We can start over again.

With God's blessing, we will make another baby."

She said bitterly, "I don't believe in God anymore."

It hit him like a fist in the gut. If he was honest with himself, he had not possessed a true faith in God for years. Because of what had happened to his *memmi*. Taken away from him like that. Murdered, there in the *kich* of their family's farmhouse. And he, a ten-year-old boy, had found her lying in a pool of blood.

He wished that his fall off Maude had drubbed that memory out of his brain. But it hadn't.

Had he, too, become godless? He had been taught that if you believed in the Lord, if you followed his commandments, if you gave your soul to his son Jesus Christ—then after you died, on the Day of Judgment, you would be raised from the grave and carried to your reward in a realm high above the earth, there to dwell in bliss with your loved ones forevermore.

But what was really up there, other than a sky that went on and on, getting colder and darker and emptier the farther you went?

"We'll never see our little boy again," True said.

Gideon made no reply. He, too, disbelieved that they would ever see David. They would struggle and die on this uncaring earth, and their bones would fall to dust. They would be forgotten. As his baby son would be forgotten. And his *memmi*. And everyone else he had ever known or loved.

True shrugged herself out of his arms and went off toward the bedroom. He didn't stop her.

He sat down in a chair, pain throbbing in his skull.

He flinched at the gray cobwebby thing hovering at the edge of his vision.

Learn with me your certain doom;
Learn with me your fate tomorrow

Chapter 3

—◦◦◦◦—

THE WAGON CREAKED EASTWARD. ALONZO DROVE. GIDEON SAT beside him on the hard seat.

The wagon's right front wheel creaked with every third or fourth turn. The sound made Gideon feel as if his brain were being wrung inside his skull, twisted one way and then the other. The irregularity of the creaking was especially hateful: he found himself listening for it, anticipating it, wincing when the loud *creeeaak* finally came.

The wagon creaked past a field where people pulled flax. It creaked past another field where two men and a yoke of oxen worked at wresting a stump out of the ground. The oxen strained into sweat-blackened collars as one of the men cracked a whip over their backs and the other man hacked at the stump's roots with an ax.

Somewhere along this road, thought Gideon, *I fell off Maude*. He could not recall having ridden this way a fortnight ago, or anything else about that day, not to mention the days or maybe even weeks preceding it.

The road to Sinking Valley. What had he been doing there?

As he considered their destination, it dawned on Gideon that Sinking Valley must have been named for the sinkholes that complicated its terrain—in one of which a body had been found.

The wagon creaked down a grade, the horses taking short steps, rump muscles bunching as they held back the rig's weight.

At a ford, Alonzo drove the wagon into the stream and stopped to let the horses drink. Gideon felt cool air rising up from the water. He wished the water would swell the offending spoke on that wheel and end its *greislich* creaking. Little chance of that.

He glanced up. The cobwebby thing hovered in the corner of his vision. He made himself look beyond it, to the long green flank of Mingo Mountain, extending northeastward, its far-reaching slope faint in the haze. On the other side of the mountain lay Sinking Valley.

★★★

At the wagon's approach, a man and a woman got up out of chairs and stood in the dappling of shade and light beneath a big spreading elm.

Twenty paces away, an open-topped box sat on a pair of trestles.

Alonzo stopped the wagon so that the team stood in the shade. Gideon looked at the man and woman standing there waiting. He looked at the neat, well-kept farmstead. He looked at the box: maybe four feet long by three feet wide by three feet high, made of rough lumber, the kind of box that might hold tools or kindling or wood scraps.

He eased himself down to the ground and made his way toward the man and woman. Out of the corner of his eye he regarded the box, from which a glut of flies suddenly lifted, whirred about in the humid air, and settled again.

He smelled it, like the dead horse on the street in Adamant: the stench of mortifying flesh.

The man standing in the shade wore a cream-colored shirt and dark trousers held up with a suspender across his chest.

These people, Gideon remembered, called themselves *Neigeboren*. It meant "Newborn."

The man held out his hand. Gideon shook it. The man's hand, smaller than Gideon's, offered a firm grip. The man was of medium height with a gray beard rimming his jaw, no moustache, trimmed gray hair showing beneath his hat. His eyes a complex color somewhere between blue and green.

"I am glad to meet you, Sheriff Stoltz," the man said, "even under these sad circumstances. I am Peter Nolf, the pastor for our congregation." His voice was open and friendly, with a middling strong Dutch accent.

Nolf nodded toward the woman standing beside him. "This is Frau Trautmann."

Gideon took off his hat and nodded.

She was tall for a woman, although she stood several inches shorter than Gideon's six-foot height. Frau Trautmann wore a plain cloth bonnet with the tie strings undone. At the bonnet's edges Gideon saw blonde hair with some gray in it. The woman's blue eyes were set wide apart in her face. She had broad shoulders and ample breasts and looked to be around forty years of age. She wore a dark blue dress and an apron, scattered with green blades of grass which she attempted to brush off with her hand, long-fingered and work-reddened. "Jonas is in the field making the hay," she said. "I haff my son sent to get him."

A breeze whispered through the elm's leaves, causing the interstices in the shade to shimmer on the ground like running water. The flickering light worsened the pain in Gideon's head.

He looked toward the box. "Do you know who it is?"

"It's Rebecca Kreidler," Pastor Nolf said.

When he heard the name, an image sprang into Gideon's mind: a pretty oval face below thick auburn hair that swept back from a widow's peak.

His heart sped up. *Do I know this woman? Do I know someone named Rebecca Kreidler?*

Gideon looked out at two men and a small brown dog approaching across a recently cut hayfield. The men and the dog entered the shade. The dog, panting, went over to the fence and lay down.

"Goot day, Sheriff Stoltz," said the older of the men. He didn't introduce himself; plainly he expected Gideon to recognize him. The man was barrel-chested and bowlegged. His face seemed somewhat familiar to Gideon. He must be the farmer, Jonas Trautmann.

Trautmann shifted his pitchfork from his right hand to his left and shook hands with Gideon and then with Alonzo.

"You remember my son Abraham," said Trautmann. He indicated the strapping young man who had come up beside him.

As his father had done, Abraham shook hands with Gideon and Alonzo.

For a while no one said anything.

Gideon turned toward the box. He had a job to do, a responsibility to fulfill. He began walking. The others followed.

When Gideon got close, the flies took off again, the air above the box darkening. The buzzing of their wings diminished as the flies landed again. Most of them landed back inside the box. Some of them lit on Gideon's shirt, others on his face. A few began exploring the corners of his mouth. Hastily he brushed them away.

The stench made his throat close. He forced himself to look.

Staring up at him were the remains of a face. The skin brown and leathery, black holes where the eyes and nose had been. White teeth behind withered black lips. Auburn hair, littered with leaves and twigs, began in a widow's peak above the morbid mask of the face. Beside the head lay a foot still in its shoe, the shoe scarcely larger than that of a child, worn and broken down at the heel. A bone angled up, a sticky-looking mahogany color. A glistening green fly climbed up the bone in fits and starts, then took off on blurring wings.

Gideon saw the flare of a hip poking through moldering cloth. Flesh on the hip appeared to be moving. Maggots churned there.

He crossed quickly to the fence and vomited over the rail. A pig came running, which made him vomit again.

The others stood looking at him.

Gideon cleared his throat and spat. His face ran with sweat. On wobbly legs, he returned to the group.

Jonas Trautmann's eyes were bright. Nothing this exciting has ever happened before in his life, Gideon thought dully.

"We found her the day before yesterday," Trautmann said. "My wife's *gschwei*." It meant sister-in-law. "The varmints had been at her." With his Dutch accent, Trautmann pronounced "varmints" with a W instead of a V. "Coons and foxes, I expect. Possums." He tapped his pitchfork's shaft against the ground. "We had to use forks to gather up the remains."

The thought of what had once been a person being collected in pieces with pitchforks made Gideon deeply sad. "The body was in a sinkhole?"

Trautmann pointed the fork's curved wooden tines toward the hayfield. "Up at the edge of the woods. A big one. She was most of the way down in it."

"Who found her?"

"Abe's dog."

To Gideon's ears it sounded like Trautmann had said "Ape's dock."

"Emma was carrying around . . . something foul," Abraham said. The boy was tall and blond, with his mother's wide-set blue eyes and regular features. "It was one of the *hex*'s hands."

Gideon swiveled his head and stared. "Are you saying this woman was a witch?"

The pastor, Peter Nolf, shook his head. "Frau Kreidler was troubled," he said. "There is no reason to call her a witch."

Abraham's face reddened.

"Show me where you found her," Gideon said.

★★★

Heat shimmered above the field. The sweet smell of cut grass filled the air. Big white clouds bloomed on the horizon.

With each step, pain pulsed in Gideon's head. He worried that he might be sick again.

Why did he seem to know this woman—this Rebecca Kreidler? Why, when he heard her name, had he seen in his mind's eye a vision of a face? A beautiful face. And auburn hair.

His memory of visiting the Trautmann farm this past spring came rushing back.

It was the time of year that some called the six-weeks' want: a time for digging the last wizened apples and shriveled turnips out of the sand barrels, cutting the last smoked meat off the bone, picking dandelions and nettles and pokeweed for the pot.

A brilliant day. The land seemed colorless beneath the sun's glare. Maude had a bounce in her gait. She wanted to go fast, but he held her back, knowing she wasn't fit after standing around for much of the winter. He remembered dismounting and leading her by the reins up the poor road that climbed Mingo Mountain. On top, he got back on; they crossed the forested ridge, then descended into Sinking Valley.

The road wound among chestnuts and oaks, beeches and basswoods, the trees thick-trunked and tall. It would be another month before they put forth leaves.

He came out of the woods, turned left on the valley road, and turned left again at the first lane he came to.

Beside the lane, two women were stooped over, picking greens. As he rode up, one of them straightened and looked at him.

He gave his name and identified himself as the sheriff.

The woman was young, maybe eighteen years old. Tall and slim. Beneath a bonnet, wisps of blonde hair framed a pretty face. The other woman was smaller; she looked up briefly, then returned to cutting a dandelion clump and putting it in her basket. Before she turned away, Gideon glimpsed dark eyes in a pale oval face.

The blonde girl grinned at him. *"Iss 'Schtolz' net Deitsch?"* Is Stoltz not German? *"Ferwas schwetzscht du Englisch?"* Why are you speaking English?

"I grew up speaking *Deitsch*," he said. "But now I live in Colerain County, and I like to be understood, so it is the common tongue that I use."

The blonde girl switched to English. "That's what the pastor says, too. We must all learn to speak the English so we can get along with our neighbors." Still grinning, she said to Gideon, "You look too young to be a sheriff."

He ignored the comment. "I need to speak with Jonas Trautmann. Do you know him?"

"Of course. I am his daughter Elisabeth." She poked her chin toward her companion. The small woman reached out with her knife and cut another clump of greens. "My *aendi*," the blonde girl said. Her aunt. "We're letting her stay with us. For now."

"Please direct me to your father," Gideon said.

"Follow me." The blonde girl put down her basket and in one quick motion took off her bonnet and slung it aside. Maude jumped, and Gideon had to grab a handful of mane. Elisabeth Trautmann laughed. She caught up her skirt in her hands and took off running, her shapely feet sending up puffs of dust.

She left him in front of a shed. Inside, a burly man held an ax to a grindstone mounted in the crotch of a forked tree trunk supported by a wooden frame. A young man turned the stone with a crank.

"Jonas Trautmann?" Gideon asked.

The wheel slowed its spinning.

"*Ja*, that's me," the burly man said.

"I am Gideon Stoltz, the county sheriff. Your neighbor, Andrew Rankin, filed a complaint against you."

Trautmann's eyebrows lifted. "What does he have to complain about?"

"He said you plowed an acre of his ground last year and planted on it corn—that you're using it as if it's your own."

Two days ago Rankin had come to the jail beet-faced and scowling. As if he expected the Dutch Sheriff would never lift a hand against another Dutchman, no matter what he'd done.

"He told me he informed you several times that you were trespassing," Gideon continued.

Trautmann lifted one shoulder. "It's not that simple. Let me show you."

Out in the sunshine Trautmann led them past a new bank barn, its stone foundation neatly mortared, its wood siding still oozing pitch. The farmer paused when he saw Maude. The bay mare stood where Gideon had looped her reins over the fence. Her coat was patchy with the spring shedding. "That's a nice mare," Trautmann remarked. "A bit small, but strong-looking, good legs and back. Is she *Deitsch* bred?"

Gideon nodded.

They walked on, Gideon and Trautmann and the young man who had been helping him in the shed, whom the farmer introduced as his son Abraham. They came to a stubble field. Scents of dried manure and sun-warmed dirt mingled, not unpleasantly, in Gideon's nose. He looked at the map Andrew Rankin had drawn on a scrap of paper. He pointed at a white oak standing beside a small stream. "Is that tree on the property line?"

Trautmann nodded.

"And the line continues on to that pile of rocks?"

The farmer nodded again.

"Then clearly you ignored the boundary when you planted all the way to the stream." Gideon walked through the stubble to the streambank, Trautmann and his son following.

"Yes, well," the farmer said in a placating tone. "I did plow onto him a little. But it's ground he can't use. It's on the wrong side of the stream for him. See?"

The patch lay in a bend where the stream pulled away from Trautmann's land, then curved back again. The streambank was steep and undercut, so that a team could not cross.

"I threw some *mischt* on it and ran my furrows to the bank," Trautmann said. "I think it gave ten bushels."

"It was more than that, Father," Abraham said.

Jonas frowned.

"Good bottomland," Gideon said. "I bet it yielded well."

Trautmann had finally agreed to reimburse Andrew Rankin for twenty bushels of corn harvested off the acre last year, and to work out a lease should he wish to use the land again. It had seemed to Gideon a reasonable solution that would promote good relations between neighbors.

Riding away, he had looked for the two women picking greens but hadn't seen them.

★★★

Walking across the close-cropped hayfield, climbing toward the sinkhole, Gideon wondered whether Trautmann and Rankin had agreed on a lease for that bottomland acre. Which now seemed of little importance compared to the fact that a woman's dead body had turned up on the Trautmann farm.

Memory flashed again in his brain, like lightning briefly illuminating a night scene: *A woman, small and slender, dark eyes in a pale face below a widow's peak of auburn hair. In a room lit by a candle.*

He staggered, caught his balance. *Herr Gott, why do I know this?*

The sun beat down. His pulse hammered in his neck. He looked across at Alonzo. His deputy carried an empty sack. Even though he was fat, Alonzo didn't seem bothered by the heat.

Behind them Gideon heard the heavy footfalls of Jonas Trautmann and the lighter tread of his son Abraham.

He looked back. The pastor, Nolf, had come, too.

The dog ran on ahead.

The men stopped at the edge of the sinkhole.

It was a big one, like Trautmann had said. Seventy or eighty feet across, maybe thirty feet deep. He couldn't see to the bottom because of the dense vegetation. Sinkholes were common in the long parallel valleys in Colerain County. Sometimes they opened up in awkward places like the middle of a cropfield or beneath a road or the corner of a barn or a house. Some sinkholes drank down entire streams of water. Some were said to open into caves that penetrated deep underground.

Gideon nodded to Abraham, and the young man led the way down a faint path through the brush.

Gideon dug his heels into the steep slope and grabbed hold of saplings to keep his balance. Deerflies orbited his head. The rank smell of the vegetation almost choked him.

He heard the stabbing alarm whistle of a groundhog. A bird called *teacher teacher teacher*. A rabbit dashed out from beneath a shrub, its white tail bobbing—then darted into the brush with the dog yipping at its heels.

Near the bottom of the sinkhole, Abraham stopped.

Gideon caught a faint putrid stench. It seemed to cling to the undergrowth. Pale flies sat on the shrubs' leaves, fanning their wings; they looked fragile, as if they'd just hatched.

"Here." Abraham tapped his boot against a greasy patch on the ground where the plants looked like they'd been singed. The dog returned as suddenly as it had vanished. It sniffed at the greasy patch and made to roll in it, but Abraham kicked at it and it shied off.

The others came pressing through the brush. They stopped and stared at the death-soaked ground.

A drop of sweat fell from Jonas Trautmann's nose. "She was up against this tree." He put his hand against a small maple. "Her legs were spread apart. Her . . . her woman's parts were pressed up against the trunk. It looked like the tree was growing out of her."

Gideon tried to visualize the maggot-ridden corpse, lying on its back on the slope, legs and feet oriented downhill, the body's slide into the sinkhole apparently arrested by the vertical tree trunk.

Instead, what came into his mind was an image of the slender dark-haired woman in the candlelit room. *Standing behind a chair, facing him. Her eyes opened wide, fine dark eyebrows arching above them. Her words tumbling out, a mix of* Deitsch *and* English.

His face twitched. This was the small slender woman he had seen in the spring picking greens along the road with Elisabeth Trautmann. Elisabeth had identified the woman as her aunt. He hadn't spoken to her then. Had he done so later?

He tried to gather his wits. *Think like a sheriff,* he told himself. *It is your duty to investigate strange deaths.*

Could Rebecca Kreidler have died from some sort of an accident? Or had something more sinister happened here? Had someone killed her, then hidden her body in this out-of-the-way place?

"We forked the parts onto an old blanket," Jonas Trautmann said. "We hauled the blanket out of the *sinkloch*. We had to tie across our faces rags, it smelled so bad, *nah*, Abe?" Trautmann looked around, but his son had gone off into the brush. The farmer turned back to Gideon. "I figured the law should know, so I sent little Jonas to tell you."

"Did you find anything else?" Gideon asked. "Scraps of clothing? A knife or a club?"

Trautmann's eyes widened. "You think someone killed her?"

"I don't know what to think." The muscles knotted across Gideon's shoulders. "Your son called her a *hex*."

Trautmann waved his hand like that was nonsense. "She went out gathering plants. She was a *braucher*."

It meant "healer" in *Deitsch*.

"She dried the plants in the bakehouse," Trautmann continued, "where she slept."

The bakehouse. The room still held warmth from the oven that opened in one wall. The candle's light flickered. Its glow illuminated the dark-haired woman standing across from him, her hands gripping the top rail of a chair. The chair between the two of them. She shook her head rapidly, the gesture emphatically saying no, no, no.

"Perhaps she poisoned herself," Nolf said. "Ate a poisonous plant by accident and then wandered here and died."

A high-pitched ringing filled Gideon's head. The gray cobwebby thing shimmered at the edge of his vision. His sight dimmed, and it seemed as if black birds flew up from the ground all around.

Alonzo grabbed his arm. "Are you all right?"

Abraham's voice came from the brush. "I found the *hex*'s other hand!"

Crushed as a moth beneath Thy hand,
We molder to the dust

Chapter 4

GIDEON SAT DOWN IN A CHAIR, HIS PULSE RACING. JONAS TRAUT-mann and Pastor Nolf had helped him clamber out of the sink-hole and walk back across the hayfield. Alonzo and Abraham were still in the sink looking for whatever else might reveal something—anything—about Rebecca Kreidler's death.

Frau Trautmann brought a stoneware pitcher from the spring-house. She poured water into a mug and gave it to Gideon, then placed the pitcher on the ground beside his chair. He lifted the mug and drank. The cool water tasted good. His pulse began to slow, and the pounding in his temples abated as he sat in the shade with the breeze ruffling his hair.

Frau Trautmann sat down in the other chair. She folded her hands in her lap and looked at them. Her husband and Nolf stood nearby. Jonas Trautmann took off his hat and used it to fan his face. The farmer was bald on top, the pale skin contrasting with his deeply tanned face. He shifted his weight from one foot to the other.

"You can go back to haying," Gideon said. "I don't have any more questions for you right now."

Trautmann put his hat back on. He shook Gideon's hand and said he hoped the sheriff would feel better soon. He told his wife, in *Deitsch*, to send Abraham out to the field as soon as he got back, and they could use her help, too, when she was free. He put the pitchfork over his shoulder and strode away, whistling.

Gideon, born and raised on a farm, knew that when grass had been cut and lay drying there was always the gnawing anxiety, no matter how fair the weather, that a shower of rain might come and ruin the hay. The hay, once dried, must be forked onto a wagon and then pitched into the barn loft, whence it could be fed to the live-stock in winter. From the animals came the *mischt*, the manure, to be put back on the land in spring, restoring the soil's fertility and making it possible to grow crops and fodder again; thus did a farm prosper from year to year.

But he had nothing to do with farming now. He had ridden away from his family's farm, leaving that life behind.

He poured more water into the mug and drank. He thought he should explain his indisposition. "I have been out of sorts recently," he said to Frau Trautmann and Pastor Nolf, "since I fell off my horse and hurt my head." A strange tingling raced out his arms to his fingertips. *I was riding back to Adamant from this very farm when I fell off Maude.*

"Riding a horse can be dangerous," Nolf said. "I prefer going by shank's mare."

Gideon tried to fight down a feeling of panic. As sheriff, he must investigate Rebecca Kreidler's death. But he felt a growing fear of what he might discover. The bizarre notion crept into his head that he himself had killed her. Killed her and dumped her body in the sinkhole. But that was *ganz narrisch*, completely crazy. He couldn't have done such a thing. It wasn't in his nature. Or was it?

He should walk away from this. Call it an accident, assume the woman had eaten a toxic plant and, sick and disoriented, staggered into the sinkhole and died there. That's what Nolf said must have happened. It made sense. The woman was a *braucher*, a healer; she misidentified a plant and made a fatal mistake. He looked again at the box holding what was left of Rebecca Kreidler. Let the *Neigeboren* bury the remains and be done with it.

But he couldn't do that. He had been ordered to bring the body back to Adamant and deliver it to the coroner. The state's attorney for Colerain County, Alvin Fish, had been quite specific. Gideon had defied Fish in the past and gotten away with it. But that had been in the service of truth and justice.

If he failed to take Rebecca Kreidler back to Adamant, would he be thwarting truth and justice?

He tried to focus on the matter at hand. Turning to Frau Trautmann, he said, "Please tell me about your sister-in-law."

The woman blinked her blue eyes. "What do you want to know?"

"How long had she lived here?"

"She came here this spring. At the end of winter."

"She was married to your brother?"

"Yes."

"Why didn't he come, too?"

"My brother is dead." The farmwife looked at Pastor Nolf, then lowered her gaze.

"It's not something the family likes to talk about," Nolf said. "Frau Trautmann's sister-in-law spent the last three years in prison."

Gideon stared at the man, dumbfounded. Then he looked back at the farmwife. "Why was she in prison?"

The woman's voice was a whisper. "She killed my brother John."

Gideon absorbed this revelation. "Tell me what happened, please."

Frau Trautmann wrung her hands. "Rebecca lost a baby—a child not yet born. She said John caused the baby's death."

"How?"

The farmwife's eyes slowly filled. "She said he struck her with his fist over her womb. My brother had a temper. When he drank, sometimes he became . . ." She searched for the word in English, then said, ". . . *gwaltsam.*"

Violent.

"Did he beat her often?"

"She said so." Frau Trautmann's lower lip trembled. "She said that he was always sorry afterward, ashamed of what he had done. He promised to treat her better and never hurt her again."

"Was he arrested? Charged with assaulting her and killing the child?"

Frau Trautmann shook her head. "He was friends with the constable." She put a bitter emphasis on the word *constable*. "John and the constable, they drank together. When Rebecca told the constable what had happened, he just laughed. He told her that a husband must his wife sometimes take in hand."

Gideon knew he would arrest a man who beat his wife like that. To strike a pregnant woman over the womb with your fist—John Kreidler must have wanted to kill his own unborn child. He couldn't imagine a father doing such a thing.

Suddenly another memory intruded: *Riding back to Adamant in the dark. From Sinking Valley. From this farm. The moon cast its light on the road. Maude picked her way around rocks and stumps. He was angry, so angry. He got a bottle out of his saddlebag, uncorked it, slugged down a mouthful. The harsh whiskey burned his throat. He kept riding and drinking. He drained the bottle, threw it away into the shadows, heard it shatter— then a sudden crashing as some beast went spooking off through the woods. Maude jumped sideways, he lost his stirrups, the ground came rushing up—*

Looking down, he saw that he was holding the mug in an iron grip, his fingers white against the brown glaze. "How did your sister-in-law kill your brother?" he asked Frau Trautmann.

"She pushed him down the cellar steps. He landed bad and broke his neck."

"A tragedy," Nolf said, "for all concerned—the husband, the wife, the poor unborn child. Frau Kreidler was convicted of manslaughter and sentenced to three years in prison. The new penitentiary in Philadelphia."

The Eastern State Penitentiary. Gideon had read about it in the newspaper. An engraving showed a huge imposing structure with high stone walls and guard towers. The state had built it at great expense to house criminals from the eastern counties; a similar prison had been constructed in Pittsburgh for criminals from the western half of the state. The article explained that the two prisons had been designed by reformers, philosophical men. Each inmate lived alone in his or her own cell, away from the malign influences of other criminals. No flogging or branding or beating with canes. No visitors, no letters from outside. The new system of solitude was supposed to foster penitence in a criminal's heart—hence the term "penitentiary."

"When Rebecca got out, she went to live with her mother," Frau Trautmann said. "She sent me a letter saying they were having trouble making ends meet. Rebecca couldn't get work, I suppose because of what she had done and where she had been. I told her to come here, live with us, and one of the *Neigeboren* become."

"It was a chance for her to begin her life anew, to become newborn in Christ," Nolf said. "As we all must do, each and every day."

Tears ran down Frau Trautmann's cheeks. "Rebecca did not join the church. She was never baptized. She never had her sins washed away. And now she is dead."

Gideon stared out at the hayfield. He thought of his own little son. David Burns Stoltz had been baptized—sprinkled—in the church he and True attended in Adamant. He remembered True holding David, swathed in a blanket so that only his little face peeked out. His eyes had widened in an astonished way when he felt the drops of water flicked from the minister's fingers. He hadn't cried. He had looked out in wonder at the world. And such an expression of love and devotion shone from True's face.

He forced his mind back to the matter at hand. To the strange death of Rebecca Kreidler. It might be an accidental poisoning. It might be something else. He wondered again why he had such vivid memories of the woman. His heart stuttered in his chest. Had he done something wicked, something unspeakable, to add to the weight of grief and pain that was crushing True?

"When did she go missing?" he asked.

"Two weeks ago," Nolf said. "The eighteenth of July. I wrote it in my diary. Right away we began to search. We looked through all the buildings on the farm, down along the creek, and in the woods. No one thought to look in the sinkhole."

Frau Trautmann dabbed at her eyes with her apron hem. "That morning, Rebecca did not come help us in the garden. I went in the bakehouse. She wasn't there. I found where she'd been sick. Jonas got the men together to look for her. Then, the day before yesterday, Abraham's dog brought back—" She bit off her words and began weeping again.

Gideon waited until she had composed herself. "Show me where she lived."

He followed as Frau Trautmann and Pastor Nolf stepped around a fenced-in vegetable garden and then past the farmhouse. Like the barn, the house was new-built: two and a half stories, tan and rose and pale green mountain stone bonded with cream-colored mortar. Behind the house, separated from it by thirty paces, stood the bakehouse. At one end of the small structure sat the beehive-shaped oven beneath its own peaked roof.

The farmwife opened the door to the bakehouse, then stood aside. Before going in, Gideon looked up. An old horseshoe had been nailed to the lintel. There were horseshoes above the doors on his family's farm: So no witch could enter. On top of the lumber that had been used to frame the door, hidden behind the trim where no one could see it, someone might have scratched a five-pointed star—a *hexafoos*, to prevent a witch from doing evil. Or, for the same purpose, left a dab of blood from a slaughtered pig mixed with that of a cow.

He went inside. Small bunches of herbs tied to nails driven into the ceiling beams. Firewood ranked along one wall. The ash rake and paddle leaning in a corner. Bread trough on the table. The oven opened in the far wall, the bricks around its mouth blackened.

A ladder rose through an opening between two ceiling beams. She would have slept there in the loft.

He went to the ladder and gripped a rung at eye level. He put his foot on the bottom rung, took a step upward, then another, reaching as he went, the ladder creaking and flexing. He climbed slowly, fearing dizziness might turn his senses topsy-turvy.

It was hot in the loft. A bed and chair. A small window, cracked open. Clothing hung from pegs: a gray dress, a dark woolen cloak trimmed in red, a matching bonnet. A cloth sack dangled from its carrying strap. He checked and found it empty.

He caught a scent: a blending of yeast and herbs and sweat.

Her scent.

A point of time, a moment's space,
Removes me to that heav'nly place,
Or shuts me up in hell

Chapter 5

Eastern State Penitentiary, November 1835

A
S IT DID EVERY EVENING, THE *NACHTEIL* CAME GLIDING DOWN IN
the waning light and landed on her bed. It folded its wings
against its sides and settled its sooty plumage with a shake.

The *nachteil* had a stubby neck and a broad head. The English
called such birds nighthawks; on summer evenings, looking up from
her exercise yard, she often saw them in flocks of twenty or thirty,
soaring and dipping, flapping their long, narrow wings as they slipped
across the sky.

Rebecca understood that the *nachteil* sitting on her bed could
not be real. There was no way for a bird to have entered her cell. The
door to the exercise yard was bolted shut. At the other end of the
room, the feeding hole was closed; she'd eaten her supper and pushed
the plate back through the opening an hour ago. Yet she had heard
the soft clapping of wings as the *nachteil* slowed itself down in flight
before landing. And, real or imagined, she could see it there clearly, a
dark shape on her bed.

The first time the *nachteil* came, she had taken its appearance as a
sign that she was going mad. Then she decided she could accommo-
date it. Together they could share the space inside the cell—or the
space inside her mind.

It came the first night they locked her in. And every night since
then, even in winter, when all such birds should have left cold, snowy
Pennsylvania and flown south or hibernated in caves or hidden in
whatever manner such creatures did to survive.

The *nachteil* stayed motionless. She interpreted its silence as a reproach: *Why did you not save me?*

She had nothing to say. She'd never spoken to the *nachteil*. It didn't seem to be the kind of thing one could converse with. But its thoughts seemed to enter her mind, and in that way it spoke to her, in this place where no one else did.

Five paces took her from one end of the cell to the other. The *nachteil*'s black shoe-button eye followed her. She turned and retraced her steps.

The dusk deepened. White-plastered walls and ceiling became pearly gray, her loom black and skeletal. Still the *nachteil* sat on her bed watching her. At some point she would look over and it would be gone—at least that was how it had been on all the other nights of her imprisonment.

She was tired from working at the loom all day. She wanted to sleep but dared not approach the bed. She sat down at the loom instead. She placed her left hand against the taut threads of the warp on the cloth she'd been assigned to weave. She turned her face upward, toward the eye of God. She looked through the round metal-rimmed skylight and searched the sky for stars. She saw none; the night must be cloudy.

With the fingers of her right hand she pinched the skin on the back of her left hand. She pulled it upward and let it go. She did it again and again. It was something that hurt, and left bruises if she persisted in it, and sometimes even bled, yet she found herself doing it over and over again.

She turned her head. Out of the corner of her eye she watched the black shadow on her bed.

This world's a wilderness of woe,
O this is not my home

Chapter 6

———— ❦ ————

FLIES CAME BOILING OUT OF THE BOX AS ALONZO DUMPED THE sack's contents into it. Late afternoon, shadows of fence and barn lengthening, the heat still intense. After leaving the bakehouse, Gideon had returned to one of the chairs in the shaded farmyard. Maria Trautmann was inside the house fixing food for their journey back to Adamant. Pastor Nolf sat in the other chair next to Gideon. Red chickens scratched in the dirt around them.

"We didn't find much," Alonzo said. "Just that hand and some scraps of cloth, probably tore off her dress by the varmints. Nothing else."

By "nothing else" Gideon understood his deputy to mean that no weapon had been found, no instrument or object to suggest a cause of death.

"Best get that box in the wagon," Alonzo said.

Gideon did not welcome his words.

"Which it's getting late," Alonzo added. "We'll have to sleep along the road as it is."

"You will be many hours traveling back to Adamant," Nolf said. "Is it wise to be so close to a dead body for that long? With the risk of effluvia and contagion? If you have finished your investigation, we can bury her here."

Gideon was tempted. Leave the body, go back to town, make excuses to placate the state's attorney. If Rebecca Kreidler's remains were buried deep in the ground, there would be no more inquiring into how she had died. It would be finished. Gradually forgotten. Including any possible involvement on his part.

He was spared deciding by hoofbeats pounding up the lane.

A sorrel horse galloped into the yard, raising dust and sending chickens scattering. Slobber flew from the horse's mouth as the rider spun it by hanging on one rein. The horse stopped, the rider sawing on both reins. The sorrel backed up, ewe-necked, shaking its head and trying to escape the pain of the bit. The rider stood in the stirrups and brought his quirt down hard on the sorrel's flank. He sat the resulting jump and spun the horse again until it stopped and stood there trembling, its eyes rolled back in its head.

The rider, a young man, looked at Gideon and scowled. "Well, if it ain't the Dutch Sheriff."

When the horse had come racing into the yard, Gideon had jumped up from his chair, ready to dash off like a scared chicken to keep from getting trampled.

The man stared at Gideon, as if waiting for a response.

"You can get more out of a horse," Gideon said evenly, "if you don't make it fear you and hate you."

"I don't recall asking you how to ride my horse." The man circled the horse again, kicking her hindquarters sideways so that Gideon had to step back to avoid being slammed into. The man spat out his words: "Bitch whore tried to buck me off at the bottom of the lane. She needed a lesson on who's boss."

Gideon kept his mouth shut. It struck him that this young man, who had arrived so suddenly and violently, might know something about Rebecca Kreidler's death. Might even have caused her death.

He noticed that the man was bareheaded; perhaps he had lost his hat during the wild ride. The fellow had a full head of reddish brown hair above a fair-complected face in which brown eyes smoldered.

The man exhaled, settling his weight into the saddle and loosening his grip on the reins.

The sorrel's eyes softened, her head lowered, and she began mouthing the bit.

The man slipped his feet out of the stirrups and swung lightly to the ground. His movements reminded Gideon of some quick supple predator like a weasel or a mink. The man was of medium height and had a lean build. Holding on to the sorrel's reins, he cut his eyes toward the box perched on the trestles. His scowl deepened, and he turned to face Gideon. "Guess you got no cause anymore to wear out that crowbait of your'n, riding her over the mountain."

Gideon felt his face flush and his jaw tighten. The man seemed to be implying that he, Gideon, had ridden Maude to Sinking Valley to see Rebecca Kreidler. And the *nidder mensch* had called Maude a crowbait. Far from it! He'd match his good little mare against any horse. He tried to swallow down his anger and push the growing apprehension from his mind.

"Your name?" he said curtly.

The young man waited long enough to let his insolence show. "James Rankin."

This must be the son of the neighboring farmer, Andrew Rankin, whose complaint about Jonas Trautmann wrongfully using his land had brought Gideon to Sinking Valley this past spring.

"Did you know Rebecca Kreidler?" Gideon asked.

Rankin nodded.

"You heard that her body had been found?"

"Bad news rides a fast horse. And you are here to learn how she died." He added in a sardonic tone, "Because you are the sheriff of Colerain County." He slapped his quirt against the palm of his other hand. "I don't believe what they're saying—that she poisoned herself. Rebecca knew her plants. She came onto our ground pretty often, looking for boneset and snakeroot and such."

"I'm told she was a healer."

"Man and horse alike. She doctored a bad cut on this mare's shoulder. Used a salve she made. She gave me a jar of it and showed me how to put it on till the wound healed. Didn't even leave a scar."

"If she didn't poison herself, how do you think she died?"

"Maybe someone killed her," Rankin said. "Maybe if you think real hard, you will figure out who killed her, and why."

"If Rebecca Kreidler was murdered, I will do my best to find out what happened."

Rankin's eyes narrowed. "I think you will hide behind your badge."

"I don't hide behind any badge." A tarnished star that had belonged to Gideon's predecessor was pinned to his vest. "I think the truth must always come out." Gideon realized he meant what he said. He felt his heart hammering so hard that anyone looking at him must see it thumping crazily as if trying to free itself from his breast.

"I wonder about that." Rankin stared at Gideon a moment longer, then footed a stirrup and swung himself up onto the sorrel's back. The horse immediately tensed.

Rankin collected the reins and walked the sorrel step by halting step toward the stinking, fly-swarming box. The mare wanted nothing to do with the buzzing, bulky thing. She threw her head from side to side and skittered her feet as Rankin used his legs to bump her on one flank and then the other, forcing her to walk straight ahead. He tightened on the reins. With the horse trembling beneath him, he looked down into the box.

Rankin stared at Gideon with hatred on his face. He spun the mare and quirted her. She tore out of the farmyard and went galloping down the lane.

Come, humble sinner, in whose breast
A thousand thoughts revolve

Chapter 7

—⟨∞⟩—

THE SUN HUNG LOW IN THE WEST, A RED ORB IN A PALE BLUE SKY
that became a serene pink at the horizon. Crickets chirped
from the grass in the glade.

Alonzo unhitched and hobbled the horses. Gideon went to the
stream trickling down the side of Mingo Mountain. He knelt, cupped
water in his hands, and dashed it in his face. The water ran down his
neck and inside his collar. He shivered, cupped more water, and
drank. The cold pure water failed to wash away the taint at the back
of his throat, of rotting flesh and death.

He came back to the glade and sat down on a log near a well-
used fire ring. It was too hot for a fire this evening. He had little
appetite, which was a pity, since Frau Trautmann had sent them off
with a sumptuous supper: slabs of smoked ham, a loaf of bread, hard-
cooked eggs, ripe peaches, half an apple *schnitz* pie. Despite the taint
in his throat and the passage of years, Gideon could still taste his
mother's *ebbelschnitzboi*—moist and sweet and tangy, with just the
right amount of cinnamon.

He stared at the circle of blackened rocks in front of him. The
rocks shimmered and dissolved, and his mind went back. His fall off
Maude had knocked a span of memory out of his head, but he had
no trouble reaching back thirteen years to that one particular day. He
told himself it was a memory he wished to be rid of. But in some
strange way he cherished it. If he was honest with himself, he
wallowed in it.

After the neun-uhr-schtick, *the nine-o'clock-snack, he works for a while raking the* ohmet, *the second cutting of hay. Then when his* dawdy *goes over the hill to scythe the field's far corner, he puts down his rake and sneaks off. He makes for the house and heads straight for the* kich. *He wants a cookie, a piece of pie if he's lucky. He can always persuade his* memmi *to give him some, even if it means cutting a slice out of a full pie. He also wants a buss on the cheek and a pat on the head, assurance that he's a good boy no matter what mean things his* dawdy *says.*

He stops before he enters the kich. *He senses that something—he's not sure what—is different. Different and wrong.*

Maybe it's the flour on the floor, the white spray across the boards where it shouldn't be. Or the quiet: He listens but can't hear his memmi *humming or singing lightly as she kneads dough or rolls out a pie crust or chops vegetables, nor any of a hundred other sounds that come from what she does in the* kich, *where he spends as much time as he can, to be with her and to get out of doing farm work.*

His nose catches a whiff of something bad. It smells like dreck.

Standing in the doorway, he feels the hairs rise on the back of his neck. He tells himself to turn around and run back to the field, because the house no longer seems like a place of warmth and comfort but one of danger. But if he goes back, his father will see that he snuck off, and before he can say a word he'll get cuffed or kicked.

Maybe it's nothing. Maybe his memmi *is up in a bedroom or down in the cellar, and there's a reason for this strange silence, this bad shit smell.*

His nose picks up another scent—tangy, like fermenting hay. No, like when they hoist the hog and slit its throat and the blood comes gushing out to fill the basin that he, Gideon, has been assigned to hold beneath the rubbery snout and whiskery jaws, to catch the blood for blutwascht, *which he hates to eat, it tastes terrible, and if he doesn't do it right and spills the blood he'll earn harsh words, a slap or a kick—it doesn't matter if other people are watching, his* dawdy *will light into him for any mistake.*

He thinks again about turning and running. But he needs to know what has happened in the kich. *He takes a tentative step. Another. Then he sees her foot, bare, on the floor. He takes another step and sees all of her. Lying on her back. Her one leg wedged up against the washbench. She doesn't move. She lies there in the middle of a big patch of red.*

The air seems to blink. Bright spears of light stab at the edges of his vision. His eyes take in her skirt hiked up around her waist, her woman's parts exposed, he knows it's wrong for him to stare, it takes a great effort but finally he forces his eyes upward, and he sees that the front of her dress has been ripped open, her breasts covered with wounds like little red-lipped mouths. A bigger mouth gapes across her throat where no mouth should be, a crude grin edged with white flecks. And all of that red.

Tightness clamps his chest. He can't breathe. And still he stares, trying to understand what he's seeing, he should tear his eyes away, but he can't, and he knows that after seeing his memmi *like this, things will never be the same again.*

The world stands still for a while. Then it heaves into motion, a new place where everything is bright and sharp-edged. He turns and lurches out into the sunlight. He trips and falls, catching himself with his hands. He tries to scream but nothing comes out of his mouth. He still can't breathe. It feels like his lungs are stuffed with gravel. Finally he catches a whooping breath. He tries to get up and run, and his legs buckle and he falls again. On hands and knees in the farmyard, he realizes he can't outrun it. He can't outrun the evil that has filled the kich, *the farm, the world.*

Gideon came back to the present, relocated himself in time and place. Sucked in a deep breath. He was no longer a terrified boy. He had become a man; a sheriff, of all things; a husband; and, for a brief time, a father as well. Now seated on a log in a glade on the side of a mountain, a week's ride away from that *kich.*

The harsh ratcheting of katydids blended with the higher-pitched chirping of the crickets. Fireflies blinked their yellow-green lights against the dark wall of the forest.

He had been ten years old when his *memmi* was killed.

Afterward, he couldn't trust his senses: A stick on the ground became a snake that coiled and struck. Crows were black shrouds blown down the wind. A scarecrow in the corn patch jumped from its pole and chased him. At night he would wake up covered with sweat, hearing the echo of his own screams.

No one was ever arrested for killing her. Over the years he came up with theories about who could have murdered his *memmi*, and none of them seemed likely. He thought of what he would do to the man who had done those things to her: he imagined many ways of killing the killer, cruel and drawn-out methods, though he could not attach a face to the body of the man he murdered in his mind again and again.

The memory of finding his *memmi's* body had never left him. Years later it had goaded him into saddling Maude and leaving his home, riding west, crossing the Susquehanna, on into the lightly settled backcountry until he fetched up in the town called Adamant. Maybe it was the memory of his mother's death that made him agree to become a deputy when the sheriff of Colerain County offered him the job. Not long after that, the sheriff died from a stroke. The county commissioners appointed him, Gideon Stoltz, as the new sheriff.

Determined to succeed, he had studied law books. Gotten help from an old judge, Hiram Biddle, who had become a friend and a hunting companion. Gideon had looked at maps. He rode all around the county, tried to learn the terrain, the streams and hollows, the hills and mountains, the forests and farms, the roads and trails. He tried to do the job he'd been given. He tried, himself, to be a good man, a good husband to the woman he married, a good father to their baby. He tried to put the past behind him.

And now what had he done?

He looked around at the darkening glade as if the answer might lie among the shadows. The katydids' ratcheting grated in his head.

He reviewed what he had learned on the Trautmann farm.

A body found in a sinkhole. The body of a woman named Rebecca Kreidler, who had arrived at the farm in the spring. An apparent victim of an accidental poisoning. Although James Rankin, a young man living on the farm next to the Trautmanns, suggested that the woman might have been murdered. While Rankin had not accused anyone of the crime, he seemed to imply that Gideon might have done it.

Which made no sense at all.

He thought hard. He had fallen off Maude on the road between Sinking Valley and Adamant around two weeks ago; that's what Alonzo said. Pastor Nolf stated that Rebecca Kreidler had gone missing two weeks back, on the morning of July the eighteenth. She must have died the evening before, July seventeenth, or in the early hours of the eighteenth.

Right around the time he had come off Maude.

He picked up a stick from the ground, broke it in half, threw the pieces away.

Why did memories of the woman keep coming to him? A beautiful woman. Had he taken up with her, had he been unfaithful to True?

Had he done something even more unspeakable?

He startled as Alonzo dropped two blanket rolls on the ground near the log. His deputy turned and clumped back to the wagon.

In the wagon's bed sat the box. They had taken an old blanket, the one Jonas and Abraham Trautmann had used to haul the body out of the sinkhole, and tacked it over the box's top. The blanket cut down on the stench and screened out most of the flies.

Alonzo came back toting a sack. With a grunt, his knees cracking, he sat down next to Gideon. He unwrapped the food Frau Trautmann had sent.

Gideon took a peach and bit into it. Saliva flooded his mouth. He barely tasted the sweet juicy flesh as he stared at the fire-blackened rocks.

Ah! What is this drawing my breath,
And stealing my senses away?

Chapter 8

⸺⦾⦾⸺

THE DAY CAME ON. TRUE LAY IN BED. THROUGH THE OPEN WINDOW she heard the creaking of the neighborhood well pump, a horse's hooves thudding past in the street, Mrs. Sayers slopping her hog and calling "Pig, pig, pig!" The high-pitched cries of children. The sounds, especially those of the children, made her feel like she was sinking into mud.

Gideon had not come home last night. He and Alonzo had to go somewhere. Something about bringing a dead body back to town. He said they might need to sleep along the road if they couldn't get back to Adamant in one day.

There had been other times lately when he hadn't come home. He told her he needed to work late, so he slept at the jail. She knew that sometimes he drank—something he had never done before. Could be he had found another woman. She asked herself if she cared and was not sure she did.

She ought to get out of bed. Her mind cast about, from the garden choked with weeds to the clothes strewn on the floor, the ashes that needed hauling from the hearth, the loaf of bread on the kitchen table thick with mold. Her thoughts veered to David, and she saw for the thousandth time the face that had been so bright and cheerful in life now slack and collapsed in death, the eyes half closed, eyes that would never see the world again, would never look into her eyes again.

She had thought it was just another cold, another childhood illness, surely it would pass. It turned out to be the influenza. She did not feel any better knowing that dozens in the county had come down with the disease; there was nothing to cure it, you either suffered through it or you died.

She sensed loss all around her. The loss of her child, the loss of her desire to care about anything, the loss of her God—maybe the loss of her husband. She stared up at cobwebs bellying down between the ceiling beams. Once she would have attacked them with a broom. Now she was indifferent.

True had been born in a cabin on the ironworks at Panther, a few miles north of Adamant. The youngest of six, with five older brothers. Schooled, even though she was a girl, until the age of twelve, so that she could read and write and cipher, which neither her father nor her mother could do. Her father was the head collier for the ironworks; her mother worked in the big house, the mansion owned by the ironmaster, at that time a man named Adonijah Thompson.

They'd sent her to work in the big house as a chore girl. Mr. Thompson was tall and strong, with the haughty eye of a hawk. A ripening fourteen-year-old, she'd caught his attention. They should have warned her about the ironmaster, she thought, protected her from him. Didn't her mother see how he watched her, pushed up against her in the hallway, the pantry? She'd been afraid to say anything. Her parents' jobs, her brothers' jobs, all depended on the ironworks. The ironmaster could send them down the road in the blink of an eye. He had finally trapped her in the cellar. She'd been too scared to fight him off. The next time he tried she screamed as loud as she could and raked her fingernails across his face. He stumbled back. His face was like iron; it didn't bleed. She stood rooted in terror at what she'd done. The ironmaster stared at her with his hawk's eyes. The moment stretched out, and she felt herself trembling, frozen in place as she grew certain that he would overpower her. But he had turned and walked away.

She thought surely he would dismiss her from service and take away her family's jobs. Every time she saw him, her heart started slamming against her ribs. But the ironmaster had ignored her from then on.

When she and Gideon married, she left the ironworks. They moved to this house that Gideon rented in Adamant. A small place, but comfortable, and she'd taken pride in keeping it neat and clean.

Now look at it.

Was it only to get away from the ironworks that she'd married Gideon Stoltz?

No, she loved him. No matter what had happened, her heart still filled with tenderness at the thought of him. Her love for him seemed like a flicker of candlelight in a vast cave. Lighting the only way she might follow to make her way out of the darkness.

Slowly she sat up. Swung her legs over the side of the bed.

She stood up with a groan and shuffled into the kitchen. She went out the back door in her dirty shift and bare feet and trudged to the outhouse. Gideon's hunting dog, a red setter named Old Dick, was wild to see her. The county's former judge, Hiram Biddle, had willed the dog to Gideon, his hunting partner and friend. Old Dick came to the end of his chain. He raised both front paws high, whimpered, and lashed his tail. True ran her fingers through the dog's fur and let him lick her face. Then she fed him his tripe and filled his water bowl from the rain barrel.

Afterward she felt so tired she thought she might as well go back to bed.

On her way to the bedroom, she passed a small table on which lay a souvenir card. Her mother had walked over from Panther and given her the card in an effort to cheer her up. The card came from the big house. They were cleaning the place out. Adonijah Thompson, the old ironmaster, was dead. The new ironmaster and his wife had their own ideas about how a mansion should be decorated.

She picked up the souvenir card and wiped the dust off it. The card had words on it in a language she didn't understand; she thought it might be French. Above the words, a picture of a hot-air balloon. The balloon was gold with a pale blue pattern. Tipped slightly to one side, it rose above a town. In the town, people perched on rooftops and clung to chimneys, smiling and waving, cheering the intrepid balloonist—who, True now saw, was a woman.

The balloonist stood in a wicker basket beneath the gold-and-blue globe of the balloon. She wore a high-collared green dress. A peaceful, contented expression filled her face. The woman held on to one of the lines that suspended the basket beneath the balloon. Birds flew around the balloon as it rose into a clear blue sky. The woman waved with her other hand. She didn't look at the people below: she looked out of the card. It seemed she looked straight at True.

True had never seen a balloon, much less ridden in one, nor did she ever expect to. She tried to imagine what it might feel like to soar above loss and fear, guilt and grief, to escape the dark cold mud sucking her down. To float. To fly free.

Buried in sorrow and in sin,
At hell's dark door we lay

Chapter 9

—⊶⊷—

"S HERIFF STOLTZ, I AM GLAD TO SEE YOU."
Gideon edged his way into the office. If Alvin Fish, the state's
attorney for Colerain County, was glad to see him, it could only mean
that Fish was in a position to inflict something disagreeable on him.

Alonzo referred to the state's attorney as the Cold Fish. Gideon
had gotten into that rather dangerous habit as well.

Fish sat in a chair facing Dexter Beecham, the doctor who served
as county coroner. The state's attorney gripped a wooden staff held
upright between his legs. His arm, with his sleeve folded back, was
thin, pale, and matted with black hair. Beecham set a lancet over a vein
in Fish's arm and tapped it with a fleam stick. The doctor held out a
basin to catch the blood that came pulsing from the incision.

Dark red blood, Gideon noted. At times he had wondered whether
the Cold Fish's blood might be clear, or perhaps a piscine green.

"I summoned you," Fish said, "to see what Dr. Beecham and I
found when we examined the corpse, or, shall I say, the disarticulated
remains of that woman who died in Sinking Valley."

Beecham, red-faced, short, and rotund, concentrated on holding
the basin as it filled with blood. "Be done here before you can say Jack
Robinson."

"I am bled weekly," Fish said. "It balances the humors and sharpens
the intellect. You should consider a similar program yourself, Sheriff."

Gideon figured that Fish would like nothing better than to open
a vein in the Dutch Sheriff's neck and watch the blood gush out.

Fish had been particularly spiteful since he'd been passed over for
the judgeship that had come open the previous autumn, following the

death, by suicide, of Judge Hiram Biddle. Fish had seniority and was an able prosecutor. The likely reason he'd been kept off the bench was that he was viewed as corrupt. When investigating a murder, Gideon had defied Fish's order to cease scrutinizing the ironmaster, Adonijah Thompson, one of the county's leading citizens; Gideon suspected Thompson of having hired an assassin to kill his own brother, whose return after a thirty-year absence could have revealed a long-ago crime. Gideon arrested the assassin for an unrelated killing. But Fish refused to let Gideon probe the man's connection to the ironmaster. A rumor spread: Thompson had bribed Fish. (Alonzo, quite the gossip, had no doubt let something slip.) The judgeship went to another lawyer.

Beecham set the blood-filled basin aside and used a pin to close the incision in Fish's arm. With a long black hair from a horse's tail, the doctor tied a figure-eight knot over the pin to hold it in place.

Fish looked along his narrow nose at Gideon. "Your report states that on or around July seventeenth, this woman, Rebecca Kreidler, is believed to have accidentally ingested a toxic plant and succumbed to its effects."

"That's what the people she was living with said." Gideon had not included in his report James Rankin's opinion that Rebecca Kreidler had been murdered, since he had found nothing to substantiate it. Not that he'd looked very hard.

Fish nodded to Beecham, and the coroner reached into his vest pocket, withdrew his pudgy fist, and held it out toward Gideon. Gideon hesitated, then cupped his palm beneath Beecham's fist. The coroner opened his fingers.

Into Gideon's hand fell three nails.

"One was in her left foot," Beecham said. "Another was in her torso, on the left side between the fourth and fifth ribs. And one had been driven into her skull."

The flesh crawled on Gideon's neck.

He stared at the nails. Their heads were squared off and tapered, their shafts stained a rusty brown. Each was about two inches long, ending in a sharp point. They looked like horseshoe nails. He found his voice. "The one in her skull. Is that what killed her?"

"Her skull was about a half inch thick where the nail went in," Beecham said. "That's fairly thick, as your human skull goes. Kind of surprising, since she was a small woman." He shrugged. "The nail penetrated the brain cavity. It could have caused her death. Or it could have been driven into the body postmortem."

"After she was dead," Fish said.

Gideon knew what it meant. He didn't say anything, not wanting the attorney to know that his comment irked.

"It is clear that this is no simple accidental poisoning," Fish said. He stared at Gideon. The state's attorney had this thing he did with his face: he let his cheeks sag and his lips go slack and his mouth fall open while he narrowed his eyes at whomever he was addressing. Gideon thought this expression was absurd but found it disconcerting nonetheless. "Tell me, Sheriff," Fish said. "How well do you know those Dutch?"

"I don't know them very well at all."

"What are they, Dunkards?"

"They call themselves *Neigeboren*. It means 'newborn.'"

Fish scoffed. "Where do these religious fanatics come from?"

"The southeastern part of the state."

"You're from down there, too, aren't you?"

Gideon had no idea why that was pertinent, but he answered anyway. "From that general area."

"What are they doing here?"

"Most of them are farmers."

"You state the obvious. Why have they come *here*, to Colerain County, of all places?"

"Where they used to live, land costs a lot. Here they can afford big farms, farms with good soil. From the limestone."

"I've heard them on the street yammering in Dutch," Fish said. "A coarse-sounding language. *Yaw, yaw!* Puts me in mind of a flock of crows." He sniffed. "They should learn English if they want to live here." The corners of his thin-lipped mouth twitched upward. "Let me tell you a story that a friend related to me. These two Dutch women are out in the garden digging up potatoes. One of them holds up a couple of good-sized spuds. 'These look chust like Chacob's balls,' the woman says. 'What, they're that big?' her friend replies. 'No, they're that dirty.'"

The state's attorney guffawed. Beecham snickered. After a while, Fish stopped laughing. "You don't seem amused, Sheriff. Maybe you don't understand the joke—don't 'get it,' as they say." Again the attorney directed his slack-faced stare at Gideon. "All 'choking' aside, I trust that you will not have any difficulty investigating this killing, even though it took place among your own kind."

"Mr. Fish," Gideon said, "Doctor Beecham pointed out that the nails may have been driven into the woman's body after she was already dead. That would more properly be considered the abuse of a corpse. And not necessarily a killing."

"Let me remind you that I evaluate any crimes committed in this county," Fish said. "Keep in mind that I am the advocate for the people. I represent them, including this woman, Rebecca Kreidler, whose remains have been presented to me in an exceedingly suspicious state. I believe she was murdered. Obviously, she no longer has a voice to tell us whether that is true. I will give her that voice, and I will give her justice. I expect you to collect the facts pertaining to this case—all of the facts, no matter what they may be."

Gideon gave a nod.

"I understand that lately you have had difficulty comporting yourself properly," Fish continued. "I heard that recently you fell off your horse on the road at night while in a state of intoxication."

Gideon blinked. How had the Cold Fish learned of his accident? Alonzo, and his loose lips. It was probably all over town.

Gideon tried again to call up some concrete memory of why he had gone to Sinking Valley that night, why he had seemingly visited

Rebecca Kreidler in the bakehouse where she lived. Two weeks ago, around the time of her death. Then, riding back to Adamant, drunk and angry, he had fallen off Maude.

What had happened at the Trautmann farm? What had taken place between himself and that woman?

He tightened his fist around the nails. Their points pricked his palm.

The state's attorney went behind his desk. He sat down in his chair and clamped a pair of spectacles onto his nose. They perched there, slightly askew, their oval lenses shrinking his eyes so that they looked like nannyberries.

"You are up for election this fall," Fish said. "I hear that at least one and perhaps several very capable men will be putting their names on the ballot for sheriff. I do not believe you have much of a chance of retaining your position." Fish gave Gideon a mirthless smile. "I doubt that the voters of Colerain County wish to have a Dutchman— and a drunkard to boot—as their sheriff."

Thy wrath lies heavy on my soul,
And waves of sorrow o'er me roll

Chapter 10

———— ∞ ————

Eastern State Penitentiary, January 1836

TUMBLERS FELL WITH A CLATTER. HINGES SHRIEKED, AND THE heavy door swung inward. Rebecca Kreidler rose from her loom as the matron and the chaplain entered the cell.

Her hands shook. She clasped them behind her back. She did not want these people to know how frightened she was on this, her last day in prison; how terrifying she had found it, to be alone in a cell within the great silent penitentiary. The matron, the chaplain, and the physician were the only people she had seen in three years. In many ways, they seemed less real to her than the *nachteil* that landed on her cot every evening. Until last night. She had sat at her loom until well past dark, waiting for the *nachteil* to occupy her bed, but it never came.

"My dear Rebecca." The chaplain was a hale, fleshy man. His moon face beamed, and his voice boomed off the walls. "You have been a model inmate. In pondering your crime, you have learned to hate it. You have opened your soul to God, and he has filled it with his grace. I have no doubt that henceforth you will obey the laws of our commonwealth, and we will never see you within these walls again."

The chaplain nodded to the matron.

Rebecca flinched as the matron put the dark cloth sack over her head.

The matron tied the hood in place, then put a hand on Rebecca's shoulder and turned her. Rebecca couldn't see a thing. Unsteadily, she followed the chaplain's footfalls, the matron guiding her from behind.

The door to her exercise yard groaned open. Cold air, crusted snow underfoot. She took short, tentative steps, afraid that she might fall. They went through the outer door into a larger open area, the breeze more active there, and she sensed other walls looming higher than the ones enclosing her yard.

The only time she had seen the whole prison was when they led her from the black windowless coach to the arched entrance gate, her wrists shackled, the shackles chained to a broad leather belt. She had looked up at gray stone walls interrupted by towers with notched tops, their sides slitted with windows.

The matron's hand tightened on her shoulder. Following the pressure, she turned and kept walking. The matron's hand slid down her back until its palm rested just below her waist, where her buttocks began their swell. She wanted to kick back like an angry horse but fought down the urge. She did not want to upset things, when she was so near to being free.

Free, after three years. One thousand ninety-five days.

When she had entered the penitentiary, she wondered who might be in the cells on either side of hers. She started to ask the matron, but the woman scowled and raised a finger to her lips. No talking. That was the rule. Over the next three years, she and the matron never spoke.

The only sign she found of prior habitation in her cell were these words scratched low on the wall: GOD WILL CARRY ME, MY WINGS ARE BROKE.

The matron's hand returned to her shoulder and gripped it. Rebecca halted. A door creaked. They stepped through the portal, pausing again as the door shut behind them. The air was warmer. The chaplain said something to another person. The matron's hand went to the small of her back, pushed her forward.

Another door creaked open and banged shut, the sound echoing before dying out. The matron untied the hood and lifted it over Rebecca's head.

She found herself standing in front of a table next to an oval mirror on a wooden stand. On the table, neatly folded, lay her gray bombazine dress and matching bonnet, and the handsome woolen cloak, charcoal gray trimmed with red, that her parents had given her on her wedding day. Beside them lay the silver cross on its fine chain, the keepsake that her friend, Old Molly, had given her. Molly was like a grandmother to Rebecca; she was some sort of a distant relation. Molly had never married. She lived by herself at the foot of Blue Mountain and healed folks using plants. Rebecca had spent summers with the old woman when she was a child and up until she married. Old Molly was a *braucher*, and Rebecca wanted to be like her. Over the years the kindly old woman had shared her knowledge of plants: how to find them, how to use them. How to speak with them and listen to what they had to tell.

The matron nodded at the clothes, then stood leaning against the wall.

Rebecca lifted the coarse shift over her head. In the mirror, for the first time in three years, she saw herself: Blue veins branching beneath pale skin. Arms and shoulders muscular from working at the loom. The dark auburn hair, with a wave to it, much longer than when she had come to the prison; unbraided, it would fall to her waist. She picked up the cross from the table, spread the chain, and put it on over her head. In terms of religion, the cross meant nothing to her. But it helped her remember Old Molly, and draw on her will and strength.

Rebecca straightened to her full height. Standing there naked, she stared at the matron until the woman lowered her gaze. She finished dressing.

An hour later she shook so hard that she had to steady her writing hand with her free hand to sign her name in their book. A guard accompanied her to the gate. He opened the wicket. She stepped through it into the world.

Assured, if I my trust betray
I shall forever die

Chapter 11

⸺◦◦◦⸺

GIDEON LEFT THE STATE'S ATTORNEY'S OFFICE. IN HIS VEST POCKET were the nails the coroner had recovered from Rebecca Kreidler's remains. Horseshoe nails, unmistakably, with big sturdy heads to hold an iron shoe on a hoof.

Something about horseshoe nails nagged at his brain—such nails driven into something, for some improbable purpose. It was a *Deitsch* practice, no doubt a superstition, from sometime in his past. He had gotten hold of some horseshoe nails and driven them into . . . what?

He plodded toward the jail. Pain throbbed in his head. A wave of dizziness stopped him. In the upper right corner of his vision hung the uncanny cobwebby thing. He tried to blink it away, without success.

His mind slid to the other worrisome situation the Cold Fish had brought up: the election this autumn. Of course Gideon knew that the office of county sheriff was coming up for a vote, but beyond putting his name on the ballot, he hadn't done anything about it. He almost laughed when he thought about getting up on a stump and giving a speech with his thick *Deitsch* accent.

At the jail he told Alonzo that he would be leaving for Sinking Valley the next morning and might not be back for a while. "Mr. Fish wants more information about the Kreidler woman's death. I'll go myself. You stay here and watch over things."

"You sure you should be on a horse, dizzy as you've been? Seems likely enough she poisoned herself, the way they said."

"The Cold Fish is suspicious."

"It's the nature of your prosecutor. Always looking to find some-body to hang." Alonzo tapped a dirty fingernail against one of his big front teeth, then wagged his finger. "Though if she did die of poison, someone else could have done it. And come to think of it, nothing says that woman was poisoned at all. She could've been strangled and dumped in that hole. Hard to tell, with the body rotten and fallen apart. Did the coroner find anything?"

Gideon got the nails out of his pocket. "He found these driven into the corpse."

"Holy hell," Alonzo said.

"There is no way of telling whether they were pounded in before or after she died." Gideon paused. "Don't say anything about this to anyone. I don't want word to get back to whoever did it."

"I'll keep it under my hat. D'you really think you should go back to that place by yourself?"

"I doubt there will be a problem."

★★★

Walking home at day's end, he thought about what the Cold Fish had said—that other men, probably older and wiser and more capa-ble than Gideon Stoltz, and no doubt better connected in Colerain County, wished to be sheriff.

Gideon had told himself that no one else would want the job. He realized now that was a stupid assumption.

Maybe he'd be voted in anyway. Hadn't he proven himself capa-ble last year by solving that murder case?

A lumberyard clerk had been beaten and robbed in Hammertown, the seamy side of Adamant. It lay on the other side of the creek, a neighborhood where saloons dispensed cheap whiskey and easy women sold their charms. The young man's skull had been fractured; after he was found, he had failed to regain consciousness before dying. No one had witnessed the attack. Yet Gideon had managed to identify and capture the clerk's assailant, one George Baker, a stranger from another town. The Cold Fish had prosecuted Baker, and a jury convicted him.

They'd hanged Baker in March, in the jail's walled-in backyard. A crew of carpenters built a gallows out of rough-cut lumber, using bolts instead of nails so it could be taken apart afterward and stored for future use.

The day had been cold and raw, with gray clouds streaming across the sky. The roofs of nearby buildings were black with spectators. The Cold Fish and the coroner and a handful of "special deputies" stood in the yard, chatting and smoking cigars that the state's attorney handed out. They quieted as Gideon led Baker up the gallows steps, his hands secured to a leather belt. Asked if he had any last words, Baker complained because his parents had not come to see his final moments. His father, Baker said, was a "cock-chafing bastard," his mother a "cock-sucking whore." The men in the yard laughed at his foul, consternated words. Baker cried out in a high-pitched voice: "Ma always said I was born to hang!" The men in the yard laughed louder.

Gideon said to Baker, "This will be quick." He placed the hood over the man's head, then the noose. He smelled urine and *dreck* as Baker lost control of his bladder and bowels.

A deep sadness filled Gideon. A human life would be extinguished by a heartless machine in which he himself was a cog—a machine that would consume Baker wholly and without pity. Not that the man wasn't guilty. Not that he didn't deserve to hang.

Gideon stepped aside. He gripped the lever that operated the trap. He looked down at the state's attorney. With his thumb and forefinger, the Cold Fish removed the cigar from his mouth. He inspected its smoldering tip. Flicked ash onto the ground. He looked up at Gideon, a smile on his face. He nodded. At that moment, committing homicide in the name of the law, Gideon hated Fish more than he could imagine.

★★★

Arriving at his house, Gideon found the door unlatched. He opened it and stood there, hoping to hear True humming or singing as she worked at cooking or cleaning.

He found her lying in bed.

As he entered the room, she heaved a sigh and slowly sat up.

"Here." He offered her his hand.

She wouldn't meet his gaze.

He took hold of her hand anyway. It felt cold and limp.

"Come," he said. "It doesn't do any good to stay in bed."

He tugged at her hand gently. She turned her face away.

"True," he said. "Please . . ." He didn't know what to say. *Please be the lively, lovely young woman I married. Please put the memory of David's death behind you. Please be my wife again.*

Finally she let him help her to her feet.

"I'll make us some coffee," he said. Then remembered there was no coffee in the house; he'd used the last of it two days ago, and neither of them had gone to the store since then.

"Come," he said again. "Let's see what there is to eat. I will cook and maybe you can choke down whatever I manage to burn or otherwise ruin."

She smiled faintly at his attempt at humor.

He seated her on a chair in the kitchen, where he found a couple of eye-sprouted potatoes and a piece of smoked venison wrapped in cloth. He sniffed the deer meat to make sure it hadn't turned. He cleaned ashes from the hearth, took them outside to the barrel. He came back in and built a fire. He scrubbed the potatoes at the washbench and peeled and cut them into pieces, then put them in the kettle to boil. While the potatoes cooked, he cubed the meat. When the potatoes were halfway to being soft, he swung the kettle away from the flames and spooned the potatoes out of the water. He put the potatoes and the meat and some butter in a skillet on a gridiron above the fire.

During all of this puttering, he failed to think of anything to say to True, and she said nothing to him.

When the food finished cooking, he put the meat and potatoes on a wooden plate. He held the plate and a fork out to her. She made no move to take either.

Did she expect him to feed her like a child? He did just that: speared a piece of venison and held it in front of her mouth. "Honey, please eat." She placed her fingers on his hand as he guided the meat to her mouth. She chewed. Lifted her eyes to his. He smiled hopefully. She lowered her eyes, swallowed.

He fed her a piece of potato.

He thought about what he might say to her. They should have a conversation; they were married, he had an interest in her life, and she had often inquired about his duties and tasks as sheriff, at least before David died. But he couldn't ask her how her day was going, that was quite apparent. Nor did he want to say anything about a woman's dead body being found; he feared it would only make her sadder.

He fed her another piece of meat. "Not so bad, is it?"

Her voice was faint. "Not so bad."

"True, honey, I'm feeling a little better myself." She didn't reply. "My head. After my fall off Maude."

She nodded.

"I still have a headache some of the time. My balance isn't so good. But I think I can ride a horse."

"I guess it takes time." She reached out and took the plate in her hands. She set it in her lap. She picked up the fork and speared a piece of potato.

"I have to go away for a few days," he said.

"Where?"

"Sinking Valley."

"I thought you just went there."

"Yes. I need to go back."

She kept eating.

He worried about leaving her in such a state.

"Have you ever been like this before?" he asked. "Sad like this? For months on end?"

She stayed quiet.

"Of course you are still grieving for David. I know I am." He looked at her. "But have you ever been stuck in melancholy like this before?"

She nodded slowly. "A few times. My gram gets this way, too. When she does, she says the black wolf is on the mountain."

True's grandmother lived surrounded by wolves and mountains. Arabella Burns dwelt by herself in a dirt-floored cabin in a lonely hollow leading north from Panther Valley toward the Allegheny Front. Gideon had visited the old woman there during the investigation he had carried out the previous autumn. And he'd dropped in on her this past spring, when his patrolling took him to that area.

True had told him more than once that her gram had "the second sight," or just "the sight": that Arabella Burns could see things, know of them from a remote distance. True thought she had the same ability, though maybe it wasn't as strong in her as it was in her gram.

"I don't feel good about leaving you," he said.

"I'll be all right."

"Will you try to keep from sleeping so much? Try to get out of bed? Do some straightening up or cleaning? Maybe work in the garden, or walk downtown?"

She seemed to ponder his request, then nodded.

He stood and took her by the arm, helped her out of the chair. He held her against him and kissed her on the lips. She pulled back a little. He kissed her again, longer and more deeply. He ran his hands down her sides. He reached around and drew her hips against his.

She seemed to freeze. "Don't," she said.

"Honey, I love you."

"I can't. Not now."

When he tried to kiss her again, she turned her head.

Tears filled her eyes. "I'm sorry, Gid." She detached herself from him and left the kitchen. She went back into the bedroom.

He considered following her and getting in bed with her and using whatever tenderness he had left in him to show that he still loved her. But he had tried that so many times. She didn't want to make love to him. Maybe because she didn't want to make another baby, didn't want to open herself up to loss again. Or maybe she just didn't love him anymore.

He sighed. He would give some money to their neighbor, Mrs. Sayers, to buy food and look in on True, make sure she got fed.

He didn't like having to ask for help. Everyone would learn that his wife was in this terrible state. Though no doubt they knew it already.

He ate the food that True had left on the plate. He cleaned up the cooking things and put them away. He looked around the kitchen. Dust lined every surface. Cobwebs hung down between ceiling beams.

A broom leaned in a corner. He picked it up and used it to swipe away some of the cobwebs. He stopped and lowered the broom. It was pointless. The whole house was full of *schmutz*.

He looked at the broom in his hands.

And realized he had gotten it from Rebecca Kreidler.

He lurched to the chair and collapsed into it. The memory came to him strong and clear.

He spotted her on High Street.

He recognized her immediately as the small, slender woman he had seen picking greens back in April on the Trautmann farm, the woman Elisabeth Trautmann had identified as her aunt. She had caught his eye then. Her graceful form, the way she shyly turned away as he sat watching from his elevated seat on Maude.

And now here she was in Adamant. Without thinking, he crossed the street and approached her. She wore a plain gray dress, a pale apron, and a simple cap. She held herself erect, even though she was carrying an armful of brooms. When she saw him, her eyes widened and she took a step back. He doffed his hat. He apologized, said he hadn't meant to startle her.

He stood on the boardwalk and groped for something further to say. Would she be so kind as to let him look at one of her brooms? After a moment's hesitation, she leaned the brooms against the store's wall and handed him one. He turned it this way and that. He remarked on the fine quality of the broomcorn, bobbl'd *on about the handsome pattern of red twine that she'd worked into the handle. Were the brooms for sale? She nodded. She said she had made them for the dry goods store. Her voice soft and mellifluous. Something about her, maybe the tone of her voice, maybe her slender figure, maybe her loveliness, certainly her loveliness, made him want to take care of her, protect her. Hold her in his arms and draw her close against himself—but of course he would not do that, he was a married man.*

Her brooms were so beautiful, he enthused, so well made. He wanted to buy one. Not from the store, but from her.

She nodded, named a price. He pulled money out of his vest and gave it to her. When he placed the coins in her hand, his fingers touched her palm, and he felt a hot current race up his arm and course through his whole body. He left his fingers on her palm until she withdrew her hand.

He did not say: This broom is a present for my wife.

He asked her name. Because he didn't know it then. After a moment's hesitation, she told him: Rebecca Kreidler.

He smiled at her. She averted her eyes, then looked back up and returned the smile. His face burned. He couldn't believe he was doing this, couldn't believe he was approaching a woman in this manner. Such a beautiful woman, and it seemed to him that she welcomed his attentiveness. He told her that, as sheriff, he had to ride all over the county. Most likely he would come to Sinking Valley before long. His heart hammered in his chest. He recalled what Elisabeth Trautmann had said this past spring: that her aendi *lived in the bakehouse on the Trautmann farm. He asked Rebecca Kreidler if that was where she dwelt.*

She looked down again, then raised that lovely face. Yes, *she acknowl-*edged, *that is where I live. He thought she must be shy, even though she was older than he—although not much older. And so* wunnerschee, *with the widow's peak above her brow from which her hair lifted back to vanish beneath her cap—her lustrous auburn hair, her creamy skin, and, beneath fine arching eyebrows, those dark almond-shaped eyes.*

He felt like he was bewitched.

He took a last long look at her, then turned and, carrying the broom, made his way back across the street. When he reached the other side, he stopped and looked back. The walk was empty. She had picked up her brooms and gone into the store.

Standing there, he realized they had conducted their conversation in Deitsch. *He hadn't spoken that much* Deitsch *in years.*

Now he sat in the kitchen of his own house and gripped the broom he had purchased from Rebecca Kreidler. He looked at the wall. On the other side of it lay True, disconsolate in their marriage bed.

He hadn't been able to get Rebecca out of his mind. He remembered riding to Sinking Valley only a couple of days after his encounter with her on High Street. Seeking her out in the bakehouse on the Trautmann farm. At night. A secret visit. He saw again the image of the woman in the candlelight, standing behind the chair, gripping its back, a frightened look contorting her face. The next thing he could remember was riding back to Adamant, troubled in his mind, angry, drinking whiskey—throwing away the empty bottle and startling some animal and then falling off his horse.

That much he remembered and no more.

While trav'ling thro' the world below,
Where sore afflictions come

Chapter 12

———— ☙ ————

Greer County, March 1836

SHE STOOD ON THE TAVERN STOOP, A WORN-OUT GRINDSTONE scabbed with mud. The tavernkeeper in the doorway looked down at her. He named a price.

"I do not have that," Rebecca said. "But I can work in the kitchen. I can help cook."

"The cook don't need any help." The tavernkeeper was a heavy-featured man with cold eyes and sparse ringlets of gray hair limp on his scalp.

"I can scrub floors, clean chamber pots."

He shook his head.

"Or the barn," she said. "I could help in the barn . . ."

"Colored boy does the barn chores."

"Please. I am very hungry. Can I have something to eat?"

He shut the door in her face.

She stood for a moment, trying to think what to do. She stepped off the grindstone and went out into the yard. For the hundredth time she wished she hadn't begun her journey so early in the year. It had been springtime at home, with flowers blooming and trees starting to leaf out, the days and nights balmy. Here in the mountains it was still winter.

Over the last two weeks she had learned that a person on foot was rarely welcomed at a tavern. But she didn't have a horse to ride or money for coach fare. She had learned, as well, that a woman traveling alone faced worse than not being welcomed. Men made kissing sounds as she passed by. Wagoners tried to talk her into their bedrolls. Drovers whistled at her, called her a whore.

The tavern stood in a clearing surrounded by drab unkempt fields. Time and weather had blackened and checked the squared logs of the tavern's walls. The road she was following led past the tavern into a range of steep, wooded ridges. Miles of walking lay ahead of her, but somewhere beyond those confused and forbidding ridges lay Sinking Valley—that's what the farmer and his wife who had let her sleep on their floor last night and fed her this morning told her.

Her sister-in-law had sent a letter inviting her to come live in Sinking Valley. A community of religious people, *Deitsch* folk, had bought farms there. It was a place where she could find a home; a place where, Maria said, she would be welcomed. She didn't know if that would be so, but she was willing to take the chance.

Her feet ached from cold and weariness. She had almost worn through her shoes. Tonight would be bitterly cold. How she wished she could go inside the tavern, get warmed up, and eat some food. Maybe even get some hot water and clean herself.

Across from the tavern stood a gristmill, its grindstones silent. The low sun glinted orange on the frozen mill pond. It tinted the bottoms of gray clouds sailing across the sky. The wind blew grains of snow across the iron-hard road. The road was rutted and dabbed with green and brown manure and studded with old rotting stumps cut off below wagon-axle height.

The tavern's sign stood atop a crooked pole. Against a faded black background, a white bird spread its wings and pointed its opened beak upward, as if crying out in defiance or pain.

Beneath the bird, the words WHITE CROW.

Old Molly had told her that every so often a crow would hatch out white. It wouldn't grow very old before the other crows, the black ones, turned on it and killed it.

She checked her purse again: three one-cent pieces and a half-cent. At a few taverns east of the Susquehanna they'd let her work for bed and board. But after she paid the toll and crossed the long covered bridge over the half-frozen river, the settlements thinned out. People were meaner and more guarded. Some nights she found shelter at farms where they let her sleep in a barn or stable or, if she was lucky, on the kitchen floor. Sometimes she had to go hungry and lie out on the ground.

She tucked her hair beneath her bonnet. Pulled her cloak tight. Something cold and hard tightened around her heart. She would never make it to Sinking Valley. She would die on this road. She wondered if that would be a bad thing or a good thing.

A small colored boy came around the corner of the tavern and took hold of her cloak's hem. He tugged it sharply, three times. "Mister Craddock, he says you come inside."

She felt a tremendous relief as the boy led her through a door into the tavern's kitchen. She took off her cloak and bonnet. A thick-set woman with a seamed face put her to work scrubbing pots. The boy went outside again. Through a small dirty window she saw him go running off in the fading light. Down the road he went, skipping over ruts and stumps.

Her stomach growled. She wished the thickset woman would offer her food but didn't dare ask. The woman brought another dirty pot and set it down in front of her. When the woman turned away, she peeled a rime of crusted food from the pot's lip and popped it into her mouth. The woman waddled to the fireplace and stirred a rich-smelling stew. She lifted the lid off a cast-iron oven, checked on the pie baking inside, put the lid back on, and shoveled fresh coals on top.

After a while, a man came into the room through the same door she had used earlier, the boy slipping in behind him. The man stared at her. He did not go on into the dining room, where she had seen several other men seated around a table playing cards and dipping drinks from a China bowl. Instead, the man came up to her. He was broad and strong-looking. Blue-eyed, with pale bristles on his cheeks and chin. He smelled strongly of tobacco. He took off his coat and hat, set them on a chair. He grinned at her. "I will treat you fair and square," he said.

Then he was pulling her by the arm into a storage room lit by a candle. The candle's flame wavered as someone shut the door behind them. The man began pawing at her.

She pushed him away. "Leave me alone!"

His grin widened. "You're a wild 'un," he said. He put his hand on her breast.

She lunged toward a shelf filled with jars, tried to pull it down and make a noise that would bring people running. The shelf was secured to the wall. The man laughed, as he might have done at a child throwing a tantrum.

He shoved her forward into a keg. Its wooden lip dug into her midriff, forcing the air out of her lungs. He lifted her skirt from behind.

Gasping, she pulled her skirt back down. She tried to shout "No!" but only a weak bleat came out.

"Give it up to me," the man said. "Give it up to me, and I won't arrest you."

She managed to dart around to the other side of the keg while he fumbled at his trousers. She got her breath back. "Arrest me? I've done nothing!"

"Nothing, you say? Why, you stole the day's receipts out of Mr. Craddock's desk." The man came around the keg and grabbed her by the hair. He bore her backward, pinning her against the stone wall. He clamped his hand around her throat and pressed his body against hers. She struck at him with her fists and tried to turn her hips aside.

"I didn't steal!" she cried out.

"I am the constable hereabouts," the man said. "I tell you, you are a thief, and you will go to jail lessen you treat me right." He kissed her hard, tried to stick his tongue inside her mouth. She clamped her jaws shut, felt his hand on her throat tighten. "Mr. Craddock runs a tippling house without a license," the man said, "but he don't get fined if he does the law a favor now and then." Still gripping her by the throat, the man used his other hand freely beneath her skirt. "You don't fancy going to prison, now do you?"

It took the will to fight out of her—knowing that if they charged her with theft, with any crime at all, she would be taken back to the penitentiary, put in that silent hell again. Where no one spoke to you. Where your wings were broke and you couldn't fly.

Her mind seemed to leave her body. Then the strong blue-eyed man was inside her, thrusting hard, banging her against the wall.

★★★

She lifted the latch and went out into darkness.

Pain stabbed between her legs. Her back ached where the man had slammed her against the stone wall. Her neck rubbed raw from his chin bristles.

There was nothing she could do to the one who had raped her. The one to whom the tavernkeeper had made of her a gift.

She limped along on the frozen road. If anyone came, she would hide in the forest. She shivered in the cold. She felt weak and dull-witted, as if she'd just gotten up from a sickbed. It hurt to move her legs, to put one foot in front of the other. She went on in this stiff, painful way for some time, the road climbing toward a notch in the ridge. She stopped and looked back.

Behind her, the clouds were lit from below. Reddish light played across their gray bellies. Lower down, a bright orange light flickered between the black upright trunks of the trees.

After the constable had gone away, the thickset woman had let her out of the storeroom and given her a mug of hot cider and a bowl of stew. The woman didn't say anything to her.

Later the thickset woman banked the fire, snuffed the lamp, and left.

Rebecca had found a rag and a pail of water and cleaned herself. She wrapped herself in her cloak and lay down on the floor next to the warm hearth. She shook all over. She feared the constable would come back, or the tavernkeeper would decide to take his turn, or they would give her to someone else.

After a while, weariness had won out and she slept. Then she jerked awake, sweat pouring from her body. It was hard to breathe. For a moment she didn't know where she was. A faint red glow from coals on the hearth. She struggled to her feet. She found some cooked meat and half a loaf of bread and a chunk of cheese and put them in the small sack she carried with her. She went to the kindling box. With trembling hands, she took out kindling. On the floor beneath the window, she crisscrossed the small pieces of wood and added big hanks of coarse tow. She found a sliver of fatwood. Knelt by the fire. Her hands shook so hard she could barely hold the sliver against a live coal. She blew on the coal. It glowed brightly with each puff of breath. The fatwood gave off black smoke. She blew some more, and it took flame. She straightened, crossed the room to the window, and set the burning sliver on the sill.

She had wrapped her arms around herself and bent over at the waist. A low keening sound filled the kitchen: after a while she realized it came from her mouth.

She had heard the soft clapping of wings. The *nachteil* came fluttering down. It lit on the windowsill, a black shadow. Slowly it shuffled along the sill. Its foot nudged the burning sliver. The sliver fell onto the pile of kindling below.

I soon shall pass the vale of death
And in His arms resign my breath

Chapter 13

⸺◦◦◦◦⸺

A s GIDEON RODE INTO THE YARD, PETER NOLF LOOKED UP FROM his hoeing. Slowly the *Neigeboren* pastor straightened from his work. He came out through the garden gate, smiling, and reached up to shake hands.

"Welcome, Sheriff Stoltz," he said in English. "I didn't at first recognize you."

"I am here to look further into Rebecca Kreidler's death," Gideon said from his saddle-perch on Maude.

Nolf nodded.

"I hope you can introduce me to people here in the valley," Gideon said. "People in your church, also the Trautmanns' neighbors, and any others who might have known Frau Kreidler."

"I will do whatever I can." Nolf cocked his head. "I thought you agreed that her death was an unfortunate accident."

"Most likely that's what it was. But the state's attorney has directed me to gather more information."

"Of course," Nolf said. "The law must be thorough."

Gideon looked about. Nolf's house was built with horizontal planks that had been freshly whitewashed. Blue and yellow flowers cascaded down from window boxes. Gideon saw no large barn, no stretch of cultivated fields. There was a low log structure that might hold fodder and shelter an animal or two, and beyond it a small fenced-in area in which stood a tan-colored cow. "You do not farm?" Gideon asked.

"I keep that *milch* cow, grow some vegetables. I have a few colo-nies of honeybees. For preaching, people give me things—hay and grain, firewood, meat, and the like." Nolf added, "My wife and I were never blessed with children to help out on a farm."

"I will be here in Sinking Valley for several days," Gideon said. "Do you know of a place where I can stay?"

"Right here, under my roof."

"I can pay for my room and board. The county gives me an allowance."

"If you wish. Please, go ahead and put your horse in with my cow. There's a good stream of water running through that lot. You must be hungry after your ride. Let's go inside and break bread together."

Gideon dismounted, unsaddled Maude, and rubbed her down with a gunny sack he found in the pastor's barn. He turned her out, and Nolf forked some hay over the fence. The pastor pointed out a rack in the barn where Gideon could put his saddle. Gideon unstrapped the carbine in its leather scabbard. Carrying the gun, his ammunition pouch, and a saddlebag of clothes, he followed Nolf out.

As they approached the house, Gideon halted. Between the door and a window, a length of tree branch had been nailed to the wall. Attached to the branch was a gray papery hornets' nest a foot and a half long. Black-and-white hornets went in and out of a hole in the bottom of the egg-shaped nest. Some of the hornets went winging off into the yard; others flew in through the open window.

"Isn't it dangerous to have those insects inside your house?" Gideon asked.

Nolf chuckled. "If you don't bother them, they won't sting you. I found that nest in the woods and brought it here. The hornets do me the favor of catching flies, which they take back to their nest and eat."

Gideon wondered how one could relocate a big nest full of angry stinging insects, but he didn't ask. His business here was more serious.

Inside the house a few hornets bumped along the walls and went wobbling across the room. The house was clean and tidy, with a few well-used pieces of furniture, the best of which was a *schrank*, or wardrobe, made of figured walnut. On one wall hung a framed piece of *fraktur* art. This *fraktur* had no brightly colored *distelfink*, the thistle finch that foretold happiness and good fortune—a common motif, and one that decorated a painting in the parlor of the house where Gideon had grown up.

The piece of art on the pastor's wall showed a different sort of bird, a fierce-looking eagle above a dire motto in an ornate script: GOTT SIEHT ALLES.

God sees all.

Nolf beckoned Gideon into the kitchen. On the table were bread, *schmierkees*, tomatoes, a joint of meat.

Gideon kept expecting Nolf's wife to come down the stairs from the house's upper floor. "Where is Frau Nolf?" he asked.

"I am sad to say that she died."

"I'm sorry," Gideon said.

"Grace passed away this spring. She had not been well for several years. She got weaker and weaker. She took to her bed, and finally she died." Nolf gave a wan smile. "We are all sojourners on this earth. Our days are as fleeting as a shadow."

The pastor gestured for Gideon to sit, then took the other chair. Nolf clasped his hands in front of his face and rested his forehead against them. Switching to *Deitsch*, he offered grace.

★★★

After the meal, the pastor suggested they walk to a nearby farm where Gideon might talk to the family and perhaps learn more about Rebecca Kreidler. Gideon would have liked to have lain down for a while and rested his aching head, but he had a job to do, so he agreed to the meeting.

The pastor set a brisk pace, striding along on a road through a stand of beech trees whose smooth gray trunks resembled the columns of great buildings. The air was cool in their shade.

"The farm where we're going belongs to Henry Harbison and his wife Sadie," Nolf said. "It borders the Trautmanns' place on the west. Henry and his brother each inherited half of their family's farm. A few years ago, Riley, that's Henry's brother, he sold his land to the Trautmanns. He loaded up a wagon and went west—to Indiana or Illinois. Or maybe Iowa. One of those places that starts with an 'I.'"

They emerged from the forest into a weedy field.

"I don't like to speak ill of anyone," Nolf said, "but Henry Harbison would rather go hunting than till his fields or spread manure and lime." The pastor winked. "He grows a lot of rye. I hear that he makes some good whiskey. He's a blacksmith, too."

Hounds began baying as they neared the farmstead. The barn was weathered gray, its ridgeline sunk in the middle. Trash and dog filth littered the yard. Boys and girls of all ages came running, then stopped and stood gawking at the *Neigeboren* preacher and the stranger with the star on his vest. The dogs slunk behind and between the children, their tails held low and their hackles raised, growling from deep in their chests. From out of the house came a lean woman in a calico dress. Like the children, she was barefoot. Gideon and Nolf raised their hats.

"Good day, Mrs. Harbison," Nolf said.

The woman's eyes passed suspiciously from Gideon to Nolf and back to Gideon. She addressed the tallest of the children. "Matthew, go fetch your pa."

Presently Henry Harbison came around the corner of the barn. He was a tall, rawboned man with broad shoulders and a big belly. His rolled-up sleeves exposed sinewy forearms covered with grime. Large hands dangled at the ends of his arms.

"Mr. Harbison," Gideon said, "I am Gideon Stoltz, the county sheriff."

Harbison made no move to approach or to shake hands.

"I'm sure you know that Rebecca Kreidler, who was living with your neighbors, died recently," Gideon continued. "Her body was found in a sinkhole on the Trautmanns' farm."

Harbison nodded. "I helped look for her when she went missing. I heard her body turned up in that sink."

"I am here to try to find out more about Mrs. Kreidler," Gideon said. "Did you know her?"

"Seen her here and there. Can't say I knowed her."

"Where did you see her?"

"She walked all over this valley. Down by the creek, up on the mountain. You might see her anywhere."

"Did she ever come onto your land?"

"A time or two."

"Why was that?"

"To pick plants."

"Did she ask your permission?"

Harbison shook his head. "Seems to me that woman did pretty much what she pleased. Leastwise she didn't bother asking before she went traipsing around on our ground."

"Where did she go?"

"Can't say for sure." He bobbed his head toward Mingo Mountain, the long forested ridge behind the farm, fencing in Sinking Valley on the north. "There's a patch of ginseng up there. I warned her off it."

"Did she leave it alone?"

"Far as I know she did."

"Pastor Nolf tells me you are a blacksmith."

"I make hinges and tools and such. I can shoe your horse." He added, in a proud tone, "I build a rifle now and then."

Gideon studied Harbison's face. It looked closed, suspicious, as if the man didn't want to give up too much in the way of information or opinion. Gideon saw that set of face a lot in Colerain County. Maybe it was because he was Dutch. Or maybe it was because people here didn't like anyone exercising authority over them, least of all a man half their age.

"I hear you are a good hunter," Gideon said.

"I keep us pretty well stocked with game. And I sell some in town." Harbison nodded at the tall son who had fetched him. "Matthew, too. I'm learning him to track and shoot. He is a tolerable shot. He knows them Dutch better'n I do"—another head bob, in the direction of the Trautmann farm. "Him and their boy Abe run together."

"Did you know Mrs. Kreidler, Matthew?" Gideon asked.

Matthew Harbison's face colored, and he looked down.

His father laughed. "Bet he wishes he could've knowed her. Little thing was pretty as a September peach."

"Such as boys will long for," Sadie Harbison added drily, then finished the couplet: "when they're hanging out of reach."

"I don't know how out of reach she was," Harbison said with a leer.

"Hold your tongue, Henry," his wife snapped. "That woman is dead and buried. You'd best hope she stays in her grave and don't come back to haunt us."

Gideon saw no reason to correct Sadie Harbison, but Rebecca Kreidler's body was not in a grave. Her skull was in a cabinet at Dr. Beecham's house, and the rest of her remains were in a covered barrel in the coroner's back yard.

A gray-haired woman came hobbling out of the house leaning on two canes. Gideon saw the halting movements of what appeared to be hugely swollen legs beneath her dress.

The woman said in a harsh voice, "That witch poisoned our dog."

"I doubt that, Mother," Henry Harbison said quickly.

Gideon lifted his hat.

"You're mannerly, for a sheriff." The old woman glared at her son, then rapped one of her canes against a cast-off rusted pail. "That woman was always pokin' around where she wasn't wanted. And I do say she was a witch."

"I talked to Mrs. Kreidler several times," Nolf said in his mild voice. "I saw no evidence that she was a witch."

"Of course you'd say that." The woman scowled at the pastor. "You Dutch stick together no matter what." She faced Gideon again. "That little viper come back here after Henry run her off. I was outside, settin' on that bench." She pointed her cane at a dilapidated wooden bench beneath a shade tree. "I told her, 'Show me what's in your poke.' She got her pretty little nose up in the air and said it weren't none of my business what she had in her sack.

"One of our dogs was with her. She said it had come up to her in the woods and followed her around, so she thought to bring it back to the house. I told her to get off our ground and never come back." The old woman brought her cane down hard. "Two days later, that dog was dead. It couldn't keep food down, and it crawled in under the corncrib and died there. I tell you, she poisoned it."

"Most likely it just took ill," Harbison said. "Might not even have been the same dog."

The old woman shook her head. "That witch was vexed at what I said to her, so she killed our dog. Lucky she didn't poison us."

"Do you have any specific reason to believe that Mrs. Kreidler poisoned your dog?" Gideon asked. "Did you see her give it any food?"

"No."

"Did you see her come back here?"

"Probably she come at night."

"You asked me about hunting," Harbison said to Gideon.

"There you go, changing the subject," the old woman cried out. "That's just like you, Henry Harbison. Now you will yarn on and on, and brag about all the wolves and panthers and bears you have slain."

Harbison ignored his mother's outburst. "I was fixing to invite these two men on a hunt," he said. "Tomorrow morning. We're getting a gang together to put on a ring hunt up in the Big Kettle. Maybe you heard about it already, Mr. Nolf."

"Yes," Nolf said.

"We'll make us some meat," Harbison said. "And we'll kill some varmints." His face darkened. "Last week a bear carried off one of Otto Ormsby's shoats. Otto didn't have a gun on him. That she-bear popped her teeth at him when he tried to run her off." Harbison looked at Gideon. "How about it, Sheriff? You come here armed, didn't you?"

Gideon figured that he could talk to a lot of people at the hunt and maybe learn more about Rebecca Kreidler. "Where do we meet?" he said.

Cease then trembling, fearing, sighing,
Death will break the sullen gloom . . .

Chapter 14

⸙

THEY STOOD AT FIRST LIGHT BENEATH TREES WHOSE BRANCHES interwove eighty feet overhead. Gideon counted more than sixty men, around half of them *Neigeboren* in their telltale homespuns with the single suspender across their chest. Most of the men carried guns; a few held spears, and one man had a pole with a bayonet lashed to its end. Gideon reckoned that the majority of the adult males in Sinking Valley had gathered here on the lip of the wooded hollow known as the Big Kettle.

Henry Harbison cradled a percussion lock rifle whose gleaming cherry stock was inlaid with a brass patch box and a silver moon and stars. His son Matthew had a rifle almost as long and slim as he was. Jonas Trautmann toted a nondescript flintlock, and his son Abraham had an even older and rustier gun. One man carried a shotgun with a flared muzzle; Gideon hoped the fellow was careful where he pointed that blunderbuss. Pastor Nolf held a battered Brown Bess with a cut-down stock, the kind of musket British troops had used during the Revolution. Gideon had the .45 caliber carbine from the jail's armory.

He spotted Andrew and James Rankin. Andrew was holding forth to a small group of men who listened to him intently. His son James stood with his rifle's buttstock on his boot, his hands resting on top of the barrel. When he saw Gideon looking at him, he straightened and frowned.

Harbison raised a brass horn and waved it in a circle. The talking ceased. "You'uns know what to do. Spread out, and when you hear the horn, start down in. Don't go too fast, keep your eye on the men either side of you, and stay in line as best you can. Call out every now and then but don't make too much noise—just enough to keep 'em moving and not so much that they run back through the line. And remember: no shooting till we get all the way to the bottom."

Harbison divided the men into two groups. Each group formed a line with their leaders facing in opposite directions. The men began walking, the two lines stringing themselves out along the edge of the Big Kettle.

Gideon followed a man wearing a hip-length smock. He let the man get far enough ahead that he could just see the pale smock bobbing out in front. On their right, the slope dropped down into the bowl-shaped valley, where daylight had yet to penetrate.

The air was cool and damp. A loud rushing came from overhead as a flock of wild pigeons took off from the trees; it sounded to Gideon as if a huge canvas tarpaulin had been suddenly ripped from the roof of the forest.

An owl hooted.

A raven sounded a series of metallic *tocks* that seemed to come from nowhere and everywhere.

Gideon startled at a loud snort followed by hooves thumping. A moment of silence, then more thumps as the unseen deer came down from its high bound and its hooves struck the earth again; then another moment of silence as it leaped farther down into the Big Kettle.

After a quarter hour, the pale smock in front of Gideon stopped. Gideon halted. He turned to face the Kettle.

Minutes passed. The light strengthened. Gideon found he could discern different shades of green on the leaves of chestnuts and maples and oaks. He tested the lock on his carbine by pulling the hammer back, then easing it down again. Once a week he and Alonzo practiced shooting mark at an ore pit outside of town. If he got an animal in his sights, he hoped he wouldn't miss.

Harbison's horn brayed in the distance.

The men started down into the Big Kettle. The slope was gentle at first. Then it steepened.

The man in the pale smock let out a yip. Another high-pitched cry came from Gideon's right, and another farther down the line.

He swung out wide to avoid an outcropping of rocks. Fighting through brush, he momentarily lost sight of the pale smock on his left and the other man on his right. But there could be no doubt in which direction to go: Down, past jackstrawed fallen hemlocks, their bark scaling off in ruddy sheets. Down, among head-high laurel whose wiry stems bent and whose glossy leaves rattled as he pushed past. Down, past twisted oaks smothered in wild grapevines, gray boulders blotched with dull green lichens and draped with viridian moss.

Faint calls came from the other side of the Kettle. Ahead of him, Gideon heard leaves rustling, twigs breaking, the heavy breathing of some beast.

He saw a flash of brown and instinctively raised the carbine. Then he remembered Harbison's admonition not to shoot until they reached the bottom. He lowered his rifle and resumed walking.

Gradually the slope leveled out, and they were at the bottom of the Kettle. All he could see in front of him were scores of black and brown tree trunks and thousands of green leaves. He startled at a sharp *crack* that echoed all around. Then a deep booming sound followed by the *slap-slap-slap* of buckshot tearing through foliage. He flinched at the thought of the lead balls streaking past.

A deer came running toward him and stopped abruptly. A buck, its tall, wide antlers covered with reddish-brown velvet. The buck flared its nostrils and twitched its ears. Gideon shouldered the carbine while thumbing the hammer back. He placed the gun's sights on the patch of white below the buck's chin. He took a breath and let some of it out and tightened his finger on the trigger. The hammer fell, the rifle roared, and the buttstock slammed into his shoulder. The buck bowled over backward. It lay in the brown leaf duff, its belly a dazzling white, its hind legs kicking. With trembling hands Gideon tipped the flask to pour powder down the gun's barrel. He rammed home the lead ball in its linen patch, primed the pan.

Shots banged from all directions. Cries and shouts. "Don't let 'em through!" "Get 'em!" "Kill 'em, kill 'em!" A big gray wolf sprinted from left to right—now in the open, now behind brush. As Gideon raised the carbine, the wolf turned and ran straight at him. Gideon could do no more than wave the gun as the wolf streaked past two steps away, pink tongue lolling over sharp white teeth, tawny eyes rimmed in white.

He heard a *boom* and the *thump* of a ball hitting flesh, then a loud bawl. A second later a huge black shape came hurtling toward him. He barely had time to cock the hammer. Holding the carbine at his hip, he pointed the muzzle at the onrushing shape and pulled the trigger. The gun bucked in his hands. The bear dropped its head. Its legs buckled.

Slowly the bear fell over onto one side. Blood poured from its mouth. Gideon smelled the tangy metallic scent of the bear's blood mingling with the acrid smell of burnt gunpowder. Heart pounding, he reloaded again. His head had begun throbbing with pain, and his stomach was jumpy.

He stepped around the dead bear. Fiery flashes erupted from one gun, then another. Smoke swirled. Men let out guttural cries as they lunged forward, beating down with their rifles' buttstocks or thrusting with their spears at the milling, darting animals—wolves and deer and wildcats and foxes. A *Neigeboren* man sank his spear into the side of a bear cub. The cub, the size of a small dog, squalled loudly. The man withdrew the spear and plunged it again.

Gideon stopped and stood panting. A wave of nausea swept over him, and he fell to his knees. At that moment he heard a sound like two hands clapped together above his head. Through watering eyes he saw a puff of smoke thirty paces away.

With a jolt he realized that what he'd heard was a ball whipping past over his head. He stared at the place the shot came from. The smoke thinned, revealing only featureless brush.

His stomach convulsed and he bent forward, vomit gushing from his mouth.

★★★

He knelt on the forest floor. Drew in a breath, wiped his mouth with the back of his hand. The shooting had ceased. Around him men were laughing, clapping one another on the back, using their pike poles and gun butts to prod and turn over carcasses.

He heard a jeering laugh. "Looks like the Dutch Sheriff can't stand the sight of blood."

Gideon put the carbine's buttstock on the ground and pushed himself upright.

James Rankin stood next to Henry Harbison. Rankin directed a sneering grin at Gideon.

"What's the matter, Sheriff?" he said loudly. "The killing get a little too hot for you?"

Harbison came up to Gideon. The big man stuck out his hand.

"You made one hell of a shot on that she-bear," Harbison said. "Dropped her in her tracks."

"What do you mean?" said Rankin, striding forward. "I killed that sow!"

Harbison barely glanced at Rankin. "You gut-shot her. I seen the dust fly off her hide." The big man kept pumping Gideon's hand. "That stock-killer would've got clean away if you hadn't shot her."

Men stopped what they were doing to listen.

"He killed a big buck, too." It was the man in the pale smock, the one Gideon had been following. "Right after we got down in the bottom."

A third man grinned. "That buck cartwheeled when the ball hit him." The man came up to Gideon and put out his hand. "You made a lot of meat, Sheriff." More men had gathered. "Where'd you learn to shoot like that?" "I'm damned glad you shot straight. I don't reckon that sow will drag off any more of my hogs."

James Rankin turned and stalked away.

Gideon swallowed down the bitter taste in his mouth. He thought about the ball that had gone screaming past his skull.

An errant shot loosed during the melee, aimed at some animal that had dashed between himself and the person in the brush?

Or had someone tried to kill him? He found himself strangely comforted by the thought. If someone wished him dead, it might mean that Rebecca Kreidler's killer wanted to prevent the sheriff from finding anything out. Which, of course, would mean that he, Gideon Stoltz, was not responsible for the woman's death.

He went to the patch of brush where he'd seen smoke from the shot. He pushed the branches aside and studied the ground. A few crushed ferns and scuff marks in the dirt. Nothing else.

Who had fired the shot? Could it have been James Rankin? Henry Harbison? Someone else?

All around him men were unsheathing knives and crouching over fallen animals. Before the hunt, Harbison had said the meat and hides would be shared equally.

The bear Gideon had killed was being skinned and quartered by three men. One of the men told Gideon that he would tote the heavy hide and the others would carry out the loin and the fore- and hindquarters.

Gideon went looking for the buck he had shot. After searching for a while, he spotted its white belly. He put down the carbine and took hold of the deer's antlers; cloaked in velvet, they felt soft and warm to the touch. He lifted the deer's head. His ball had entered the buck's neck just below the chin and exited at the rear, severing the spine.

He had never cleaned a deer but figured it could not be much different from what you did when you slaughtered a pig or beefed a cow. He rolled up his sleeves. With his knife he made a slit up the buck's belly. Intestines, paunch, and liver bulged from the cut. He reached inside and severed the deer's windpipe, then cut the organs free. They slumped out of the body cavity and lay glistening and steaming on the ground.

"Did you kill this deer?"

He looked up. Nolf stood over him. It was the first he had seen of the pastor since the two lines of men had separated to surround the Big Kettle.

Nolf gave a low whistle. "Lots of good *haschfleesch*. We'll be eating venison for days. Here, I will help you drag him." A rope was wound around Nolf's waist. He untied it, then knotted it around the buck's neck. The pastor straightened and leaned into the rope to test the weight. He whistled again. Then, putting one foot in front of the other, he began to pull the deer up the slope.

Gideon picked up Nolf's musket. With the carbine in his other hand, he walked beside his companion.

"You must be a good shot." Nolf smiled. "Someone told me you also killed a bear. All I managed to do was miss."

After about ten minutes the pastor stopped, drew a kerchief from his pocket, and mopped his face. Gideon handed the rifles to Nolf and prepared to take his turn dragging.

Before they resumed climbing, he looked down into the Big Kettle. Green and hazy in the morning light, to all appearances the hollow was a peaceful, untrammeled place. Yet an hour ago it had roiled with violence and bloodshed and rage—rage against the wild beasts, perhaps against the forest itself, the wilderness that made men and their efforts seem puny and futile.

Gideon thought again about the ball that had whipped past his skull. Probably just an accident. He'd been lucky. Lucky that someone was not now dragging his corpse out of the forest, to be carted back to Adamant and presented, stinking and bloated, to his wife.

He wondered if True would care.

★★★

They divided the meat and hides in the spot where they had gathered to begin the hunt. Harbison made a show of giving Gideon the hide of the big bear and recounting again the shot Gideon had made to kill the charging bruin. After that, Gideon asked if he could speak to the group.

"I won't take much of your time," he said. "As most of you know, I am the sheriff of this county, and I have come to Sinking Valley to learn about a woman who died here several weeks ago. Her name was Rebecca Kreidler. At the time of her death, she was living on the farm of Jonas Trautmann."

He scanned the faces turned toward his. Jonas Trautmann looked sober. James Rankin scowled. Other visages bore expressions of curiosity or that much-seen guardedness. Gideon noticed no one who appeared truly ill at ease, nor any man who failed to meet his gaze.

"If any of you know anything about Rebecca Kreidler, I want to talk to you. Things she might have done or said, places she went, people she spent time with."

"I heard she poisoned herself by accident," a *Neigeboren* man said.

"I have heard that, too," Gideon replied. "It may be true. However, as sheriff, I serve the state's attorney, and he has directed me to gather as much information as I can."

A gruff voice spoke. "You must figure someone killed her, to come all the way back here and snoop around."

"Not necessarily," Gideon said. "If any of you have anything you wish to tell me, I am staying at the house of Pastor Nolf at the west end of the valley. I will also be riding around, and I may visit you where you live."

Afterward, no one came to talk with him. He reckoned they all wanted to get their meat home, to be rubbed with salt and hung up in smokehouses, the pelts fleshed out and laced to stretchers or nailed to walls to cure.

Two wagons waited on the faint trace leading away from the Big Kettle. The men loaded the meat and hides and the wagons trundled off. Gideon and Nolf walked with the others down off the mountain.

It was mid-afternoon by the time they reached the pastor's house. They salted meat and hung it in Nolf's smokehouse. They flensed the bear hide and managed to stretch it out and secure it to the side of Nolf's small barn. Gideon was worn out. He barely had enough energy to eat a light supper, and was asleep in bed before the sun went down.

Soon my spirit, flutt'ring, flying,
Shall be borne beyond the tomb

Chapter 15

⸺⸱⸻

THE NEXT MORNING GIDEON SADDLED MAUDE AND RODE TO THE
Trautmann farm. He felt considerably improved: his head didn't
throb as fiercely, and his stomach wasn't queasy. The filmy, cobwebby
thing still lurked in the upper right corner of his vision, but it seemed
to have gotten smaller and fainter—or maybe he was just used to it
and it didn't bother him as much.

He decided to question the Trautmann family members separately.
He asked that two chairs be placed outside again under the elm in the
same patch of shade where he had sat resting, recovering from nausea
and lightheadedness, on the oppressively hot day when he and Alonzo
had come to the valley and collected Rebecca Kreidler's remains.

The first person he talked to was Elisabeth, the eldest daughter.
"How did you feel about your aunt coming to live with you?"
Gideon asked.

Elisabeth Trautmann took off her bonnet and placed it in her lap.
Her blonde hair was braided behind her head. She lifted her comely
face and regarded Gideon, seated in the other chair four feet away.
With an innocent look, Elisabeth said, "How did I feel about having
a murderer come live with us?"

"Rebecca was convicted of manslaughter, not murder. There's a
difference."

Elisabeth shrugged. "I guess she had to live somewhere."

"Did you know Frau Kreidler before your family came here to
Sinking Valley?"

"I knew her, but not well. She is—she was—much older than I am."

"How old was Frau Kreidler?"

"I don't know exactly. I think about thirty years old."

"And you are . . . ?"

"Eighteen."

Eighteen and unmarried, Gideon thought. Even though Elisabeth Trautmann was a beautiful young woman.

"When your aunt came here," he said, "did you enjoy learning from her? How to make those brooms she sold? Or how to use plants to cure sickness?"

"I have no interest in those things."

"Did you ever go with her to gather plants?"

"No."

"When I came here in April, I saw the two of you picking plants along the road."

"Spring greens. For food. I never went with her when she picked those other plants, the ones she used for medicine. Anyway, I think she wanted to be alone."

"Your brother called her a *hex* the last time I was here. Others have said she was a *braucher*. Was she a witch, or was she a healer?"

Elisabeth remained silent.

"Or was she neither?" Gideon asked.

"Why don't you ask the people who called her those things?"

"I will. I would also like your opinion."

"She seemed to know a lot about plants. She made them into poultices and salves. She used them to make tea. Some of them she ate." Elisabeth sniffed. "Maybe she didn't know as much about plants as she thought she did."

"You believe, like the others, that she died from accidentally eating a poisonous plant?"

"Of course," Elisabeth said without hesitating.

"What kinds of conditions did she treat with plants?"

Elisabeth looked off to the one side. "Female conditions."

The subject made him uncomfortable, but he pressed her. "Please explain."

A red flush covered Elisabeth's cheeks. "I'd rather not."

"Did she ever give you anything to treat a female condition?"

The flush became deeper and more general on the young woman's face. She looked up with a defiant expression. "No."

"Did you see your aunt the day she died?"

"Probably."

"Did you see her on the night she died?"

"No."

"Is there anything else you want to tell me?"

Elisabeth looked at him with her wide-set blue eyes. "There was something my aunt had—a cross made of silver. It was very beautiful."

"A piece of jewelry?"

Elisabeth nodded. "She wore it on a chain around her neck. It has a dark stone in the center, where the arms of the cross come together. A red stone. A ruby, I think."

"How big is this cross?"

She held her fingers about two inches apart. "This tall. The silver had vines and flowers carved into it. Mother and I looked for it in the bakehouse, but we could not find it. The cross was not with her body."

"Maybe it's still in the sinkhole."

"Father and Abe looked all around where she lay. They would have found it."

"I take it you want the cross for yourself."

The young woman blushed again.

"That's all for now," Gideon said. "Please tell your brother to come out."

Elisabeth Trautmann rose and crossed the yard toward the stone house, her back straight, her nose in the air.

As he sat waiting, Gideon tried to remember what had happened between himself and Rebecca Kreidler. Why had he gone to visit her? He feared he knew the answer. And the timing: it was frightening to think that he had seen the woman so soon before her death. Maybe even on the night of her death.

A shiver ran through him. Again he asked himself, *Did I kill her? Drive nails into her body? Dispose of her corpse in a sinkhole I didn't even know existed?*

Abraham Trautmann coughed, and Gideon looked up.

The young man seated himself in the other chair.

Gideon tried to order his thoughts. He greeted the Trautmanns' eldest son, then said, "I understand you are quite a hunter."

Abraham smiled shyly. "Who told you that?"

"Henry Harbison. He said that you and his son Matthew range around in the woods together."

"Whenever we can get away from work, Matt and I go out and see what we can shoot or trap." Abraham was grinning now. "I saw you kill that bear in the Big Kettle. You didn't even aim. You just pointed your gun, and it spouted fire, and that sow fell down dead."

"Yes, well. I was lucky. Did you shoot anything?"

"I shot a panther! The pelt's not so thick, since it's summer, but it was a big cat. We nailed its hide to the corncrib. Do you want to see it?"

Gideon wondered if Abraham had witnessed the shot that sent a ball screeching past his head. Then he wondered if the Trautmanns' eldest son had fired the shot himself. Looking across at the young man's eager, open face, he didn't believe it.

"Congratulations," Gideon said. "You probably know there's a twelve-dollar bounty on a panther. Same as for a wolf. You need to bring the scalp with the ears on it to the jail." He straightened in his chair. "Last week, when my deputy and I came to get Frau Kreidler's body, twice you referred to her as a *hex*. Why?"

"I don't know."

"There must be some reason."

Abraham shrugged. "She was different."

"How so?"

"She would go off by herself, wander around. Talking to herself, or maybe talking to the plants. Like she was *verrickt*, you know? Touched in the head. Matt and I saw her in the woods all the time."

"Gathering plants?"

"Yes."

"Talking to plants?"

"That's what it looked like. Muttering and mumbling."

"So you called her a witch."

"Matt's grandma said she was one—sometimes she'd ask me, 'Why do you Dutch let that witch live with you?' So Matt and I started calling her that. It was sort of a joke between us."

"Did you ever hear of her casting spells or putting a curse on anyone?"

Abe shook his head. "I don't believe in *hexerei*. Yes, I called her a witch, but it didn't mean anything."

"How well did you know your aunt?"

"I didn't have much to do with her. She worked with the women, and in the bakehouse. I work in the fields and the barn."

"Frau Kreidler killed your mother's brother. What do you think about that?"

"I wish it hadn't happened."

"Did you hate her for killing your uncle?"

"My uncle—he was not an easy man to get along with."

"Did anyone hate her for killing John Kreidler?"

"She served her prison time." Abraham blanked his face, as if that settled everything.

"Do you know of anyone who might have wished to harm her?"

Abe's eyebrows rose. "Not everyone liked her, but I don't think anyone wanted to kill her."

"Who didn't like her?"

Abe squirmed in his chair. "She never joined the church. That upset some people."

"I'm thinking about something more personal and specific than not joining the church," Gideon said. "Tell me who didn't like Rebecca Kreidler."

"The Harbisons didn't like her."

"Because she went on their land without permission. I was told she stopped doing that after she was warned off."

Abe gave a half-nod. "I guess so."

"Anyone else?"

"James Rankin was sweet on her," Abraham said. "Before she came here, James spent a lot of time with my sister. Elisabeth was not happy with our *aendi* when James started looking at Rebecca more than at her. But Elisabeth would never have done anything to hurt her."

"James Rankin courted your sister? What did your parents think of that?"

"They didn't know. He wasn't really courting her."

"Is your sister in love with James Rankin? He doesn't belong to your church."

"No, he doesn't," Abe said. "I don't know if she loves him or not. Maybe she just likes to flirt with him."

To Gideon it sounded as if Abe wasn't quite as pious as the *Neigeboren* wanted their young people to be. Nor was Elisabeth.

"So your sister was displeased with your aunt because she attracted James," Gideon said.

"I don't think she *tried* to attract him. She gave him some salve for a cut his horse had gotten. Other than that, I don't think she paid much attention to him. It was more the other way around." Abraham ran his finger around inside his collar. "I guess he thought she was beautiful. Lots of men did."

Gideon decided to change the subject. "Tell me again how you found her body."

Abe repeated the story he had told earlier. How his dog brought home the decomposed hand; how he followed the dog back to the sinkhole and discovered the corpse; how he fetched his father and together they used hay forks to pick up the remains.

"All right," Gideon said. "You can go now. Though I may want to talk to you again later."

Abraham got up, shook hands with Gideon, and left.

Gideon looked at the house. Frau Trautmann should be coming out next. No doubt the farmwife would have harbored at least some hard feelings toward her sister-in-law, who, after all, had killed her husband, Frau Trautmann's brother—although Frau Trautmann had freely admitted that John Kreidler had been a violent, abusive man.

He stood up and stretched. He had arranged to interview the family in this order: first, Jonas Trautmann. Gideon had confirmed his opinion that the farmer was basically a simple man who wanted others to like him, even though he wasn't above bending the rules a bit—such as farming a piece of ground he didn't own. Jonas had imparted no new information to add to Gideon's understanding of Frau Kreidler's situation or her death. Next, Gideon had questioned Elisabeth Trautmann, then her brother Abe. The younger children— six of them—Gideon had decided he didn't need to talk to.

Suddenly a memory flooded his mind, so vivid that he almost lived it. *He is clutching a hammer in his hand. He brings the hammer down hard, striking a nail on its head, BANG. He is full of anger. He strikes with the hammer again and again, driving the nail deeper with each blow.*

The memory dimmed and faded. Gideon rubbed his hands harshly across his face. Why had he been pounding in that nail? What was he pounding it into? He thought hard but couldn't bring the memory back. Maybe it was nothing. Maybe it hadn't even happened.

He looked up as Frau Trautmann approached. She wore a dark blue dress, her steps calm and unhurried, her eyes level, her posture erect.

Gideon forced himself to smile at her. He thought the smile she returned looked forced as well. Perhaps out of annoyance at having to interrupt her workday to be questioned by the sheriff. Or out of nervousness or guilt?

He held the chair for her as she sat, then reseated himself across from her.

"Thank you for agreeing to talk with me," he said, "and for letting me speak with your daughter and your son. I know this is not convenient, and not pleasant for you or your family. But I have to ask these questions. The state's attorney wants to be absolutely certain about how your sister-in-law died."

"I think it is very clear how Rebecca died," Frau Trautmann said.

Gideon lifted his hand and opened his palm, as if to say "Go on."

The farmwife looked off across the hayfield. "Rebecca picked a plant and ate it for some reason. It turned out to be the poisonous kind, and it killed her. I feel very sorry for my sister-in-law."

It sounded rote to Gideon. He decided to ask something that might startle the woman. "Do you think Rebecca was justified in killing your brother John?"

Frau Trautmann jerked her face back, her eyes wide. "I . . . I don't know. The Bible says 'Thou shalt not kill.'"

"Did you forgive her for what she did?"

Frau Trautmann blinked. "We are supposed to forgive others—so that our heavenly Father will forgive our own trespasses."

"Indeed." Gideon drummed his fingers against his leg. "Did you go to Rebecca's trial, when she was convicted for killing your brother?"

"There was no trial, just a hearing before a judge. She said she was guilty."

"Did you attend the hearing?"

"No. I had things to do on the farm and with the children. And I didn't want to see her then."

"Did you visit her while she was in prison?"

"They don't allow visitors."

"Of course, I forgot. Would you have gone if it was allowed?"

"It would have been far to go—all the way to Philadelphia. I don't know that I could have left the farm and the children."

"When my deputy and I came to get her body, you mentioned that you were the first person to notice that Rebecca had gone missing—when she didn't turn up in the morning to help you in the garden."

"Yes."

"And you believe she died the night before that?"

"I do now. At first I thought she had just gone away."

"She had worked with you in the garden the previous day, correct?"

"Yes."

"Did you see her that evening?"

"No. It was late afternoon when I saw her for the last time. In the evening I was in the house, cooking and serving supper, cleaning up afterward, and putting the young ones to bed. Then I went to bed myself."

"Rebecca did not eat at your table?"

"Not often. And not on the night she died."

"She ate by herself?"

"She seemed to prefer it."

"Was that all right with you?"

"It didn't matter to me where she ate. Sometimes she wanted to be alone. She had been through so much pain and sorrow. I think her time in prison . . . it made her strange."

"How so?"

"At times, I would say something and she wouldn't seem to hear me. She wouldn't answer back. Or she would just start talking about something completely different. Not even talking to me, it seemed like. Talking to herself, or someone else."

"What kinds of things did she say?"

"They didn't make sense. Sometimes she seemed to be speaking to someone named 'Molly.' I remember her crying out once, saying, 'My wings are broke, I can't fly.' It didn't even sound like her own voice speaking."

"How did that make you feel?"

"It made me afraid. Another time we were in the bakehouse rolling out the dough. She put down the rolling pin. She held on to the table and started swaying. I thought she was going to faint. Then she started pinching the back of her hand. Talking to herself, the words tumbling out. I tried to calm her, get her to stop. Finally I got her to sit down in the chair. I held her by the shoulders and talked to her until she would look at me. Then she seemed to come out of it. Like waking up from a bad dream."

"Did she ever tell you what it had been like, to be in prison?"

Maria shook her head. "She never talked about the past."

"She lived alone in the bakehouse. Whose decision was that?"

"Jonas decided it. We didn't have room in the house. And I didn't want her with the children."

"Because . . . ?"

"Because of what she had done."

"You mean killing your brother?"

"Yes."

"Were you afraid she might harm you or your children?"

"No, I didn't think that."

"Day to day, how often did you see Frau Kreidler?"

"Almost every day. She helped with whatever we were doing, indoors or out. Sometimes she went off on her own and gathered plants. And in the evenings she stayed in the bakehouse making her brooms. The money she got for them, she gave to Jonas to pay for living here."

"Did she ever receive visitors in the bakehouse?"

Maria shook her head. "Not that I am aware."

"She was a widow, and still of marriageable age. One would think some of the men hereabouts might have courted her."

"If they wanted to do that, they would have come and talked to my husband first. As far as I know, no one asked Jonas if they could court Rebecca."

"I heard that James Rankin, your neighbor's son, was attracted to her."

"I don't know about that."

"Did James Rankin also court your daughter Elisabeth?" he said.

Frau Trautmann shook her head. "We would not permit that. The Rankins, they have a different religion from ours." She swallowed. "Why do you bring up these things? I don't see that they have anything to do with Rebecca poisoning herself."

"As sheriff, I have to follow certain procedures," Gideon said. "Do you know why your sister-in-law didn't join the church?"

"I hoped she would join. I hoped she would humble herself and become one of us. But she wouldn't do that."

"Could she have poisoned herself on purpose? Taken her own life?"

"I have asked myself that question many times. I don't know the answer, but I think it is possible."

"You said you found where she had been sick inside the bakehouse."

"Yes."

"And you cleaned it up."

"Yes."

"Was there anything strange in the vomit?"

"I don't recall anything."

"Any plant matter?"

"I don't remember."

"What do you remember?"

"A chair had been knocked over. Some of the baking things were scattered about, like she had thrashed around after poisoning herself."

"Do you know what Rebecca ate on the night before she went missing?"

"I don't know that."

Gideon noticed that tiny beads of perspiration had formed on Frau Trautmann's upper lip. It was a hot day; he was sweating himself.

"Was Rebecca taking any of her own preparations?" he asked. "For an illness, or for her general health?"

"I don't know."

Gideon asked the same question he had posed to the Trautmanns' daughter. "Did she ever give you one of her potions to cure any female condition or complaint?"

Like her daughter, Frau Trautmann blushed and would not meet his eyes. As Elisabeth had done, she replied, "No."

"Are you sure about that?"

"Yes, I am sure."

"Rebecca must have talked to you about the plants she picked and used."

"No."

"Did she ever mention dangerous plants, ones that must be avoided?"

The farmwife shook her head.

"So you have no idea what she might have eaten when she poisoned herself? When she became so sick that she vomited, and thrashed around in the bakehouse, and wandered all the way up across that big hayfield and went down into the sinkhole and died there?"

Frau Trautmann raised her hands with their palms up and let them fall slowly to her lap. Sorrow lay on her face. She used her apron hem to wipe perspiration off her cheeks and upper lip. "We never talked about plants. I don't know what could have killed her."

"Does anyone around here know about medicinal plants?"

"I know a little. I grow in the garden some herbs. *Raude, grodebalsem, kamille, warmet.*"

Rue, sage, chamomile, wormwood. Common plants for home remedies. Gideon's own mother had grown and used those herbs.

"Does anyone know more than you?" he asked. "Who do the *Deitsch* folk here in the valley turn to when they get sick or need help?"

She hesitated, then said, "Sometimes people go to Pastor Nolf."

★★★

Gideon trudged up through the hayfield. No breeze to relieve the heat. He had to stop now and then to catch his breath and fight off dizziness. The sky was white, without depth or definition. A dead sky, alienating in some strange way. On one of his pauses, Gideon looked down at the Trautmanns' house and barn and outbuildings: springhouse, corncrib, wagon shed, woodshed, chicken coop, pig sty, smokehouse—a good, self-sufficient, carefully kept *Deitsch* farm— and at the stone-built bakehouse where, until three weeks ago, Rebecca Kreidler had lived.

On one side of the Trautmann farm, separated from it by a stretch of forest, lay the tired weedy acres owned by Henry Harbison; on the other side, also beyond a forested tract, was the Rankins' prosperous farm, which included a gristmill.

The view from the high field revealed Mingo Mountain to the north and Dark Mountain to the south, the two parallel forested ridges that fenced in Sinking Valley. The ridges merged at the west end of the valley in a broad uplift. At the eastern end of the valley, barely visible through the haze, the ridges also ran into one another, a rugged terrain that included the Big Kettle.

He made his way to the sinkhole. He stared down into it. Weeds and vines and briars and shrubs and spindly trees cloaked the steep slope. Plants occupied every inch of the declivity, thousands and thousands of them, in their scores if not their hundreds of kinds. Heat rose from the depression like the breath of some huge beast. A faint trail led down through the greenery to the spot where the body had been found—the path down which, so the people here wanted him to believe, Rebecca Kreidler had made her agonized way before collapsing and dying.

Why was there a trail into the sinkhole? Had animals made it? Had humans ever followed it? If so, for what purpose?

Why hadn't the people searched here when trying to find Rebecca?

When questioning the Trautmanns, he had felt that both Maria and her daughter Elisabeth knew more about Rebecca than they were willing to say. Maybe they relied on her knowledge of plants to deal with embarrassing or life-swerving situations. Even he knew that certain plants could be used to start a woman's monthly bleeding if she was overdue. Some plants could cause a pregnant woman to miscarry.

Gideon thought again about the nails that had been driven into Rebecca Kreidler's body. Either when she was alive, or when she was dead. Driven into her living body with great cruelty and perhaps a burning rage, or driven into her corpse with callous indifference.

She appeared again in his mind, the beautiful oval face with its pale clear skin, the almond-shaped eyes below fine arching eyebrows, thick auburn hair extending back from a widow's peak—with a sense of shame, he realized he could recall Rebecca's visage more clearly than he could summon up the face of his own wife, True.

He could not deny that Rebecca had attracted him greatly. That he had felt for her a fierce and perhaps irresistible lust. What had happened between them in the bakehouse? Had she taken him into her bed? Or had she spurned his advances, sent him away—that would explain why he'd been so angry during his drunken ride back to town.

Should he wonder if, because of that rejection, he had killed her? Driven nails into her? It seemed so utterly impossible.

He searched for that memory again, of himself driving nails into something—but couldn't connect with it. Everything in his brain seemed cloudy and gray.

Tension gripped his guts. He tried to relax by breathing in deeply, then letting the air flow out in a long whispered exhalation. His head had begun throbbing again. And that *verdammt* cobwebby thing was hovering there in his vision.

He focused on the northwest horizon. On the far side of Mingo Mountain, Adamant lay in its broad valley.

He had been gone from True for two days. Was she keeping herself fed? Or was she lying in bed, sunk in despair?

A thought entered his mind, one he'd been staving off ever since he had ridden off to Sinking Valley.

Maybe True had done something to herself. Something desperate, something that couldn't be remedied. He should go back home, go to his dear wife, make sure she was well.

But he couldn't abandon what he was doing here. Not yet.

He hadn't learned much. Yet he felt strongly that people were holding back, purposely telling him nothing he didn't already know—and maybe lying to him.

He looked back into the sink. He stared at the indifferent seethe of plant life. The sinkhole was a green hell. A place to get lost in. A place to hide a body in.

Like one alone I seem to be,
Oh, is there any one like me?

Chapter 16

———⚬⚬⚬———

Sinking Valley, Midday, July 17, 1836

BETTER IF SHE'D BEEN A MONSTER. YOU SAW THEM IN PHILADELPHIA and Lancaster, even in the small town where Rebecca had grown up and where she went to live with her mother after they let her out of prison.

When monsters left their houses they hid their faces behind scarves and shawls, with only their shame-filled eyes peering out. If they uncovered themselves, children screeched and ran and adults shrank back or turned away.

The monsters were men and women. Some had purple growths sprouting like roosters' combs from their foreheads or mushrooming out from their cheeks or chins. Some had clefts reaching upward from their mouths, livid slits from which spittle roped down. Some had faces cratered and disfigured with pockmarks and scars.

She knew a monster. Frau Schuster lived next door to Rebecca's family. One day when she was cooking, an ember popped out of the hearth, skittered across the floor, and touched her petticoat's hem. Flames raced upward and turned her into a twirling, screaming torch. The flames burned her clothes off and melted the skin on her face and neck. She must have wished a thousand times that she had died. But she lived, a monster formed by fire. When Rebecca was little, she saw Frau Schuster once without her shawl. Her mouth was a red-rimmed hole with white pegs of teeth pointing in all directions. Glossy pink skin banded her chin to her neck so that her head was pulled down and sideways. She looked at Rebecca through eyes that had no lids.

Rebecca screamed and ran.

She had never burned herself like Frau Schuster. She had never come down with the smallpox or sprouted tumors or developed a crusty rash.

No. Her curse was that she was small and pretty and drew the awareness of men like a fledgling *schpetzli* catches the eye of a hawk. Men who were fathers and husbands and sons. Shopkeepers and farmers and blacksmiths and preachers. Innkeepers and constables. Men who smiled at her, who whispered sweet words as they edged near.

She had thought their attentions would end when she married John. For a while, her husband had been polite and respectful, and she believed that, as a proper *hausfrau*, with a child growing in her womb, her time of being harassed by men had ended. John said he would take care of her forever. But then he started drinking. She didn't know why. Maybe he was afraid that he couldn't provide for a family. Maybe he got tired of her, or didn't like the way the child changed how she looked. His drinking got worse. It brought out the suspiciousness and cruelty in his heart. Once, in his cups, he accused her of inviting other men's attentions. *The way you cock your head at them*, he said. He grabbed her by the arm. *The way you smile, the way you stick your* diddies *out.* He swore that the child she was carrying was not his; she must have gotten pregnant by some other man. She pleaded, saying she had only been with him. He held her by the arm and balled up his other hand and hit her in the stomach. Hit her hard. Again. He threw her down on the floor and stormed out of the house. She vomited and wept and bled from between her legs, and there was no one to help her when she struggled out to the privy and crouched over the stinking hole and felt a great rending inside her. After, she used her underskirt to stanch the bleeding. She never knew if it would have been a boy or a girl. The notion formed in her mind that if it had been a girl, if it would have grown up to become a small, slender, *wunnerschee* woman, then it was lucky it had never been born.

That night she lay alone in bed. Thinking how she would stick a knife on him. Put poison in his food. Wait until he wasn't looking and crush his skull with a hammer.

In the end, it hadn't been difficult. He had slapped her across the face for some offense, then turned to go down into the cellar for a jug. Without thinking about it, she shoved him from behind. He tumbled headfirst down the steps. She stood at the top, watching. Down there in the dim light he lay with his head in the dirt at an odd angle. His eyes half open, his mouth ajar. He seemed to be looking up at her. She stared at him for a long while. He didn't blink. She could tell that he was no longer breathing. She walked down the steps and spat in his face.

Now she had come to this new place, Sinking Valley. She could go out in the woods and gather plants, the ones Old Molly had shown her. She could be by herself, alone with her thoughts and memories and with the *nachteil* if it came to visit her. Then the boy from the next farm happened by. His horse had a cut. She gave him some salve from the *schwarzwatzel*, the plant the English called comfrey. Something Old Molly had shown her, how to mix the leaves with honey to make a healing salve. After that, the boy came often. He asked her to go walking with him. She should have refused, but she was afraid to do that; she didn't want to anger him. It would be all right, would it not, just to go for a walk? As they strolled, the boy bragged about himself, his family's farm with its profitable gristmill, how rich he would become. He made little quips to display his wit. He walked close to her and let his hip graze hers. His elbow touched her side, her breast. He stopped and turned to her, smiling, and took her in his arms. He tried to kiss her. She pulled back and turned her face away. She didn't speak harshly to him or demand that he leave her alone, because she was afraid.

There were others, too, in this community of people who considered themselves to be pious and "newborn"—men who looked at her in the same avid way. Because she had a pretty face. Because she was small and slender and *wunnerschee*. Because men always did that.

The first time she had seen the young sheriff, she was with Elisabeth. In the spring, in the month of April, not long after she had come to her sister-in-law's farm. She and Elisabeth had been gathering *bettseecher* and *pokbeer*, the new greens pushing up along the lane. Rebecca felt the anger and resentment rolling off her niece as the girl looked at her with narrowed eyes, muttered under her breath, snicked her knife through a sprout and tossed it backhanded into the basket.

The sheriff rode up on his horse. He looked down on them. The way he stared made her legs feel like broomstraws. She was sure he had come to arrest her. He must have learned about the fire at the tavern. He would carry her off to jail, and then they would put her on trial for arson, or for murder if someone had died in the fire. If they didn't hang her, they would take her in the windowless coach to the big penitentiary, back to the cold stone floors, the thick iron doors, the long days of silence. They would lock her away for the rest of her life.

But the sheriff had not come for her on that spring day. He was there to speak with her brother-in-law Jonas.

She had seen the young sheriff again just two days ago. She'd gone in to town with her brooms. A crisp blue-sky day. The kind of late summer day when you could almost believe the world was a benign and welcoming place. She rode in the back of the wagon; Jonas drove, and Maria sat next to him, turning around now and then to chat. Elisabeth had been left at home, sulking, taking care of the young ones.

The wagon followed the narrow bumpy road up and over the mountain and into the broad valley. Past deep woods, brushlands, an ore pit, farms. Finally they came to the town—she had found it very different from the towns back home, where shops and stores and houses shared walls between them, lining the well-traveled streets, with tall spreading trees to provide shade. Adamant was raw and dirty. It sprawled over several hills from which the trees had been cut. It was full of people and livestock and loud sounds and sharp smells. A big stone schoolhouse sat on one hill; a cemetery covered another hill; the courthouse with its copper roof stood at the foot of a third hill, and a building that looked like a jail sat higher up on that same hill.

Jonas left her off, and he and Maria drove on. She was about to take her brooms in to the dry goods store when the young sheriff came up to her, and her heart flailed in her breast because she knew that this time he would surely arrest her. But it turned out he was just like the others. He wanted to draw near to her. He wanted to see if she would welcome and return the ardor that glowed from his face. She reacted in the only way that she believed might ensure her safety—she tried to make herself small. She looked down and said no more than was needed. She tried to be pleasant without flirting. She wanted the encounter to end quickly and without furtherance. The sheriff was hardly older than a boy, but she could see that he was strong and powerful, even if he didn't realize it. She wanted to flee, but she kept her feet planted and hoped it looked like she was paying polite attention as he talked, her heart pounding and her stomach churning all the while. Finally he bought a broom from her. He said something about how he rode around the county, and how he sometimes came to Sinking Valley. Then he left her there in front of the store. She hoped it would be the last time she would see him. All she wanted was to go back to Sinking Valley and be alone.

But a short time later he was standing outside in the darkness, tapping on the bakehouse door.

I'm fettered and chained up in clay;
I struggle and pant to be free

Chapter 17

———⊶∞⊷———

TRUE LAY IN BED AS LIGHT SLOWLY FILLED THE ROOM. SHE HAD tossed and turned most of the night before falling asleep toward morning—a sleep that seemed no more restorative than her sweating wakeful hours wrestling with the sheets.

Outside, someone split wood for a morning fire. She heard the *thump-thump-thump* of a butter churn.

Her body ached. Her brain felt sodden. Something dark clotted in her head behind her eyes.

She considered her own death. An event perhaps not so far off. The idea gusted over her that she could make the pain go away. She could go into the kitchen right now, take up a knife, and plunge it into her breast.

She clutched the sheet. The very notion that she would have such a thought made her heart flutter in her chest.

Gideon wasn't here. Away on sheriff's business. Why had he abandoned her, left her all alone?

Suddenly she thirsted to look at something beautiful. The souvenir card that her mother had brought to her, the picture of a woman dressed in green, borne aloft beneath a gold-and-blue balloon. Her mother had thought of her, cared enough for her, to walk all the way from Panther and give her the card.

She rolled her legs out of the bed. When her feet hit the floor, it felt like what little energy she possessed drained down through them, through the floor and into the mud beneath the house. The cold mud that was slowly sucking her down.

The card, where was the card? The last she remembered seeing it, it was on the small table outside the bedroom. Clumsily she stood. One step at a time, she lumbered across the floor. She grabbed the doorjamb to hold herself up. The card wasn't on the table. She shot her eyes around. Someone had stolen it. Someone had come into the house and stolen the card, the beautiful card. She felt filled with despair. Yet she could not muster enough anger to curse the thief.

She had to use the outhouse.

She needed to feed the dog.

She made her stumbling way to the kitchen. Looked around for the card. It wasn't there. Maybe she'd burned it on the hearth. No, she hadn't had a fire in days.

A knife lay on the counter. Its handle was made of little rings of polished leather, and its blade was long and thin. Gideon kept it razor sharp. She began to tremble. She turned away so she couldn't see the knife. She wrenched the door open and ran out into the back yard, into stifling heat.

Old Dick was happy to see her. It melted her heart to watch him shake his head and twist his body and lash his tail. She sat down with him and held him close. The red setter pressed against her, whimpering, washing her face with his tongue. "You poor thing," she said. "You poor, poor thing."

She unhooked him from his chain. He followed her, tried to crowd inside the backhouse with her.

In the heat the privy stank to high heaven. It needed hearth ashes dumped down the hole, but she was too weary for that.

When she finished, she went back into the kitchen. Old Dick came, too. She thought she would give him the scraps from last night's meal. Mrs. Sayers had brought ham and beans and cornbread. True figured she'd cut the rest of the ham off the bone and feed it to the dog.

She reached for the knife on the counter, then pulled her hand back as if the blade spouted flame. She edged sideways until the ham bone on its platter lay between herself and the knife. She grabbed the bone, threw it on the floor. Old Dick pounced.

She returned to the bedroom. She had to find the souvenir card. She got down on her hands and knees and looked under the bed. Only dust and dirt there. She struggled back up and checked the bed itself. One corner of the card poked out from under the sheet like a pale blue pond in a snowfield.

She snatched the card. Sat down on the bed and stared at the woman in green occupying the basket beneath the balloon. Birds flew all around the woman as she was borne aloft by the beautiful balloon carrying her off into the heavens.

One halting step, then another. Old Dick hung back, then came up with her, bumping her leg with his shoulder and wagging his tail and looking up at her as they went.

Somehow she had managed to get out of her shift and put on a dress and walk through the kitchen without looking at the knife and go out the door with Old Dick and shut it behind them and continue on into the street, where she hadn't ventured in weeks.

One step, and another. Her breath was short. She had to stop and rest. She took the card out of her skirt's front pocket, held it in a trembling hand, and looked at it. Put it back again.

One block, another block, struggling in the heat. She realized she hadn't put on her shoes. She passed people who seemed not to see her and others who stared at her and one person who spoke her name, but she kept on going, trying to hold her destination in mind. On and on she went. There. The barn, big and red. On its ridge it had, incongruously, a fat copper pig as a weathervane instead of a stylish trotting horse. The barn had a limestone lower level where they kept the horses at night. A long wagon shed branched off at an angle. The wagon that Judge Biddle had willed to Gideon would be in the shed. The gelding that Judge Biddle had willed to Gideon would be in the dirt lot along with the other horses. She decided not to take the wagon for the simple reason that she didn't know how to drive one. She had never ridden a horse, either, only sat on Maude when Gideon led her about. But Gideon said the gelding, Jack, was used to being ridden, and that he was placid under saddle.

The hostler, a colored man, came up to her. "Ma'am?" He regarded her with surprise.

"I am True Stoltz. The sheriff's wife."

"Yes, ma'am. I recognize you. How can I help you today?"

She asked the hostler to get Jack and saddle him for her. She had brought money to rent a saddle.

"Jack," the hostler said, "now that's a nice horse. You planning to ride him somewhere? That horse will take care of you. Sheriff Stoltz, he rode out of here on his mare the other day with his own saddle. I see that you don't got a saddle with you, but we can fix you up, cash or credit. Do you prefer a lady's saddle?"

She shook her head, thinking she'd just slide off one of those fancy side saddles that high-class women used when riding.

"A regular saddle then," the man said, and wandered off.

Old Dick sat down in the dirt. True stood and waited for a while. She felt tired. Then she sat down in the dirt next to the dog and folded her legs along her side.

Presently the man came back leading Jack, a saddle girthed on the black gelding's back. Jack looked tall to True. She got up from the ground, and he still looked tall. The horse blew through his nose, nodded his head up and down, and whinnied. True asked the hostler how much to rent the saddle and tack. She paid him using coins from a small pouch she extracted from her skirt's pocket.

He looked at her and then adjusted the stirrups. "Ma'am," he said, "can I suggest something? Make it easier for you to ride in that skirt." The hostler bent low and reached his hand down and back between his legs. From this crouched position he looked up at her. "Take holt of the back of your skirt and draw it forward and up, like this." He straightened and brought his fist forward from between his legs as if holding a bunched-up skirt.

Then he wove the fingers of both hands together, bent low again, and held out his cupped hands. It took True a moment to realize that the man was offering to help her mount. She reached back through her legs and gathered her skirt. She started to put her right foot in his hands, then realized it was her left foot that needed to go there, otherwise she'd end up seated backward on Jack.

She found herself smiling at the notion. It felt strange to smile; it almost hurt her face.

She had to put her bare foot in his bare hand. No doubt it was very improper. She didn't care. She set her left foot in his cupped hands, and he boosted her up. She threw her right leg over and across Jack's back and let go of her skirt and settled herself in the saddle. Behaving as a true gentleman, the hostler looked aside so as not to view her ankles and calves as she fitted her feet into the iron stirrups and pulled her skirt down as far as it would go.

"You have to get off anywhere," the hostler said, tightening the girth another notch, "why, you just find yourself a rock or a log to stand on and you should be able to get back on him again."

She asked, "Do I need a whip?" Gideon had said something about Jack being lazy.

"I don't believe so," the hostler said. "No, Mrs. Stoltz, you do not need a whip. Jack here is not the fastest horse in the stable. But he will get you where you want to go." The man looked at the sky. It was a pale gray, almost white. The air hot and damp and still. "How far you planning to ride?"

"As far as I need to go."

He nodded. "Looks like it could rain." He touched his hatbrim. "Have a nice ride." He patted Jack on the rump. "Be good for this lady," he said.

True clucked to Jack the way Gideon did when driving him. Jack stood there. He pointed his ears back.

"Giddup," she said.

Jack didn't move.

The hostler walked away, whistling. True marshaled her strength. She took her feet out of the stirrups, turned her heels inward, and walloped Jack in the ribs. He looked back at her as if to say, "Well, if you insist," and stepped forward.

A solemn darkness veils the skies,
A sudden trembling shakes the ground

Chapter 18

———⚬⚬⚬———

MIDGES SWIRLED IN GIDEON'S FACE. HE WISHED FOR A BREEZE TO scatter them and liven up the sullen air. In the west, dark clouds bulked above the ridge. The sun, setting behind the clouds, made their edges blaze.

He used a fingernail to scrape a midge out of his ear. At least the *verdammt* things didn't bite.

Nolf appeared unconcerned about the midges and the heat and the gathering storm. He leaned on the top rail of the zigzag fence. His cow and Gideon's mare stood peaceable in the dry lot. Gideon leaned against the rail next to the pastor.

"Who did you talk to today?" Nolf asked.

"The Trautmanns, and some of the other people you suggested."

"Did you learn anything new?"

"Not really." Gideon waved a hand, temporarily dispersing the midges. "The other day at the Harbisons' farm, that old woman accused Rebecca Kreidler of being a witch. You said that you'd spoken with her several times and found no reason to think she was one."

Nolf smiled. "Odd, how people still believe in witches, even in this day and age."

"Did Rebecca ever talk about witchcraft, about *hexerei*?"

"She never said a thing. People who claim to be witches always want to talk about it, perhaps to make others fear them or hold them in high regard. Nothing Frau Kreidler said or did made me think she wanted that kind of attention. Or any attention at all."

"How often did you speak with her?"

"Three or four times, I suppose. I visited her at the Trautmanns' farm soon after she came here. And I spoke with her on a few occasions when I met her out walking."

"What did you talk about?"

"I invited her to join our church, but she chose not to do so." The pastor shook his head. "Tell me, Sheriff. Are you a religious man?"

Not long ago, Gideon would have said yes. Now he wasn't sure. "My wife and I go to church in Adamant."

"Which one?"

"The Methodist."

"I don't believe I've seen it."

"You wouldn't think it was a church if you did. It's just a log building on a back street."

"We *Neigeboren* don't have a church. We hold our services in people's homes. It's simpler that way. Were you brought up Lutheran?"

"Yes."

"So many *Deitsch* folk belong to that church. But you have embraced a different denomination."

"My wife's doing."

Nolf nodded. "You will probably finish your inquiries in Sinking Valley and will go back to Adamant soon. But if you're still here on Sunday, feel free to come and worship with us."

Thunder rumbled down the valley. The clouds in the west billowed higher. The sun hovered just above the horizon, its rays knifing between the gray and purple cloud columns.

"Do you think Rebecca Kreidler was disturbed in her mind?" Gideon asked.

"Yes. I think she was badly disturbed." Nolf's brow knit. "I asked her what it had been like, to be in the penitentiary for three years. At first, she didn't want to say. But finally she told me that it had been very hard on her—all alone, kept away from other people. Caged up like an animal. Not allowed to talk with anyone or have visitors or even to receive letters. Tell me, how is that a good way to reform a person who has committed a crime?"

Gideon couldn't answer that question. "When you spoke with Frau Kreidler, did you ever talk about plants or healing?"

Nolf shook his head.

"I understand that you are knowledgeable in how to use plants."

"I don't want people thinking I'm a *braucher*. I'm just a man who has been called to serve God and this congregation. But it's true that I have some understanding of plants and medicine."

"You didn't talk about this with Frau Kreidler, knowing that she was interested in the medicinal uses of plants? Even when you met her out walking, when she was probably collecting plants?"

"I don't recall that it came up."

"How did you come by your own knowledge?"

Nolf smiled. "You ask a lot of questions, Sheriff."

"I'm sorry. It's the only way I know to do my job."

"If you want to find out how I learned about plants, you will be in for a long story."

A crack of thunder split the air and went echoing down the valley. The mountains to the west disappeared behind a wall of rain. Tall trees beyond Nolf's house thrashed in the wind.

The midges, Gideon realized, had vanished.

"Let's go inside," Nolf said.

★★★

With the windows shuttered, the pastor's house felt snug in the storm.

Nolf brought a jug from the cellar and filled two glasses.

"Tell me if you like this."

The cool drink tasted tangy but agreeably so. "It's good," Gideon said. "What is it?"

"I make it from the fresh bobs of the *shumack*. There's honey if you want to sweeten it."

Gideon stirred a spoonful of honey into the drink, then sat down in a rocking chair. Nolf sat in a second rocker. Lightning struck nearby: brilliant light flashed, and a thunderclap followed a moment later. Rain beat on the roof.

"Have you ever felt ashamed of being *Deitsch?*" Nolf asked.

"No." After his knee-jerk answer to the unexpected question, Gideon thought to himself that he did feel ashamed at times, especially when he considered some of the superstitions his people held onto. Although superstitions and other backward beliefs—in witches, ghosts, and the second sight, which True claimed she possessed— were hardly limited to people of German descent.

"I was ashamed of being *Deitsch* when I was a boy," Nolf said. "We lived in Maryland, just south of the Pennsylvania line. We had a nice farm. For years we worked to make it fertile and profitable—my father, my mother, my four sisters, and me.

"One day, we went in to town. A crossroads town called Rising Sun, on the road between Baltimore and Philadelphia. We were Brethren, *Schwartzenau Brudergemeinde*—Dunkers, they called us, because we baptized by immersion.

"That day they were holding an election out in front of a big stone tavern—the tavern was called the Rising Sun, just like the town. The drink flowed freely. Some *Eirisher* bullies saw us and decided to have a little fun. There were four of them. First they called out lewd remarks to my mother and my sisters. Father told us to ignore them. Then one of them grabbed Father's hat and put it on his own head. You can imagine how his friends howled at that. Of course, the constable was nowhere to be seen.

"Father had some English. He asked politely for his hat back. The men just laughed. It looked like Father was going to lose that hat—not such a terrible thing, I guess. But it got worse. The man who had snatched his hat made a fist and struck Father in the face, knocking him down. One of the other men had a whip. He began using it on our *dawdy*.

"Have you ever seen a man whipped? My father writhed in the dust as the lash rose and fell. I was thirteen years old. I wanted to run and help him, I wanted to fight those bullies. But my mother held me back. She thought I'd get the same treatment, and no doubt she was right. The blood welled up where the whip cut through Father's shirt. But more painful to me was the way he begged those thugs to stop. I can still hear his screams. His pleas for mercy."

Another bright flash of light pulsed through the shutters, another thunderclap detonated outside the house. In the moment of brilliance, Nolf's face appeared both sorrowful and serene. "Finally they tired of their fun," he said. "The one with the whip coiled it and hung it over his shoulder. The man who had taken Father's hat skimmed it so that it landed next to Father in the dirt. Mother let go of me. But I did not rush to help my *dawdy*, even though she and my sisters did. No. I was ashamed of him. I was ashamed of being Brethren, and ashamed of being *Deitsch*.

"I was even more ashamed when Father sold our farm. He said he wouldn't live in a place where a man could be attacked in public like that. He was afraid, of course. They could have killed him. No charges were ever brought. And he was right to be afraid. The people we lived among, many of them hated us. They thought we were self-righteous. They resented the way we would pool our money and buy out their neighbors' farms, so that our young people could get a start in farming. They saw how we could take a worn-out piece of land and make it bountiful again. We were smarter than they were. Smarter and willing to work hard. They envied us. And envy breeds hatred.

"After selling the farm, we moved to Philadelphia. We rented two rooms in an old house. Father went to work as a laborer. Sometimes I worked alongside him. My mother and sisters cleaned other people's houses and took in laundry. For three years we hung on, barely able to feed ourselves and pay the rent. Then they all died within a week. From the yellow fever. How they suffered. The blood ran out of their eyes and mouths."

Nolf fell silent. The light in the room was now so dim that the pastor was nothing more than a shadow.

"All because of that day in front of the Rising Sun." Nolf's voice caught in his throat.

"I am sorry," Gideon said.

"I didn't catch the fever," Nolf said. "Afterward, a man named Thomas Houseman took me in. I'm not sure how it was arranged; someone in our church may have done it. Mr. Houseman was a Quaker, a learned man, and very kind. A botanist and an herbalist. He sent me to school, where I learned to read and write and speak English. I worked as an apprentice in his apothecary shop. I went with him into the countryside to pick plants. He taught me how to identify medicinal plants and to make the preparations he sold in his shop."

"With your knowledge of plants," Gideon said, "can you guess what Rebecca Kreidler may have eaten to cause her to die so suddenly? And so painfully, it seems?"

Nolf took a while before answering. "There are many plants that, if you take them in small doses, can cure different ailments. But if you ingest too much of them, or the wrong parts, they can hurt you and in some cases even kill you."

"Can you name some of them?"

"Indian hemp, foxglove, baneberry. You can eat the fresh green shoots of pokeberry in the spring, but in summer the roots and leaves of the mature plant become toxic. Some mushrooms can cause rapid, painful death. Even garden plants can be dangerous. Rhubarb stalks are good to eat, but the leaves of the plant will make you very sick and can even kill you." He paused. "It could have been any of a number of different plants. Some people call them the devil's feast."

Nolf got up, crossed the room, and opened the door. Outside, the storm had abated, although rain still fell. A cool breeze came flooding in. Gideon actually shivered—for the first time in weeks, and it felt delicious.

The pastor used a stone to prop the door open. He refilled their glasses with the *shumack* drink and sat back down in his chair. "Now tell me about yourself."

"There's not much to tell," Gideon replied.

"Why does a *Deitsch* man leave his home and come here?" Nolf asked. "For us, this congregation, we came to settle on good farmland purchased at an affordable price. But you, Gideon Stoltz—what brought you to Colerain County?"

"I wanted to see what it was like to live in a different place," Gideon said. Which was true, as far as it went. "I did not want to farm. My younger brother wanted to take over our family's farm, so I made my father's choice an easy one."

Nolf waited, clearly hoping to hear more.

Gideon had never told anyone in Colerain County about what had happened to his *memmi*. How that searing and somehow shameful event had finally driven him to saddle Maude and leave his home. He didn't care how many times they tried to scrub away the bloodstains on the kitchen floor. Those stains would always be there. You could cover them with rugs, you could tear up the floorboards and lay a new floor, but the *kich* would still be a defiled place, a place that evoked terror and pain. Even as he thought of it now, he felt his shoulders stiffen and his head pull down like a turtle's head drawn into its shell.

"Something terrible happened," he said. "When I was a boy. My mother was killed. Someone murdered her. In our house." He could hardly believe it—he was telling this calm, quiet man something he had never even shared with his wife.

"I was ten years old. I found her."

A long silence. Then Nolf said, "What a horrible thing. Losing your family to a plague, that's an awful experience. But to lose your mother to violence? So needless. So sad." The pastor shook his head. "How was she killed?"

"With a knife. No one was arrested. I doubt they ever will be."

"Did leaving your home help you overcome that tragedy?"

"I have made a new life here."

"How did you end up in Adamant?"

Gideon knew it would sound ridiculous but admitted it anyway. "I saw the name on a map. It made the town seem like an interesting place."

"And how did you become sheriff?" Nolf said. "You're young. An outsider. And you're *Deitsch*."

"Soon after I came here, I was hired as a deputy by the old sheriff, a man named Israel Payton. I guess he didn't care that I was *Deitsch*. I could read and write, and had my own horse, and that was enough. Then he died from a stroke of apoplexy and the county commissioners gave me his job. At least until this fall, when there will be an election. I don't know if the voters will keep me as sheriff or not." Again the reality that he might lose his job hit him. If he could find out what had happened to Rebecca Kreidler, mightn't that persuade the people to keep him on as sheriff for the next three years?

Unless, of course, he had killed her himself.

"Your head injury," Nolf said. "When you fell off your horse. How are you feeling now?"

"I'm getting better."

"Those kinds of injuries can take a long time to heal. What are your symptoms? Perhaps I can be of help."

"I get headaches. It hurts to look at the sun. My balance, sometimes it's bad. I get dizzy. And I get tired, sometimes it seems like all of my strength suddenly gets used up."

"Have you had any loss of memory?"

Gideon nodded.

"From the time of your accident?"

"Then, and going back a ways."

"It must be hard for you to keep your thoughts sorted out. To do the work of a sheriff."

Gideon didn't want to talk about himself anymore. "Pastor Nolf, where did your congregation live before you came here?"

"In Berks County. In a valley with shale soil, not very productive for farming. We heard about Colerain County, and a group of our men journeyed here and looked around. They found this valley, where people were willing to sell land. We began moving here six years ago."

"Your church, the *Neigeboren*. I've not heard of that religion before."

"Years ago we split off from the Brethren. You know, the usual reasons—we differed on interpretations of the Bible, as well as certain expectations about how Christian folk should live. We are not a large church. But I believe we are a Godly one.

"Like the Brethren, we don't have a bishop or a group of leaders; there's no formal church authority. The people chose me to be their pastor twenty years ago. But other men also make decisions and lead services. Like the *Brudergemeinde*, we take the word of God to heart: 'Be not conformed unto this world.' And so we dress simply and keep our traditions plain."

"Can outsiders, people from other religions, join your church?"

"If they aspire to a gentleness of spirit, then yes, we welcome them as *Neigeboren*. They must want to be born again into God's saving grace through baptism as adults. We follow Jesus's teaching that to enter into the kingdom of God, one must be born of water and of the Spirit."

"Can *Neigeboren* men and women take wives and husbands outside the faith?"

"That's one of the points on which we differ from the Brethren. Our people are not permitted to marry outsiders. If they do, they are asked to leave the church. Unless, of course, the outsiders themselves join."

Nolf continued, "You asked earlier if I thought Rebecca Kreidler had a disturbed mind. I told you yes, I did sense that. I also sensed in her a deep anger and a black despair. As *Neigeboren*, we work to purge from our lives that which would not be pleasing to the One we serve, including anger and despair.

"One thing I have been considering since her body was found: I think it's very possible that Frau Kreidler took her own life. That she purposely ate a plant she knew would kill her, and in a way that would inflict severe pain."

Gideon thought about the nails in the woman's corpse. They made it hard for him to believe she had committed suicide. No, she had been murdered. Who could have done it? He forged ahead in his thinking, not letting himself consider any involvement on his own part.

Nolf knew a lot about plants, including poisonous ones. The pastor didn't seem to be the kind of man who would take another person's life. And what motive could he possibly have had to kill Rebecca Kreidler?

Gideon wondered if he should tell Nolf about the nails. To see if the pastor might say something that would move this investigation forward. Or whether a shocked or guilty expression might claim his face. But the room was dark; he couldn't see Nolf's features. He also sensed that it was not yet time to make that revelation.

Nolf was saying something, but Gideon didn't apprehend the pastor's words. A memory had emerged from the fog in his mind.

He is standing in darkness. He looks around and sees a glow in the east. He reaches out and touches the rough bark of the tree. The pear tree, in the orchard above their scheierhof. *He hasn't been able to get hold of any coffin nails, but the* hex *said brand new horseshoe nails would work, too.*

He stole three horseshoe nails from the farrier Biedermeyer.

The glow in the east strengthens.

The sun peeks over the horizon.

He holds the nails up, clasping them between thumb and forefinger. The sun's rays strike the nails, burnishing them. He recites the incantation the hex *man told him to say:*

"O Dieb, ich binde dich bey dem ersten Nagel, den ich dir in deine Stirn und Hirn thu schlagen . . ."

"O thief, I bind thee by the first nail, which I drive into thy skull and thy brain . . ."

With the hammer he drives the nail into the pear tree. With each blow he feels the tree shudder, hears its leaves make little shushing sounds. It might be for naught, the hex *said you had to grease the nails with fat from an*

*executed criminal or some other sinful person, and how could he ever get that?
He only half-believes in the spell anyway, though he'd given two bits for it.*

*". . . to return the saddle thou hast stolen; thou shalt feel as sick and as
anxious to see the place thou stole it from, as felt Judas after betraying Jesus.
I bind thee by the other nail, which I drive into thy lungs and liver."*

He pounds the second nail into the tree.

The thief filched the saddle right out of their barn.

"The third nail I drive into thy foot . . ."

*His brand new saddle that he'd saved for two years to buy. He planned
to use it on his filly, Maude.*

*"Oh thief, I bind thee, and compel thee, by the three holy nails that were
driven through the hands and feet of Jesus, to return the saddle to the very
same place from which thou stole it . . ."*

A crash of thunder jerked Gideon out of his reverie. Repeated
lightning flashes lit the room, and a volley of sound filled the air. He
saw Nolf staring at him, puzzlement and concern on the pastor's face.

Gideon gasped and dropped his drink on the floor. The liquid
spilled as the glass rolled at his feet.

Storm is gathering in the west
And you are so far from home

Chapter 19

—⊷⊷⊷—

J ACK WALKED.

True felt like she was sitting on a broad stool that moved in a strange and unfamiliar way beneath her.

It took Jack a long time to carry her out of town. It seemed to True as if the gelding were an old man out for a stroll, pausing to lean on his cane and look at this, look at that. Pottering. Old Dick trotted along with them, making forays into the brush and coming back and rejoining them on the road.

Jack walked past thick-trunked sycamores with their parti-colored bark and ranks of smaller birches with their flaky coppery bark, the trees lining the banks of Spring Creek, whose flow, glimpsed between the trunks, coiled murkily and lazily in its bed. The road passed through deep woods, past hills scalped by the colliers, and over a stretch of flat streamside land known as Bald Eagle's Nest, named for an Indian chief who had once kept his camp there. True's brother Jesse had told her once that Bald Eagle was murdered by the settlers; they laid his body in his canoe, stuffed a piece of johnnycake in his mouth, and set the canoe adrift in the stream. Jesse said that Bald Eagle's restless spirit flew back to his nest and haunted the place to this day, Jesse naming her a 'fraid baby and scaring her witless with this and many other such tales.

Jack stopped. He took the bit between his teeth and threw down his head, pulling the reins out of True's hands. He grazed, his head moving from side to side, his teeth making little ripping sounds as he cropped the grass. True sat on Jack's broad back as he ate. He lifted his head, looked around, lowered his head again, and tore off more grass.

When he had finished eating, he resumed walking.

True picked up the reins again.

They met an ox-drawn wagon filled with iron bars. Then a man striding along wearing a battered top hat, a bulky sack thrown over his shoulder. Jack stopped and regarded each in turn as they approached and passed.

The road and the stream cut through the gap in Muncy Mountain.

When the road emerged into Panther Valley, True looked east toward the ironworks. She heard the faint clang of the forge hammer and the thump of the blowing tubs; saw the yellowish gray soot smudging the air above the furnace. At the ironworks was the cabin where she had been born, where her parents still lived, in the shadow of the ironmaster's mansion.

Jack walked across the covered bridge spanning Panther Creek, his hooves thumping the planks. They left the bridge's shaded interior and came back into glare. The air was hot and the sun beat down. True hadn't worn her bonnet; it had seemed like too much work to find it and put it on.

At the fork, she tugged on the left rein, and Jack turned away from the ironworks and headed west down the valley.

Reddish rocks peeked through dirt in the road. Muncy Mountain made a long green wall on the left. On the right, a series of narrow hollows climbed toward the Allegheny Front, distant and pale in the haze. One of the side hollows farther down the valley was called Burns Hollow, because that was where her forebears had lived and farmed in those long-ago days and where her gram, Arabella Burns, still resided.

When Jack came to the first run flowing down out of a side hollow, he lowered his head and drank. Then ate some grass growing on the stream's bank.

"Let's go!" True cried out. "Jack! A little faster, please."

A grinding sound as Jack grazed.

Finally he lifted his head and walked across the ford. The stream came up to his knees. On the other bank, he continued down the valley.

True worried that she might not recognize Burns Hollow when they came to it. She hadn't been there in several years. One of her aunts lived on a bottomland farm at the hollow's mouth, and the farm had a small log barn with many racks of deer antlers nailed to its gable end; the branch road up Burns Hollow departed from the main road and went north between the antler-ornamented barn and her aunt's farmhouse.

True feared that, even if she found the right road, her gram might not be home. She might have gone away somewhere.

Or she might have died and passed on to her reward.

True swallowed. Her throat was dry. Why had she gotten out of bed this morning? Why had she left the house and fetched Jack and ridden him out of town?

She needed to relieve herself. But Jack was walking, and she didn't want him to stop, and despite what the hostler had said, she worried that if she got down off the gelding she wouldn't be able to get back on again.

Jack walked.

He walked when Old Dick barked and raced past his legs and ran ahead until the setter was just a red dot on the road, then not on the road, he had gone off into the brush.

A covey of young mountain pheasant came cheeping and fluttering on stubby wings out of the brush like bees disturbed from their hive. Jack stopped and stared at them, then resumed walking.

He walked down the road through a forest of tall trees. He walked across marshland on a section of corduroy road, the logs tipping beneath his hooves, tea-colored water welling up between them. Jack walked through a stand of great laurel, the shrubs taller than True's head, the air cool in the deep shade, shiny leaves rattling as she brushed them in passing. Mixed in with the laurel were thickets of hobblebush, the wayfarer's tree.

True came to a clearing in which sat a small log schoolhouse, vacant at this time of the year.

A church with unpainted plank siding at the mouth of a hollow that was not Burns Hollow.

Deer trails fingering into the woods.

Ahead of her she saw a man on horseback. The man rode toward her on a small horse, pale gray in color. The man stopped his horse at a wide place in the road and let her come up to him. A dove-colored slouch hat sat on the man's head; he took the hat off in a deliberate, formal manner, as if it were a crown. He held it over his heart. He was tall and rail-thin, with hair the same pale color as his horse. He had a broad brow and a long narrow nose, his face further attenuated by a thin beard that straggled down from his pointy chin.

"Good afternoon, miss," he said.

True considered informing him that she was a ma'am and not a miss but it seemed unimportant to do so.

Jack walked up to the gray horse. He arched his neck and looked down at the smaller animal. The man, being tall, sat eye-to-eye with True. He was very close to her. She noticed that he wore no buttons; long, straight thorns pinned his blouse shut. His eyes the color of denim cloth washed many times. "You are a wildwood flower," he said, smiling at her. "A precious bloom waiting to be plucked."

True thought it an odd thing to say. She did not bother answering.

Jack walked past the man on the gray horse and continued down the road.

★★★

Where was Old Dick? True hadn't seen him for some time. What would befall him if he got lost? Would a bear eat him? Would a pack of wolves tear him limb from limb? What if she met with such dangerous beasts? She turned and looked back, suddenly afraid that the man on the gray horse had followed, but no one was there.

Thunder growled in the distance.

The forest trees seemed to lean in over her. The sky darkened. The wind rose, and the leaves showed their pale undersides. True felt dizzy and weak. She had eaten very little in the past days. She had not drunk water in a while. Why not get down at the next stream crossing, have a good long drink, and relieve herself? But if she got down and Jack ran off, she'd be done for. The man on the gray horse, perhaps insulted by her lack of reply to his greeting, such as it was, might come and attack her. Strangle her or knock her over the head. Leave her corpse to be scavenged by bears and buzzards and skunks.

Thunder crackled high overhead, and Jack startled beneath her.

"Let's go, Jack!" she cried. "Faster!"

Jack walked.

The first drops of rain rattled in the trees' leaves. Some of the drops found their way down through the forest canopy and splatted on the road.

A surge of drops, a brief cessation in the rain, and then it was pouring. Thunder boomed above Muncy Mountain. True crouched low in the saddle. The rain pummeled her back. Suddenly Old Dick materialized on the road, sopping wet, wagging his tail and grinning up at her.

Thunder rolled up and down the valley. Trees creaked and groaned as if spirits imprisoned inside their trunks were trying to fight their way out. The rain soaked her dress and plastered her long black hair over her shoulders. She began to shiver.

It rained harder. She could see a scatter of trees beside the road and a few dark trunks standing beyond them. The rest of the forest was a confusion of greens and browns and blacks.

She felt like she was weeping, but no tears came—or if they did, the rain washed them away.

She closed her eyes.

Jack placed his feet carefully, avoiding rocks and roots and stumps. In one spot he made his way off into the woods to bypass the many-branched crown of a tree that the storm had broken off and thrown down on the muddy road.

True jerked awake. She'd been asleep, though that hardly seemed possible with the way she was shivering, and the rain bucketing down. She stared at the road leading onward through the forest. Her eyelids grew heavy again.

She dreamed she was holding David, he was burbling and waving his arms, reaching out to her with his perfect little hands, and she pressed her cheek against his, cooed to him, laughed with him, kissed his dear little face, smelled his fresh baby scent.

She woke. Wept. Wailed.

Jack walked.

She looked around and had no idea where they were, other than on a mud-bogged road in the dark woods in a driving, strength-sapping rain. Her shoulders quaked. Her body shook. She closed her eyes again.

She knew she should remain alert so as to descry the barn with its bristle of deer antlers, because if she missed it she would keep riding and never come to anything else again. True recited to herself: Turn right, between the antler barn and the farmhouse, and follow the track up the side hollow. But she was too tired, too weary in mind and limbs and soul. She wanted to sleep, and dream of holding David in her arms again, and never wake up, her little boy accompanying her to wherever life took her, or death.

Jack walked.

And stopped.

The rain had scanted to a drizzle. True opened her eyes. It was almost dark. She dared let go of the reins and use her hand to wipe the rainwater off her face, push strands of hair out of her eyes. All around her, wood thrushes sang their evening lays.

Jack had somehow turned off the valley road, carried her up the side hollow, and stopped in front of the cabin where her gram lived.

The cabin's door opened and out stepped Arabella Burns.

There is rest for the weary;
There is rest for you

Chapter 20

———✦———

THE AIR IN THE CABIN WAS WARM. GRAM BURNS PEELED OFF TRUE'S clothes, wrapped her in a quilt, and eased her onto the bed.

As True drowsed, she heard the fire crackling, the crane creaking as the old woman swung a kettle over the flames.

A tub clunked across the floor toward the hearth.

True drifted into sleep. She dreamed of galloping on a black horse down a road that went arrow-straight through the forest, the horse's hooves reaching far out in front, pummeling the ground, trees rushing past on each side. She wanted the horse to slow down and walk, it could even indulge itself by eating grass if it wanted to. But she had no control. All she could do was sink her fingers into the horse's mane and hang on for dear life as it pounded down the road.

She cried out in fear.

She woke to find Gram Burns seated on the mattress next to her, stroking her forehead. The room smelled faintly of smoke.

The old woman helped her get off the bed and cross the floor to the tub. Gram Burns took hold of the quilt, and True stepped out of it and into the tub; she sat, feeling the hot water rise up to her breasts. Narrow filigreed leaves floated in the water, and a spicy scent mingled with that of the smoke.

With a poker, Gram Burns nudged a stone out of the fire and onto the hearth. She dipped her hand in a pot, sprinkled water on the stone. The drops hissed and spat and recreated themselves as a cloud of steam.

Gram Burns tested the bath with her gnarled fingers and added more hot water from the kettle.

"That smoke you smell? Comes from rabbit tobacco," she said. "It will keep any spirits out from under this roof; you will sleep easy tonight. I rubbed down that horse of your'n and gave him all the hay he could eat. Your dog seems happy enough in the barn."

True leaned back against the warm wood. She hadn't had a tub bath in ages—had lacked the energy or the gumption to haul water and heat it.

Gram Burns poured hot water into a teapot. "We'll let this steep for a while. Rattleweed. It will chase away the black wolf. It's good for black-haired women like yourself." Somehow True understood that Gram Burns had been a black-haired woman, too, though her grandmother's hair had been white for as long as True could remember.

Gram Burns dipped a rag in the bathwater and gently rubbed True's forehead, her temples, behind her ears. "Set up straight." Gram Burns rubbed the rag over True's shoulders and under her arms and around and over her breasts.

"You are a skinny thing," Gram Burns said. "Fever thin. 'Cept you don't have a fever, not to the touch, anyway.

"I think you are wandering between worlds. Like a ghost in search of another ghost. You should be back here in this world. Your husband needs you."

"I don't know where he is."

"He is wandering himself." Gram Burns had True stand. She cleaned her all over with the rag, front and back, her arms and legs and her private places.

"Set back down again."

The old woman poured dark steaming liquid from the teapot into a mug. She tasted it, grimaced, and passed the mug to True.

True took a sip. "So bitter," she said. "It tastes like dirt."

"Life is bitter. And it ends in dirt."

The old woman used a crooked finger to tuck True's hair behind her ears. The rag in her other hand approached True's face. True closed her eyes, and Gram Burns brushed them in a slow circular motion.

"Drink some more of that tea," Gram Burns said. "When you are feeling better, I'll learn you about plants. I'll show you the ones you should know. A whole tribe of plants."

"If I'd known more about plants, I could've saved David."

"What did you do for him?"

"All I could find was mint. I remembered that you used to dose me with it when I was sick. I brewed some tea and got him to drink a little of it."

"That was good to do. You have the instincts for plants. Honestly, I doubt anything could have kept him here on this earth."

Tears welled up in True's eyes. "I miss him."

"You'll miss him forever," Gram Burns said. "Tell me. Did you meet anyone on the road coming here?"

True nodded through her tears. "An old man."

"On a gray horse?"

"Do you know him?"

"Everyone comes to know him by and by."

"Who was he?" True asked.

"No more questions. Drink the rest of that tea. I'll pour some more hot water in your bath. Stay in it as long as you want."

Ah! we're much to blame, we're all the same—
Alike we're made of clay

Chapter 21

THE DAY DAWNED CLEAR, THE AIR WASHED CLEAN BY THE STORM. In the night Gideon had lain awake listening to the rain on Nolf's roof and mulling over his memory from the evening before: his youthful self driving nails into a pear tree to make a thief return his saddle.

A stupid act. A backward superstition. Of course he'd never laid eyes on that saddle again.

His memory was still spotty, but portions of it were becoming clearer. Yes, he'd been in the bakehouse with the Kreidler woman, and he had a good notion of why. He still didn't know if she had refused his advances or accepted them. But could he have murdered her? Lost control of his emotions for some reason, killed Rebecca Kreidler, and, as he had done to the pear tree years ago, driven nails into her corpse?

He told himself to quit worrying and do his job. In time, the truth would come out. Let it. Help it. Whatever that truth might be.

The road he followed traversed forested and cleared land, linking the farms in Sinking Valley to one another—and to the gristmill, owned by Andrew Rankin, where the different farmers' wheat and rye were ground into flour, their oats milled, their corn turned into meal. Rankin took a portion of the grain as payment for grinding it. Freighted to Adamant and sold, it had made him the wealthiest land-owner in the valley.

As the day wore on, Gideon spoke with people in fields and houses and gardens and barns. The English folk, many of them, answered his questions reluctantly. He ended up conversing in *Deitsch* with most of the Germans, since they seemed more comfortable using that language, although it was not easy for him because their dialect differed markedly from the one he'd grown up speaking.

What he was told amounted to rumors and innuendo and nonsense.

"Witch or thief? Maybe she was both. Someone snuck into our storeroom and stole a wheel of cheese. It was her, I'm sure of it."

"She tried to tempt my husband. I saw the way she looked at him when we passed her on the road."

"I was out walking one night when I felt something brush against my face—like the wing of a bat, or a night bird. I'm sure it was her. I ran home as fast as my legs would carry me."

"She looked at me out of the corner of her eye. After that I couldn't eat, I couldn't sleep, I had shooting pains all up and down my one leg for a week."

"I found a piece of paper rolled up in a little scroll, tucked between two logs in the wall. It had letters written on it in the shape of a cross. Some kind of a curse or charm she put there. No, I don't remember what I did with it, lost it or threw it away."

"I heard a shriek in the night from the roof of the house. It was her or some animal under her control."

"One morning I found three feathers stuck in the top of a fence-post. Dark feathers, the color of soot. The witch must have plucked them out of some bird and put them there. A spell of some sort. We were very careful after that. Praise be to God, nothing bad happened."

"She was a murderer with a black soul. We shouldn't speak ill of the dead, but if you ask me, she got what she deserved."

★★★

The Rankins' three-story mill sat next to a pond backed up by a dam built of the same mountain stone used to construct the mill and the family's large handsome farmhouse.

A kingbird hawked for flies above the pond. The mill's overshot wheel spilled water. No wagons were lined up; likely there were days scheduled for milling the different grains, thought Gideon, and this was not one of them.

He dismounted and looped Maude's reins over the hitching rail. He went through the door into the mill. Hearing voices from above, he climbed the stairs.

In the big open room Andrew Rankin and his son James were dressing the millstones. They had hoisted and dressed the runner; now they were working on the bed stone, a wheel five feet in diameter fixed to the floor. Andrew squatted on his hams, watching as his son, kneeling, recut the grooves between the bed stone's lands. The younger Rankin held a mill bill, a sharp steel chisel fixed in a heavy wooden thrift. His forearms rested on an old sack filled with bran or some other steadying substance; he lifted and dropped the thrift, producing a regular percussive sound.

"Gentlemen," Gideon said. James stopped cutting. The Rankins slowly got to their feet. In Colerain County, people sometimes said "Every man is sheriff of his own hearth," and the looks the Rankins gave Gideon expressed that sentiment.

Gideon said, "I am here to gather information about—"

"We know why you're here." Andrew Rankin was a short man with a touch of gray in a full head of hair that was the same reddish brown as his son's. "We heard your speech at the Big Kettle. We had anything to say, you'd have heard it then."

Gideon looked at James Rankin. "At the Trautmanns' farm last week, on the day when my deputy and I came to get Rebecca Kreidler's remains, you told me you didn't believe she had picked and eaten a poisonous plant by mistake. You said you thought someone had 'done her in'—killed her."

"What are you driving at?" Andrew Rankin snapped. "That woman poisoned herself. We have work to do here. Now get out."

"Mr. Rankin, this past spring I helped straighten out the problem you were having with Jonas Trautmann using that acre of your land without permission. I was doing my job then. I'm doing it now. I will be on my way as soon as your son answers my questions."

"Then ask your damned questions and get out of my mill. Rye and wheat will be coming in soon. These stones won't sharpen themselves."

"Were you friends with Mrs. Kreidler?" Gideon asked James.

James Rankin nodded.

"Were you courting her?"

"You should leave right now," Andrew Rankin cut in again.

"I can leave if you want me to," Gideon said. "I can go back to Adamant and tell the state's attorney that you and your son refused to provide me with information, and he will subpoena you to come to the courthouse and answer my questions under oath. It's the slow way of doing things, but we can handle it that way if you want."

The older man scowled.

Gideon restated the question: "Were you conducting a romance with Rebecca Kreidler?"

"I could ask you the same thing," James said.

"Answer me, please."

"My answer is that it's none of your damned business. But since you are threatening to drag us in to Adamant, I will tell you that no, I was not romancing Rebecca Kreidler."

"Did you want to?"

James's eyes flickered downward.

"Did she turn you down?"

James said nothing.

"Did that make you angry enough to kill her?"

Rankin looked up, his eyes blazing. "I did not kill Rebecca Kreidler."

"This has gone far enough—" Andrew Rankin said.

"Returning to your statement," Gideon went on, still addressing the younger man, "about how you thought someone else might have 'done her in.' Did you have anyone in mind?"

"The people she lived with. The Dutch."

"Anyone in particular?"

"Some of them called her a witch. You could look there. You don't have much trouble poking your nose into other people's affairs, Sheriff. What about your own? I hear you're a married man. Yet you were chasing that filly yourself." James sneered. "I saw your horse tied to a tree near the lane to their farm one night. I waited around and watched you leave her house and get on your nag and ride off."

If Gideon had any doubts about his visiting Rebecca Kreidler, James Rankin's statement destroyed them.

"We're talking about you and Mrs. Kreidler," Gideon said. "I understand that you were also keeping company with the Trautmanns' daughter Elisabeth."

Andrew Rankin's face swiveled toward his son. "I told you to leave that wench alone."

James glared. "There's nothing going on between us."

"But there was," Gideon said, "until Rebecca Kreidler came to live with the Trautmanns. Isn't that so? Elisabeth Trautmann is pretty, maybe there was something going on. Though maybe you weren't planning on marrying her. Why buy the cow when you can milk her for free?"

James raised the thrift and took two steps forward.

Gideon stumbled back. His heel caught on a block of wood on the floor. To keep from falling, he grabbed hold of the runner stone where it stood upright, secured by an iron clamp. He looked up to see Andrew Rankin struggling with his son, holding on to James's arm.

"Damn you," the elder Rankin spat at Gideon. "You come here with your insults and accusations, looking for a fight, and a fight you will get. Put that thrift down," he ordered James. "Go outside and teach this Dutch bastard some manners."

James lowered the mallet. He was panting, and his face was red.

"There will be no fighting," Gideon said.

"You're a coward," Andrew Rankin said.

"No." Gideon felt cold all over. "I'm not a coward. But I didn't come here to fight—or to goad your son into committing assault on an officer of the law. I am here in this valley investigating an unexplained and untimely death." He looked back at James. "I apologize for my remark about your intentions toward Elisabeth Trautmann. No doubt she is a fine, decent young woman." He could see that his apology took both of the Rankins aback; clearly they'd expected a belligerent response.

"I will ask you again," Gideon said. "Were you conducting a romance with Elisabeth Trautmann until her aunt came here? And did you then end it because you were attracted to Rebecca Kreidler?"

"I refuse to answer," James said. "You want to drag me in to Adamant, go ahead. I will tell your state's attorney that the sheriff of Colerain County abused his office by preying on a woman who couldn't defend herself. I will tell him that you forced Rebecca Kreidler to commit adultery with you. And I will swear under oath that I saw you leaving the bakehouse on the night she died."

★★★

Gideon rode with his hat brim low to block the setting sun. A splitting headache had returned. Either from the day's glare—or from James Rankin swearing that he'd seen Gideon on the night Rebecca Kreidler died.

He felt worn out and confused. He didn't know what to believe about the Kreidler woman's death. Had she poisoned herself, either on purpose or accidentally? Or had she been killed by someone who feared or hated her, someone who thought she was evil, a threat, a dangerous witch? And try as he might, he still couldn't remember what had gone on between himself and the woman.

"Can you tell me what happened?" he asked Maude.

She twitched her ears back at him.

He needed a rest from the hard work of questioning people. He decided to leave Sinking Valley and return to Adamant tomorrow, even though he had no new information—or at least no information he wished to share with the Cold Fish.

He wanted to see True. He wanted to hold her in his arms and have her wrap her own arms around him.

The world recedes, it disappears,
Heav'n opens on my eyes, my ears,
Lend your wings! I mount! I fly!

Chapter 22

———✀———

Sinking Valley, Evening, July 17, 1836

HER HEART POUNDED LIKE THE HOOVES OF THE FOUR HORSES THAT had hurried the heavy coach through the cobbled streets: a black airless juddering womb that had carried her to prison, to that silent isolate hell.

Rebecca grabbed hold of the chair as the room spun around her. The bakehouse on her sister-in-law's farm in Sinking Valley.

She didn't know what was wrong with her. She was scared.

Sweat started on her face and ran down her sides under her dress. Her shoulders shook. She felt lightheaded. She looked at the bowl on the table, empty now of her supper, a sweet-tasting stew. The brown wooden bowl went in and out of focus; it became two bowls, then four, then on and on until dozens of bowls receded in a pulsing shimmering haze.

Her breath rasped in her throat. Her knees wobbled. She held onto the chair—if she lost her grip she would fall into a powerful stream that would sweep her away. Her stomach cramped, and she groaned. Her heart beat faster, louder, faster yet.

She fought for breath. Her sight cleared momentarily. She seemed to lean over and look down into a well.

Faces. So many faces.

She saw her husband John lying dead. She leaned over and spat in his face.

More faces, familiar and strange, kind and cruel, pleasant faces that warped and melted into devils' masks.

Her mother and father, young again, and she looked up into their smiling loving faces. Frau Schuster with her burn-ravaged face. Old Molly with a wen on her chin, deep seams on either side of her mouth, looking with kindly eyes. The prison matron. The innkeeper who let the strong man rape her. The strong man with his tobacco stench and his wolf's grin. The pastor Peter Nolf. James Rankin. The young sheriff from Adamant. Jonas Trautmann. Abe Trautmann. Elisabeth, her mouth tight, her eyes sharp and mocking. Maria, an angry look on her face, as she tried to explain to her sister-in-law that John had forced her to it, what else could she have done but protect herself by pushing him down the steps? Once more she saw John's face, and when again she spat into it he suddenly rose up from the cellar floor and grabbed for her. She scrambled away, ran deeper into darkness.

Her vision faded.

Her heart trailed off, became faint. It missed a beat.

She let go of the chair and ripped at the collar of her dress. She thrust her hand inside, grabbed the cross.

Her knees buckled. She fell and lay on her back. The stream carried her along. She floated in it, looking up, holding onto the cross. Fragments of memories skittered through her mind. Thoughts became colors, orange and blue and red. The colors faded and slowly darkened.

From far off she heard a hollow clapping of wings. Closer and closer it came. A shadow fell across her face, her breast. The *nachteil*. Its shadow covered her. She felt the strength of its wings, which were now her wings. She beat her wings and flew upward into light.

The fearful soul that tires and faints
And walks the ways of God no more

Chapter 23

—∞∞∞—

GIDEON PAID NOLF FOR HIS LODGING AND SAID GOODBYE TO THE
pastor. He was eager to get home, anxious about True. But
before he could head for Adamant he needed to have Maude shod.
Her shoes were thin, the nail heads almost worn off. On a long fast
ride, she'd surely lose one.

Approaching Harbison's forge, he heard a hammer ringing against
iron.

The smith listened to Gideon's request and set aside the hinge
he'd been making. "Anything for our sheriff," he said.

Gideon couldn't tell if the man was mocking him or not.

Harbison pulled Maude's shoes. He took one in his hands, gave it
a wrench, and bent it like sheet tin.

The blacksmith got out bar stock of the correct length. He
worked the bellows; it sounded like a giant's heavy breathing.
Harbison heated the bar in the forge until it was red. Clasping the bar
in the middle with his tongs, he quenched one end in the slack tub,
then the other end. With hammer blows he began shaping the bar
over the anvil's horn.

As he worked, Harbison talked about the recent circle hunt. "We
killed a panther." He brought the hammer down, *BANG*. "Two
wolves." *BANG, BANG*. He flipped the shoe back and forth on the
anvil, hammering it flat, the blows dull and muted on the heat-
softened iron, louder and sharper-toned as the metal cooled and
hardened. "We made plenty of venison." *BANG*. "And you killed
that stock-killing she-bear." *BANG, BANG, BANG*.

The hammering made Gideon's head ache.

Harbison held the shoe over the hardy hole and punched the nail slots. He set the finished shoe aside and got out another iron bar.

"I need to tell you about something I remembered," the black-smith said. "Back in the spring, April, it was. A stranger showed up here. His horse threw a shoe, so I made him a new one." Harbison hacked deep in his throat and spat. "He asked did I know of a woman, she would've come here in the last week or so. He called her a 'pretty little thing.' Said she was Dutch. I didn't know then that the Kreidler woman had moved in with them people bought my brother's farm. So I had nothing to tell the man."

Harbison lifted his grimed arm and pointed his hammer at the ridges surrounding Sinking Valley. "You have to climb over a mountain to get here, no matter what direction you come from. Which means you need a pretty good reason to come to this place. I asked the stranger why he was looking for that woman. He said he wanted to ask her some questions."

"About what?"

"He didn't say."

"Did he give his name? Or where he was from?"

Harbison shook his head. "I've been trying to remember."

"What did he look like?"

"A little older than you. Short hair. Solid and strong. I gauged myself against him; a blacksmith will do that, you know. I tell you, I wouldn't want to tangle with that one."

"What about his horse?"

"Dark bay, same as your'n. Taller, though. A jumper, had to twitch him to get that shoe on. Another thing: That fellow smoked a little black cigar while he watched me make that shoe. Had a tobacco stench all over him. You couldn't have taken him in the woods, the game would've smelled him a mile off."

"Do you know if he went anywhere else in the valley?"

"I can't say." Harbison wiped sweat from his face with the inside of his forearm. "I remember that he had a fancy saddle. It had a letter tooled into the leather below the cantle. I think it was a *K*. And beside it, a little pine tree."

Harbison lifted one of Maude's hind feet, held it between his legs, and trimmed it. He put her foot down, banged the shoe for that hoof into its final shape. He fetched nails from a jar, put some in a pocket in his leather apron and others between his lips. He picked up the shoe with his tongs and reheated it in the forge. He lifted Maude's leg again and pressed the shoe against the hoof. The hoof hissed and gave off pungent steam. Maude crow-hopped, and Harbison hung on.

The blacksmith nailed the shoe in place.

Harbison finished his work: four shoes tidily fitted, the nails set high and well-clenched.

"You make a good shoe," Gideon said, "and nicely shaped nails. Can I buy some to take with?"

Harbison handed him the jar. "Take what you need."

Gideon paid for the shoeing and the extra nails. He got on Maude. With this new knowledge of a stranger come to Sinking Valley, perhaps looking for Rebecca Kreidler, he wondered if he should go back to the Trautmanns' farm and ask more questions. Harbison said the stranger had been here in April; perhaps he'd gone there. Had he come back more recently?

But something told Gideon he should get home to Adamant right away.

"Hold on," Harbison said. "I just remembered where that stranger said he was from. A place called McDonald, or something like that. The other side of the Seven Mountains."

★★★

Gideon arrived at his house that afternoon. The door was unlatched. He let himself in. He called out and got no response. Ever since he'd found his *memmi*'s body, he hated going into silent houses by himself. And this house was silent as the tomb.

True wasn't in the kitchen or the bedroom. The bed was unmade, the house as dirty and cluttered as he'd left it.

She wasn't in the garden or the back yard. He saw Old Dick's chain lying on the ground.

"They ain't here." Mrs. Sayers peered at him over the fence. "She weren't here yesterday when I went over with a pot of bean soup and a peach pie I'd baked special. Your dog was gone, too."

"Do you know where she went?"

The woman shook her head.

Gideon got back on Maude and rode to the jail. Alonzo told him he hadn't seen True, either. "Some letters came that you should look at," his deputy added.

"What about?"

"Legal folderol from Harrisburg, a couple of bills for runaway slaves."

"They can wait."

"The Cold Fish sent a message. Of course he'd never come to the jail himself, he had to send a boy with a letter. It says you are to report to him immediately."

"If he asks, tell him you haven't seen me."

Gideon told Alonzo about the few things he had learned in Sinking Valley. He briefly described the circle hunt but didn't bother saying that he'd almost gotten shot. He said he had no real suspects yet. And he mentioned the stranger from south of the Seven Mountains.

When he left the jail, Alonzo followed him outside.

Gideon swung back up on Maude. "Maybe True went to Panther to be with her kin. I'm going there now. Sorry to make you stay and do all the work, but I need to find her."

"That's all right, I'll hold the fort."

Gideon thought he would leave Maude at the livery and ride Jack—until the hostler informed him that True had taken the gelding. "She left here Thursday in the late forenoon," the hostler said. "The day that big storm came through."

"She has never ridden Jack before," Gideon said. "She doesn't know how to ride. Why did you let her take him?"

"She told me to saddle the horse. She rented a saddle and tack. What was I supposed to tell her? 'Ma'am, you are not permitted to ride your own horse'?"

"Jack's not her horse, he's my horse." Gideon realized how stupid that sounded. "Did she say where she was going?"

The hostler shook his head. "I asked her how far she was planning to ride. She said 'As far as I need to go.' I remember that." The man shrugged. "Last I saw, she was on the road to Panther."

★★★

At the ironworks, Gideon found no one home at the Burns's cabin. He led Maude to the grassy common around which the workers' dwellings clustered. He took off her saddle and let her nibble on grass that had been grazed hard by livestock. He rubbed her topline as she picked at the sparse blades. She was sweaty and tired. He hoped he wouldn't have to ride her farther.

A bell clanged. Men converged on the pyramidal stone furnace whose brick stack belched smoke and soot. A pour of iron was about to take place: the molten metal run out of the furnace into channels in the casting shed's sand floor to make pig iron, the big central sow with smaller side branches creating ingots that looked like nursing piglets.

Gideon hoped True's mother would soon return from her work at the ironmaster's mansion. For an hour his worry grew.

"Brother Gideon."

Jesse Burns's voice normally grated on Gideon's nerves, but now he welcomed it. He turned, and there stood his brother-in-law, along with Davey Burns, Jesse's and True's father.

"Have you seen True?" Gideon asked.

"Not lately," Davey Burns replied.

"Don't tell me you've gone and lost my sister." Jesse Burns was a tall sturdy man with smallpox scars cratering his sun-browned face. His smile made it plain that he found Gideon's discomfort amusing.

"She took our wagon horse Jack and rode off on him," Gideon said. "The day before yesterday. The day of that storm."

"Why'd she do that?" Davey Burns asked.

"I don't know. I was away in Sinking Valley. She hasn't been well lately. She's been spending a lot of time in bed."

"Still grieving that baby," Davey Burns said.

Jesse chipped in: "Maybe she got tired of living with a man who's away all the time, poking his nose in other people's business."

"Where do you think she might have gone?" Gideon asked his father-in-law.

"My ma's house." Like his son, Davey Burns enjoyed needling his Dutch son-in-law, but now he looked genuinely concerned.

"Maybe she went off with another man," Jesse said.

"Jesse, quit running your god-damned mouth," Davey Burns said. He looked at Gideon. "She always liked to be with my ma, even when she was little. Always pestering us to take her there."

"I'm going there now."

"Your horse looks done in. You'd best stay here tonight."

"No. I need to find her."

He left the ironworks and rode west down Panther Valley.

He knew how to find True's grandmother's cabin. He'd gone there the previous autumn to ask the old woman about an event that had taken place in Colerain County three decades ago: a trial and hanging whose reverberations, down through the years, he suspected of causing his friend, Judge Hiram Biddle, to commit suicide. True's beloved Gram was a quirky old soul. First, she'd almost shot him. Then she'd fed him and served him coffee so strong it would have melted iron. She had given him information that helped him solve several crimes. And she had peered through the severed clenched foot of an owl to glimpse the future—then wouldn't tell him what she saw.

He'd stopped in to see her again this past spring, while patrolling in the Panther Valley, at least partly to get a cup of that invigorating brew.

As he rode, the sky turned from milky white to glistening silver to dull gray.

From the woods a screech owl sounded its down-slurred whinny.

The heavy wingbeats of turkeys flogging up to roost.

Above an opening in the forest, a dozen nighthawks flitted back and forth hunting insects. Their strange sideslipping flight made it look as if the birds were limping through the air. White stripes like bandages glinted from their long narrow wings. Their weird buzzing calls drifted down.

The ridges on either side shaded into blackness.

Maude tripped and fell forward, but Gideon gripped the reins and leaned back, and she braced against the bit and regained her balance.

He tried to focus his mind on the death of Rebecca Kreidler, in a different valley miles to the east. Things people said about her, held against her. The stranger from beyond the Seven Mountains who had come hunting for her.

It was no use. Thoughts tumbled through his mind. He was too weary and shatterbrained to set them in order. Too worried about True.

Maude tripped again, caught herself before she fell.

He got off and led her. When they came to a stream coursing down from a side hollow, he took off her saddle. She drank from the stream. He let her have a good roll, then hobbled her. He spread out a ground sheet and his blankets and lay down. He put his head against his saddle and slept.

The woman is commanded, her husband to obey,
In every thing that's lawful, until her dying day

Chapter 24

⊸⊶⊷⊶⊸

TRUE STOOD AT THE BARN DOOR AND WATCHED GIDEON RIDE INTO the farmyard. Her husband looked exhausted. His eyes had gray half circles beneath them. A growth of beard darkened his face. When Gideon dismounted, Maude heaved a sigh and dropped her head.

Gideon stood holding the reins in one hand and rubbing his face with the other.

True found herself observing Gideon instead of putting down her egg basket and rushing to greet him as a loving wife should.

She asked herself, *Do I know this man? I have shared his bed. I have shared my thoughts and hopes and dreams with him. My fears and griefs. I have been honest with him—up to a point. I have not fully or truly shared my past. Just as he hasn't shared his past with me.*

The red setter came up beside her. Seeing the man and horse, Old Dick raced out of the barn, growling. When the dog recognized his master, he wagged his tail and let out excited yips. Gideon knelt down and rubbed Old Dick behind his ears and ruffled the fur on his neck. Then he straightened and looked around.

True moved out of the shadows. Gideon came up and clasped her arms in both his hands.

"I was so worried about you," he said. "I'm glad I found you."

"Sorry I left like I did. Not telling you or nobody else. But I had to do something, Gid. Coming here seemed like the one good thing I could do. And it was. It was the best thing."

He embraced her. His arms enfolding her seemed to strike a small spark off a cold hard core at her center.

★★★

True followed her grandmother. The old woman leaned on a stick. True carried a grubbing hoe and a sack. They'd left Gideon at the cabin. He had told Gram Burns about his fall off Maude and his hurt head. The old woman got out some dried plants, made tea from their leaves, and had Gideon drink a cupful. Then he had lain down on a pallet, and her gram had ordered True outside.

"I gave him skullcap," Gram Burns said. "It should ease his mind and let him rest." She went along slowly, tapping her stick on the ground. "Some call it mad dog skullcap; they say it will cure the hydrophobia. Thank God I never had to use it for that."

The trail led up the hollow. Shafts of light came down through the trees; tiny flying insects danced at different levels in the shafts. "Soon I won't be able to walk this path," Gram Burns said. "It's harder and harder for me to get out of bed in the morning. Your aunt Peg wants me to come down hollow and live with them. I'll do it when I have to. Or maybe I'll die in the woods here. Wouldn't be a bad way to go."

"I don't want you to die," True said.

"Everyone dies," the old woman retorted.

They continued on. "I'll show you skullcap," Gram Burns said. "And I want to pick some rattleweed. Look for a plant that's two, three foot tall, with pointy stalks that are even higher, and white flowers up and down them like candle flames. Pretty as they are, the flowers stink. My ma showed me that plant. She learned it off a woman who was half Indian, who probably learned it off her own ma."

"Why is it called rattleweed?"

"In the fall when the wind blows, the seeds in the pods make a rattling sound. You would think the woods was full of serpents."

They went among moldering stumps. True wondered if the trees that had once stood here were now the walls of her gram's cabin and barn. The smells of growing and flowering and dying and rotting rose from the earth. Plants covered the forest floor, a green quilt stitched together from leaves of different sizes, textures, shapes. Plants clustered along the woods' edge where the trail bordered a field.

Gram Burns named them and explained how to identify them and use them for healing. Bloodroot and boneset, birthroot and aguweed, motherwort and moccasin. Solomon's seal and skullcap. Joe-pye-weed lifting its high purple plumes. "Up on that bony ridge," the old woman said, pointing her stick, "you'll find sweetfern. I put its leaves in the water when I gave you that bath; that's why it smelled so good. Tea from the leaves can stop the runs, and the juice will dry up a poison ivy rash."

True found a clump of plants with tall flowering spikes. Dazzlingly white, they seemed to draw all of the dim forest light unto themselves. She looked inquiringly at her gram. "Is this rattleweed?"

The old woman nodded. "It's got some other names, too. Cohosh and black snakeroot and bugbane." She pointed out the lush dark-green leaves and sharply toothed leaflets, three to a stem. "It's the roots we want," she said. "Go ahead and dig."

True sank the hoe into the dark woods soil. The roots, spidery and black, tangled like some wild woman's hair. Reluctant to give up their hold on the earth. True dug all around the plant and finally freed it.

"Now wash the dirt off."

With her gram hobbling behind, True carried the plant to the stream that trickled down the hollow. She dunked the roots, rubbed them between her hands.

"The tea from these roots is what helped bring you back to the light," Gram Burns said. Not only did rattleweed chase away the black wolf, she said, it also relieved skin-crawling sensations and eased the pain from the monthlies and the hot flashes that came with the change of life.

When the roots were clean, the old woman had True shake off as much water as she could and put them in her sack.

Walking back to the cabin, Gram Burns asked her granddaughter, "What's he like, that man of yours? Does he treat you right?"

True nodded. "He has never raised a hand to me."

"He's Dutch. I'm surprised you'd marry a stranger like that."

"I never thought of Gideon as a stranger." All her life True had heard her grandmother say things like "Put the stranger near the danger" and "The stranger is for the wolf."

"Well, I guess he ain't a stranger anymore," Gram Burns said. "Although he does talk funny. I suppose you could have done worse."

"I knew he'd take me away from Panther. I didn't want to stay there."

"Do you talk together, you two? Or does he just order you around like most men will do? Expect you to wait on him quiet-like and with no complaints."

"We talk together. Or at least we used to." She fell silent for a moment. "There are things I don't know about him. I can tell. Things from his past."

"We all have things that haunt us."

"It's something bad. He never told me what it is."

"Maybe he will someday. And maybe you will share with him the burdens you bear."

★★★

For supper True and her grandmother scrambled hens' eggs. In a separate pan they seared butterfly chops from the backstrap of a yearling buck that, Gram Burns said, "wandered in front of my gun." They boiled a pot of carrots and baked biscuits in a Dutch oven. Gram Burns set out fresh-churned butter and a tub of blackberry jam to go with the biscuits.

Gideon had napped and rested the whole day through. He thought the food was delicious. He ate and ate and finished his meal with a slab of blueberry pie.

Gram Burns brewed more skullcap tea, sweetening it with liberal amounts of honey.

They took chairs outside and sat sipping the tea and watched the sun go down. Frogs croaked from the marshlands and stuttered and chirped from the woods. A whip-poor-will's call echoed down the hollow. It was late in the summer for the bird to be calling; instead of filling the evening with its chanting, it repeated its name a few times, then fell silent. Far off, a wolf howled.

Gram Burns built a small fire in a pot, making a smudge of smoke to keep off the mosquitoes. "When did you fall off your horse?" she asked Gideon.

Reflexively he reached up to touch his head. "It's been three weeks."

"How do you feel?"

"Right now I feel fine. But I get dizzy at times. It's worse when I'm tired. Or when I go out in the sun." He shrugged. "I don't know how else to do my job, without patrolling and riding around."

"You should try to rest and not do too much," Gram Burns said.

"I found rattleweed today," True said. "Gram says it's a powerful plant. She showed me plenty of others, too." She smiled sheepishly at her grandmother. "I doubt I'll remember one in ten of them."

"It takes years to learn the plants and how to use them," the old woman said. "They can be dangerous if you don't know them well enough."

Gideon had avoided telling True of the strange death of Rebecca Kreidler. But here he was with Arabella Burns, who knew so much about plants. He would be remiss if he failed to draw on the old woman's knowledge.

He described his investigation into Rebecca Kreidler's death. He explained that she had lived on the farm of her in-laws, the Trautmanns, in Sinking Valley. "It's a good farm. The land lays nice. You come down off Mingo Mountain, and where the mountain road meets the one in the valley, you turn left. The first lane you come to is theirs. The Trautmanns have built already a new house and a barn, also a bakehouse. That's where Frau Kreidler lived."

He said he'd been told that the woman, known to use wild plants in healing, likely had eaten a poisonous plant by mistake. He related what he had learned about her final hours: the apparent sudden onset of illness, evidence of vomiting in the bakehouse, and her body turning up in a sinkhole above the farm where a hayfield bordered the woods.

He then named the plants that he remembered Pastor Nolf mentioning as possibly causing her death: Indian hemp, foxglove, baneberry.

"Indian hemp," Gram Burns repeated. "Some call it dogbane, claiming it will kill a dog. I have used a tea from its roots and flowers to strengthen a weak heart. Foxglove has beautiful purple flowers. Tea from the leaves can also help a failing heart. I suppose that drinking too much tea from those plants could kill a body—but it wouldn't be a quick death like what you described. And you wouldn't be likely to eat the plants themselves.

"Baneberry is also called doll's eyes. The berries are white with a dark spot; they really do look like the eyes on a fancy baby doll. Tea from the roots can ease pain during childbirth. I've never heard of anyone dying from it.

"The one plant that comes to mind as a surefire poison is cowbane. It grows in wet places; I could pick some now down by the creek. The roots look like parsnips. It's possible someone might cook them as a meal, not knowing what they were. Cowbane will kill you quick. All you need to eat is a tiny piece."

"If the woman ate cowbane," Gideon asked, "could she have left her house, walked several hundred yards up a hill, and gone down into a sinkhole before dying?"

"Once the poison hit her, I doubt she'd have had the time or the will to make it out the door."

"That woman," True said. "Did people like her? Or did they take against her?"

"Some of them feared her," Gideon said, "They called her a witch."

"Why?"

"She didn't have much to do with others. She never joined their church. She went around by herself gathering plants."

Gram Burns snorted. "I've been called a witch. And my ma before me. People can be downright ignorant. Mind you, I'm not saying there aren't witches in this world. But people are too fearful by a long shot. Too quick to judge."

As the darkness deepened, the katydids tuned up their scratchy voices and began calling. *Katy-did, she didn't, she did.* The sound swelled, became raucous.

"They say the katydids tell a story," Gram Burns said. "Two sisters fell in love with the same man, and Katy was the one who didn't win his heart. Later, the man and the other sister died—they were poisoned. The insects in the trees kept saying 'Katy-did!' because Katy was the one who murdered them."

It was full dark. The stars swarmed in the black sky.

Gideon said to True, "I should leave here tomorrow. We could ride home together."

She didn't reply.

Gideon did not want to be parted from his wife. He wanted True's companionship, and he needed her to take care of their household. It was a wife's duty. He considered ordering her to accompany him back to Adamant; he knew plenty of men who would do just that. But he didn't know if it was the right thing to do. And he was not sure she would obey him.

It had been hard for her, after David's death, staying by herself in their quiet house. Here at least she was with someone she had known all her life, someone she loved and trusted. She was in much better spirits than when he'd ridden off to Sinking Valley, leaving her alone almost a week ago. So he said nothing.

★★★

They bedded down on pallets on the floor. Starlight came in through the window. Gideon heard Gram Burns tossing and turning on her corn-shuck mattress in the small room at the end of the cabin. He wanted to take True in his arms, but he sensed she wouldn't welcome it.

"Honey, you were brave to ride here on Jack. How did you manage that?"

She turned her head and looked at him. "He took care of me. First there was that strange man we met on the road; Jack walked right past him."

"What strange man was that?"

"A harmless old soul, I guess. Gram seems to know of him." She continued, "Then the storm came. But Jack just kept walking, even though the rain poured down and the thunder crashed and the wind knocked branches out of the trees."

"Jack is a steady horse. Rather lazy. Though he'll go fast if you cut a switch and let him see it."

"I went to sleep sitting on him. Or maybe I just closed my eyes and went inside myself. I was tired and confused. Scared. But Jack knew where to turn to get here, even though he'd never been to this place."

"Maybe you saw the turn and looked that way, and he felt you move in the saddle."

"No. Jack knew in his own mind where I needed to go."

Gideon nodded. "Horses can sense a lot of things." He didn't add that, in fact, Jack had been to Gram Burns's farm: Gideon had been riding Maude and ponying Jack when he'd stopped to see the old woman and get a cup of her powerful coffee this spring.

"People can sense things, too," True said. "If they pay attention to what's around them and what's inside them."

Gideon stayed quiet.

"You're good at using your head," True continued, "at figuring things out. But you only believe in what's standing in front of you and nothing else. There's other ways of seeing, other ways of knowing. Maybe someday you'll figure that out."

This woman she was taken from near to Adam's heart,
By which we are directed that they should never part

Chapter 25

⊷

IN THE MORNING GIDEON ASKED TRUE WHEN SHE MIGHT COME HOME. Her answer was blunt. "I don't know."

"Take good care of yourself then. And remember that I love you."

He went to kiss her. She turned her face and he ended up giving her a peck on the cheek.

He rode off on Maude. To take his mind off True's rejection of him, he mulled over what he had learned about Rebecca Kreidler, her last days and her past. The unkind things people in Sinking Valley had said about her, accusing her of being a thief, a seductress, a witch. Would the *Neigeboren* really have welcomed a former prisoner and a convicted killer into their midst? The Trautmanns, the Rankins, Harbison, the stranger who had come to Sinking Valley this spring— had one of them killed Rebecca? Or was it someone he hadn't considered yet? Someone he hadn't even met?

It was a puzzle with no clear solution. And then there was his own involvement with the woman.

A Bible verse came to him, from the Book of Matthew: "Whoever looketh on a woman to lust after her hath committed adultery with her in his heart." He had done that, at the very least. The apostle went on in his zealous and absolutist way: "And if thy right eye offend thee, pluck it out and cast it from thee."

Had someone plucked Rebecca Kreidler out and cast her away because they feared or hated her or were repelled or angered by her presence? Or because they lusted after her?

★★★

At midday on a Monday Adamant bustled with rigs and horses in the streets, people chatting on the board walks and patronizing the shops. Some would have come to the county seat yesterday for church, then stayed over to buy supplies. Soon they would leave the town and return to their farms and villages, on horseback, in wagons, and on foot.

Gideon checked with Alonzo and learned that nothing notable had occurred while he was away, with the exception of two elderly men, one fat and one gaunt, rolling around in the street fighting on Sunday morning. "I beat on the ground next to them with my stick," Alonzo said, "which that impressed the old gents enough to quit whaling on each other and shake hands and apologize for disturbing the peace."

With Maude hitched at the rail, Gideon brought the carbine inside and put it in the jail's armory. He fetched his saddlebag, intending to replenish the shot and gunpowder he'd used during the circle hunt.

He opened the saddlebag. As he removed his powder flask, something in the bottom of the bag caught his eye.

He reached in and withdrew the object. His heart flailed.

A silver cross two inches tall, the metal carved with vines and flowers, a red stone inset where the arms of the cross met.

The cross Rebecca Kreidler had worn. The cross Elisabeth Trautmann described when she asked about the piece of jewelry her aunt had owned, wondering if it had been found.

Why was it in his bag?

Had he taken the cross from Rebecca? After raping her, killing her, driving nails into her?

No. He closed his fist around the cross. He couldn't have done those things. He tried again to remember what had happened in the bakehouse the night he went there. Nothing came to him.

Alonzo entered the storage room with a piece of paper in his hand. Gideon stuck the cross back in his saddlebag and strapped the bag shut.

"Another message from the Cold Fish," Alonzo said, handing him the note. "Wants to see you in his office right away. He's got his drawers all twisted because you haven't reported to him on what you found in Sinking Valley."

Immediately Gideon left the jail and strode to Lawyer's Row.

Anything to avoid thinking about what he had just found in his saddlebag.

Fish made him cool his heels while he finished writing a brief or doing some other lawyerly thing at his desk. Gideon stood with his stomach clenched and his mouth dry, trying desperately to remember what he had done with or to Rebecca Kreidler in the bakehouse.

The state's attorney set aside his pen and raised his pasty, cadaverous face.

"Sheriff Stoltz." In pairing the title and name, Fish loaded his voice with sarcasm. "If you will, please review for me the progress you have made in discovering the person or persons who murdered that Dutch woman."

In as calm a tone as he could manage, Gideon explained how he had interviewed more than three dozen people in Sinking Valley, both *Neigeboren* and—he paused, confused over how to denominate the folk who were not Dutch, finally calling them "English."

"Have you found anyone with the motive and opportunity to have killed the woman?"

Gideon hesitated. "I talked to several people who may have held grudges against her."

"Have you identified a primary suspect?"

"Not yet."

"You were there for a week. And you are no closer to determining who killed her?"

Gideon didn't explain to Fish that he had only been in Sinking Valley for four days and part of a fifth before going off in search of his wife, since the latter was not only embarrassing but might be interpreted as a dereliction of his duty.

"Everyone I interviewed thinks Frau Kreidler poisoned herself by accident, or possibly on purpose," he said. Then he added, lamely, "I know that doesn't explain the nails in her corpse." Gideon reached into his vest pocket. He laid on Fish's desk one of the nails he had bought from Henry Harbison. "I got this from a blacksmith in Sinking Valley." He placed one of the bloodstained nails that the coroner had recovered next to the new shiny nail. "See how the head of each nail is finished, flat on top, with a little taper to the head and then more of a taper down the shaft? These nails look pretty much alike. I think they were made by the same blacksmith."

"The man's name?"

"Henry Harbison. He lives on the next farm to the Trautmanns. But he doesn't seem to have had much contact with Rebecca Kreidler, and no reason to want her dead. He didn't look nervous or uneasy when I asked him to sell some nails to me. Maybe someone else bought nails from him and used them on the woman. And the person who drove the nails into her body may not have killed her. Maybe she was already dead from poisoning herself—"

"We've been over that ground before," Fish said in a withering tone. "The woman was murdered. It is your responsibility to collect the evidence that I will then use to convict her killer." Fish wagged his head. "By God, you are ineffectual. You lack the skills and the mature judgment to carry out this job to which you have so unwisely been appointed."

Gideon stayed mute. He tended to agree with Fish. He picked up the nails.

The attorney pressed his spectacles down on the twin grooves they had worn into the bridge of his nose. He leaned back in his chair. "After Sheriff Payton died, the county commissioners directed you to finish out his term. They can just as easily remove you for gross incompetence and appoint someone else to act as sheriff until this fall's election."

He stared at Gideon. "I am prepared to go before the board of commissioners and recommend your dismissal. You have one more week. Find out who murdered that woman or start looking for a new job."

★★★

It was too late in the day to ride to Sinking Valley. And despite the dead-line Fish had given him, Gideon knew he must let Maude rest. He led her to the livery. The hostler said he'd rub her down and give her plenty of hay. Gideon also arranged to rent an extra horse for tomorrow.

At the chief clerk's office in the courthouse, Gideon asked for a map of Colerain County. He unrolled the chart on a table. Since becoming sheriff, he had pored over the map many times, trying to learn as much as he could about the lay of the land in the county he served.

The map had been created in 1820 as part of a statewide survey of all the counties in Pennsylvania. In one corner, text in a flowery script stated that Colerain County had a population of 10,490. It had grown since then: the last census, conducted in 1830, listed 14,120 residents.

Gideon blinked. He had pulled that recent census figure out of his brain with no difficulty. Were his faculties returning? Would he soon realize that he had done nothing to harm Rebecca Kreidler?

The map's text noted that Colerain County contained 1,360 square miles. Adamant was listed as having 1,052 residents. The map displayed symbols for churches, mills, manufactories, iron furnaces, mineral deposits, dwellings, even "water sinks" where streams flowed out of the mountains and drained into sinkholes—such as the one in which Rebecca Kreidler's body had been found.

Not just found. Dumped. Fish had been right all along. Someone had murdered the woman. Driven nails into her body. Hidden her corpse in a place where they thought it would never be found.

Someone else had done that. Not him.

He stared at the map, wishing it could reveal Rebecca Kreidler's killer.

What it told him was that Colerain County had a shape at least as odd and irregular as its inhabitants, roughly triangular with a sharp point knifing out eastward and a rippled northern edge where it bordered the West Branch of the Susquehanna River. On the chart, hash marks stood for mountains. Streams were meandering black lines. Gray double lines indicated roads, including the one the stagecoach followed where it threaded its way south through the Seven Mountains to adjacent Greer County. Gideon knew there were other traces through the mountains, unrecorded on the map. Like the one he had followed three years ago when he came to this place. On that track he had met three robbers and almost lost his life: when he fled on Maude, a pistol ball just missed him and took off the tip of his mare's ear.

He asked the clerk for the corresponding map of Greer County and was pleasantly surprised to find that the oftentimes parsimonious Colerain County commissioners had authorized purchase of that adjoining chart.

The Seven Mountains ran from northeast to southwest, a diagonal slash across the map. The name "Seven Mountains" wasn't on the sheet, though that was what everyone called those rugged, roughly parallel ridges. He studied the land along the southern edge of Jacks Mountain, the southernmost of the Seven Mountains. His eyes stopped on the name "McDonough." Maybe that's what the stranger had told Harbison, when asked where he hailed from; it could have sounded like "McDonald" to the smith's ear. McDonough bore the starlike symbol for a mill. Next to it, a small square and the label "White Crow Tav." A tavern, then. He should go there.

Later, he sat on a bench in front of the dry goods and supped on store-bought bread and cheese and summer sausage. Then he walked to the Methodist church. That evening the church was hosting a singing master from Connecticut, who had been in Adamant for two weeks teaching congregations how to sing harmoniously. Gideon wanted to take his mind off finding Rebecca's cross in his saddlebag.

And because if True were here, and not laid low with grief, she'd have insisted they attend.

When he went in the door, conversation in the room ceased. In the wavering lamplight he felt eyes fix themselves on him: it seemed as if everyone studied him, some with smug satisfaction that the Dutch Sheriff had arrived alone. No doubt the rumors were rife. One man had the gall to say to him, "None of my business, Sheriff, but I heard your wife left you." Gideon nodded. "You are right, it's none of your business." The man smirked. Gideon felt like punching him in the nose.

Instead he sat down in his usual place with the tenors. It felt strange to look across the hollow square and not see True seated among the trebles.

In the open center of the square stood the singing master, with a bald dome and gray locks dangling down the sides of his head to brush against a high starched collar.

In a clipped Yankee accent, the singing master discussed aspects of technique. "Let the mouth be opened freely, so as to let the sound come straight from the lungs. The bass should be sounded fully and boldly. The tenor is regular and distinct. The counter is clear and plain, the treble mild without being faint."

The singing master worked from an oblong tunebook, copies of which he distributed. This was "shape note" music: in addition to standard ovals, the printed notes included diamonds, triangles, and squares, the different shapes making it easier for common people to read music.

The singing master announced a hymn and cited its number. The singers turned to the page in the book. The singing master pitched the starting notes up and down the scale. He began beating out the tempo, moving his hand up and down in a slow chopping motion.

The first time through, the people sang the notes printed in the tunebooks: *sol* and *faw* and *law* and *me*, a strange and yet melodious intermingling of syllables, which differed for all four parts. Then they launched into the words.

They sang a dozen hymns, the singing master stopping them now and then to teach some musical rudiment.

He announced the next song, "Windham." The poetry, written a hundred years ago by the famous English cleric Isaac Watts, was arranged as a slow, magisterial anthem in the minor mode. Gideon knew "Windham" by heart. As with many of the hymns, the lyrics pierced his soul.

> *Broad is the road that leads to death,*
> *And thousands walk together there;*
> *But wisdom shows a narrow path,*
> *With here and there a traveler.*

The road to Sinking Valley could not be called broad. Would it lead him to his death? Or did death lurk along some narrow track through the Seven Mountains?

> *The fearful soul that tires and faints,*
> *And walks the ways of God no more*
> *Is but esteemed almost a saint*
> *And makes his own destruction sure.*

The words caught in Gideon's throat. He knew himself for a fearful soul, a man who walked the ways of God no more.

He would never be mistaken for a saint. He was a sinner. An adulterer.

Again he thought about the silver cross in his saddlebag.

Why was it there?

He didn't know. But if his own destruction took place tomorrow, he believed he would spend eternity in hell.

My steadfast heart shall know no fear;
That heart shall rest on thee

Chapter 26

———⊸∞⊶———

"WHO HAVE I SOLD NAILS TO LATELY?" HENRY HARBISON furrowed his grit-specked brow. "Aside from you, nobody." The blacksmith cracked a lopsided smile at Gideon. "I might have *traded* some nails. For stuff like hay and corn and spiritous liquids in jugs.

"Andrew Rankin got a bunch of nails this spring for something he was building. I believe he took some horseshoe nails, too." Harbison rubbed his chin. "Jonas Trautmann." He reeled off more names. Watson, McVey, Moffett. Reitz, Scheckler, Deiffenbach.

Gideon had spoken to those last six men earlier, found no particular links to Rebecca Kreidler, and held no suspicions toward them or their kin.

Harbison was making a blade for a knife, filing its edge. A heavy blade about ten inches long and three inches wide, with a pointed tip. It would be a fearsome weapon. The blacksmith picked up the naked blade by its tang. He held its point uncomfortably close to Gideon's neck. "Why do you want to know?"

"The coroner in Adamant found three of your nails driven into Rebecca Kreidler's corpse."

Harbison's eyes widened. Slowly he lowered the blade.

Gideon got out one of the nails the coroner had recovered and handed it to the smith.

Harbison inspected the nail. "Looks like my work." He gave the nail back. "I didn't do nothing to that woman."

"I didn't say you had."

"Does this mean she was murdered?"

Gideon didn't answer. He got back on the chestnut gelding that he had rented from the livery. He held the gelding's reins in his left hand and Maude's lead rope in his right hand. The carbine sleeved in its leather scabbard, a pistol loaded and primed in his saddlebag, and the handle of a hickory club poking out. In the bottom of the bag, wrapped in a piece of linen, lay Rebecca Kreidler's cross.

"If you hear anything, I'll be staying at Peter Nolf's house." Gideon clucked to the chestnut and moved out.

He met Abraham in the Trautmanns' farmyard.

Abe grinned. "Back so soon, Sheriff?"

"Hello, Abe. Are your father and your mother here?"

Abe's face got sober. "My *dawdy* is in the shop. *Memmi* is in the house."

Gideon dismounted and tied both horses to the fence. He beckoned for Abe to accompany him. Inside the shop, Jonas Trautmann was rubbing grease into harness leather. Abe went and stood next to his father. The farmer's first reaction on seeing Gideon had been to frown. Now he arranged his features in a neutral expression. Gideon asked Trautmann if he had bought or bartered for any horseshoe nails from Henry Harbison.

Trautmann nodded. "A few months ago." From his tidy work bench he picked up a small box and held it out. "Not many of them left."

"Have any gone missing?"

Trautmann shrugged. "I'm not sure. Why do you want to know?"

Gideon told Jonas and Abraham about the nails the coroner had found in Rebecca Kreidler's body.

The farmer's face froze. Abe's jaw dropped.

"What does this mean," Trautmann stammered, "that she had nails driven into her?"

"I was wondering if you could tell me."

Sweat stood out on Trautmann's face. He put down the harness leather and wrung his hands.

"Do either of you have any knowledge of *hexerei*?" Gideon asked.

Both men shook their heads.

"What? You know nothing about *hexes* and witchcraft?"

"No," Jonas said. "I mean, there are people who are supposed to be *hexes*, and a few spells I have heard of."

"Abe, you called your aunt a *hex* when I came here to get her remains," Gideon said. "Later you told me you didn't mean anything by it. I will ask you again: Why did you call Rebecca a witch?"

"It was all in fun. Just a game we played, me and Matt Harbison. We knew she wasn't a witch, she couldn't have been one."

"Why not?"

"She just wasn't! I mean, she was strange, she was different, but she wasn't a witch."

"Is anyone else around here reputed to be a *hex*?"

Again the men shook their heads. They told Gideon that no *Neigeboren* person would have anything to do with *hexerei*.

Jonas Trautmann sat down heavily on a stool. "Those nails," he said. "Evil, in this valley. Here on our own farm." His eyes shifted about in a panicky way. "Who could have done this?"

"That's what I need to find out." Gideon waited, but neither father nor son offered anything further. "Henry Harbison said that a man came to Sinking Valley this spring looking for someone who sounded a lot like Frau Kreidler. This was not a *Deitsch* man. Harbison said he was strong-looking. Maybe smoking a little black cigar. And riding a bay horse."

"Yes," Jonas Trautmann said. "That man came here."

"Did you know him?"

"I had never seen him before in my life. I didn't like the look of him. I wanted him to go away. So I acted like I didn't have much English. I told him, 'Here no *frau* like that.' He rode off and I didn't see him again."

"Why didn't you tell me about him earlier?"

"I didn't think of it. Was that right or wrong?"

"Did you tell your wife and Rebecca about the man?"

"Of course. Both of them. Maria didn't know him, Rebecca said she didn't know him, either."

Gideon nodded. "Now I will talk to Frau Trautmann."

Jonas started to get up from the stool.

"No, you stay here," Gideon told him.

Crossing the farmyard, Gideon considered the two men's reactions when he mentioned the nails. Both had appeared deeply surprised and upset. And who wouldn't be upset, to learn that a person might well have been murdered on your own farm? He would have been more suspicious if they hadn't looked shaken. Did they look guilty? He wasn't sure.

He tried to focus his thinking. He was determined to succeed in this investigation. Not because the Cold Fish had threatened to remove him from his job if he failed to identify Rebecca's killer. But because Rebecca Kreidler deserved to have justice done. And maybe because his own mother had been so cruelly used and killed. Thirteen long years ago. And still he couldn't escape it.

He knocked at the farmhouse door and was shown in to the kitchen by one of the Trautmanns' young daughters. Frau Trautmann and Elisabeth were preparing the evening meal. It was warm in the *kich*, and neither woman wore a cap. Their blonde hair pulled back and braided. Their blue eyes regarded him out of broad, handsome faces. Elisabeth's stare seemed sullen and aloof. Frau Trautmann looked startled. A little bit afraid?

He asked Frau Trautmann to send her young daughter out of the room. "Elisabeth, you can remain," he said. Then he told the two women about the nails.

"What do you know about this?" he said to Frau Trautmann.

"Only what I told you before." Frau Trautmann's voice was pitched high, her words rapid. "I found where she had been sick in the bakehouse. Everyone searched for her. Then much later, Abe's dog found her in the *sinkloch*." She took a deep breath. "I do not know why those nails should be in her body."

Gideon shifted his gaze to Elisabeth. "I don't know, either," she said. "I would swear it on the Bible."

A single tear coursed down Frau Trautmann's cheek. She wiped it away with a finger.

Her daughter's face looked ashen.

He wouldn't let them off so easily. Who would have had the greatest opportunity to poison Rebecca Kreidler? The women who prepared food for the family, of course. Perhaps one or both of them had made a deadly meal and taken it to the bakehouse. Each of these women begrudged Rebecca: Maria Trautmann because Rebecca had killed her brother John, Elisabeth because her aunt had stolen the heart of James Rankin, her apparent love interest.

He might not get an answer from them now. But he was planting seeds. Seeds that would cause fear to grow and flower. Fear of discovery that might make a culpable person blunder, say something revealing.

"Did either of you poison Rebecca Kreidler?"

Both women shook their heads emphatically.

"Answer me. I want to hear you say it. Yes or no."

"No, of course not," Elisabeth said.

"No! None of us would do anything like that!" Maria said. She began weeping. Beneath the track of her tears, the skin on her left cheek twitched.

Gideon remembered True telling him once, joking or maybe not, that a twitchy eye meant someone was trying to bewitch you.

"Tell me about the meal Rebecca ate on the night she died."

Both women shot their eyes around. The skin on Frau Trautmann's face twitched again. She raised her shoulders and let them fall. "I don't know. She cooked it herself."

"And you, Elisabeth?" Gideon asked. "What do you remember?"

At the moment when his gaze shifted from the elder to the younger woman, Gideon thought he caught Elisabeth shoot the barest sideways glance toward her mother.

Now the young woman raised her eyes to meet his. "Rebecca made her own meal that night."

Gideon wasn't sure he believed either woman. He let silence reign for a while. Then he said, "A man came here this spring. He may have been looking for Frau Kreidler. It was a week or so after she arrived. Did she ever say anything to either of you about who he was, or why he would have been looking for her?"

Both women averred that she had not.

"All right," Gideon said. "That's all for now. But I will be back. And I will keep coming back. Until I find out the truth about Frau Kreidler's death."

"You wanted her, like all the other men," Elisabeth blurted. "You came here at night. You were inside the bakehouse with her. Do you really want to find out the truth about her death?"

Gideon felt awash in shame. "Yes. I want to find out the truth about her death. I *will* find out the truth about her death." He sought to recover his composure. "You say 'all the other men' wanted Rebecca. Who do you mean?"

Elisabeth's pretty face was mottled, her features compressed. "She attracted men like a bitch in heat brings in the dogs."

"Elisabeth!" her mother cried.

"Tell me who," Gideon said.

"You, for one."

"Who else?"

Elisabeth shook her head: one abrupt snap to the right and then the left.

"I hear that James Rankin came to see her."

"I cannot say," Elisabeth replied.

"And that he was interested in you until he saw your aunt."

Elisabeth kept her mouth shut.

"I will leave you now," Gideon said. "I am going to Pastor Nolf's house. If you want to tell me anything, you can find me there."

He left the kitchen with the sound of Maria Trautmann's renewed sobbing in his ears. Crossing the farmyard, he caught sight of the bakehouse. Suddenly he felt an urge to go inside.

It looked much the same as the last time he had been here, on the day when he and Alonzo had come to fetch the corpse.

He sniffed the air, picking up scents of yeast, flour, wood ash. A disagreeable fustiness from mice. The bakehouse was a place where women baked bread, prepared the staff of life. In this case, also a place of death.

He sat down in a chair. Shifted his eyes around the room. Tried to imagine Rebecca Kreidler thrashing about in agony. It came to him, as it did all too often, the terror that had drenched him when he found his *memmi*'s body lying on the kitchen floor. And, much worse, he imagined his mother's own terror during the last moments of her life. He felt his breath seize up, felt it all coming back.

He stood up. He couldn't afford to revisit that memory now. He had a job to do.

He strode outside. He untied the horses and mounted. Tapped his calves against the chestnut gelding's sides. They went quickly down the road, Maude's head at his leg, a little slack in the lead rope.

Word of the nails would not have reached Nolf yet. Though it wouldn't be long before everyone in Sinking Valley knew.

Yes, ev'ry secret of my heart
Shall shortly be made known

Chapter 27

⸙

"L IEBER JESU." NOLF STARED AT GIDEON, DESOLATION ON HIS FACE. "Nails? In her body?"

"In her foot, her torso, and her skull."

"Dear God. I can't fathom this."

"But it is indeed the case that the coroner found those nails. Horseshoe nails. Someone had to drive them in."

Nolf clapped both his hands over his mouth, drew them downward.

"I am convinced that Frau Kreidler was murdered," Gideon said.

"God have mercy on us all." Nolf gave a long exhalation. "What's to be done now?"

"I will find out who killed her and bring that person to justice. I hope you can help me."

"Do you suspect anyone?"

"I just came from the Trautmann farm. Everyone there denies poisoning Frau Kreidler and driving nails into her body."

"Do you believe them?"

Gideon let the question hang in the air. He surveyed the room, with its beautiful walnut wardrobe and its *fraktur* wall decoration depicting a fierce eagle rampant above the message GOTT SIEHT ALLES. God sees all.

Does he really? Gideon wondered. *And if so, does he care?*

Several hornets buzzed past, hunting flies, apparently doing a good job of it since there were no bothersome houseflies in the sitting room.

Nolf broke the silence. "How can I help?"

"Keep your ears open. Listen to what people say. Soon everyone in Sinking Valley will be talking about this. As pastor, you may hear something that will reveal important information concerning Frau Kreidler's death."

Nolf indicated a chair. "Please. I still can't take this in." When both men were seated, Nolf said, "I am very sad for Rebecca. And I'm afraid."

"It's a horrible thing," Gideon replied. "A deliberate poisoning, most likely. And the nails. Could the nails be part of some spell? Some form of *hexerei*?"

Nolf frowned. "I don't know about that. And I'm not sure you should assume that a *Deitsch* person did this. Other people, they have their superstitions and curses, too." He went on, "It's terrifying to think we could have a poisoner in our midst. Someone so unfeeling as to take a life like that. And the nails . . . Sheriff, my fear goes beyond what happened to poor Frau Kreidler. We *Neigeboren* must live here with our neighbors. We are different. Some view us as a threat. We come here with money. We buy farms. We are changing this valley, perhaps in ways that the people who have lived here for generations do not want or like. Even now, members of our church are getting letters from relatives back home, other *Neigeboren* families asking their kin to find them land to buy. I know of two families from Berks County that have just bought farms farther down the valley. They will be here next spring.

"I told you what happened to my family when I was a boy. How my father was horsewhipped, how we were driven from our home. Because of our beliefs. Because of the way we dressed, the way we spoke. Sheriff Stoltz, I fear that others in this valley could use this unfortunate death as an excuse to persecute us. Especially if they think someone caused it using witchcraft."

"Nevertheless," Gideon replied, "it is my duty to uphold the law and to find out who committed these crimes."

"Of course. Whoever did this must be held accountable for their acts."

"The last time I was here, you gave me the names of several plants that could kill."

"Indeed. Many plants are poisonous if they're used carelessly or incorrectly."

"What about a plant called cowbane? I don't believe you mentioned it, but I understand that it's very deadly."

Nolf nodded. "It is also called water hemlock."

"Does it have any medicinal use?"

"Long ago, when I apprenticed at the apothecary in Philadelphia, I remember my Quaker master using it to treat a man for *grand mal.*"

"You mean epilepsy?"

"Yes. *Die falletgranke.*"

"Does it grow in this valley?"

"It's common almost everywhere. It grows in marshy places. But I have not seen it here."

Gideon decided to switch tacks. "I have learned that a man came here this past April, apparently looking for Frau Kreidler." He repeated Harbison's description of the man. "By any chance, did he talk to you?"

"Yes. I remember it well. A beautiful spring day. I was in my garden, getting it ready for planting, when the man rode up on his horse. I was suspicious of him, as you might imagine. A stranger asking questions about a woman."

"Did you know then that Rebecca Kreidler had recently moved in with the Trautmanns?"

"Yes, I did know that. She seemed to fit the description the man gave. I found out from him that he had talked already to Jonas Trautmann, who had not revealed that Rebecca had come to live with them. I knew about the woman's crime and her punishment. I did not think the poor soul needed anyone or anything from her past to come and haunt her. And, at the time, I hoped she would become newborn in God, become part of our community. So I lied to the man. I told him I didn't know of any such woman."

"Did anyone in the valley tell this man about Frau Kreidler?"

"I would be surprised if they did. Over time, we *Neigeboren* have learned not to say too much—not to rile things up. Do you think this man could have returned and killed Rebecca?"

"I don't know. But I want to talk to him. Assuming I can find him. Did he give you his name or say where he was from?"

Nolf shook his head. He put his hands on the tops of his thighs and pushed up from his chair. "I must go milk the cow. We will have some milk with our supper. Will you be staying here tonight?"

"If that's all right."

"Of course." Nolf gave Gideon a wan smile. "You are always welcome in my humble home. I think I'd be insulted if you went anywhere else."

★★★

While Nolf prepared the evening meal, Gideon made himself useful by chopping firewood. Using a file and a stone, he sharpened the pastor's woefully dull ax. He chopped lengths of oak into billets, then knocked the billets apart along their grain. Afterward, he went down to the stream and washed up.

Supper was smoked trout, sweet peas, and boiled potatoes in a milk sauce. Gideon found the meal delicious. Nolf had grown the peas and potatoes in his garden; someone in his congregation had given him trout caught in a weir. Later the two men sat outside in the soft evening light. Pink-and-gold clouds slowly drifted from west to east down the valley. A raven rowed across the sky, its broad wings making a soft cuffing sound. Another raven, hidden in the woods, called out in guttural *ronks*, metallic *tocks*, odd-sounding gurgles and rasps.

Nolf asked Gideon about his head injury, whether he still had headaches and if his memory had returned.

Gideon thanked Nolf for his concern and explained that he was feeling much better. He brought up again the death of Rebecca Kreidler, the nails in her corpse. But all he could get out of the pastor were expressions of sympathy toward the poor woman's suffering, and how, if he were able, Gideon might perhaps downplay the discovery of the nails, since it could put the *Neigeboren* into a bad repute with their neighbors. Nolf also strongly suggested that Gideon find and question the mysterious stranger from south of the Seven Mountains. "Perhaps he is your villain," the pastor said.

★★★

The next day, Gideon rode around Sinking Valley on the chestnut gelding, leaving Maude in Nolf's pasture.

He came to a field where a line of six men swung their scythes. In front of the men the grass rolled in the breeze like a green sea. The scythes cutting the grass sounded like a chorus of people coughing rhythmically. When the men took a break, he talked to them. They told him nothing new.

He conferred with Dutch and English folk repairing equipment, weeding gardens, traveling on the road, driving wagons and carts.

To all he revealed the fact that nails had been found in Rebecca Kreidler's decomposed body. He gauged the people's reactions. Shock, of course. Concern and worry. Fear. But he saw nothing that suggested guilt. Although, he reflected, people could be very good at hiding their thoughts and acts.

He went to the Rankins' farm at midday. A gray-haired woman answered the door. She showed him in to the dining room. Andrew Rankin sat at the dinner table, along with three children who looked at Gideon with great curiosity: this strange man barging into their home. Rankin did not bother to rise from his chair. When asked if his son James was in the house, he simply said, "Out somewhere on his horse."

Rankin stiffly introduced the gray-haired woman as his sister, Thurza, who, following his wife's passing some years ago, had come to live with them, keep the house, and raise the children. The farmer gave out near-monosyllabic answers to Gideon's questions. To the revelation of nails found in the Kreidler woman's corpse, Rankin frowned and said, "You came here and ruined our meal for that?"

At day's end, Gideon rode back to Nolf's house. He was exhausted. His eyes hadn't liked the day's glare. The cobwebby thing had come back, in a slightly different position. It hadn't startled him, but it grated on his nerves.

About all he'd learned was that farther down the valley a seldom-used trace climbed through a gap in Dark Mountain, the ridge hemming in Sinking Valley on the south. He was told this by a man he recognized from the circle hunt in the Big Kettle, the fellow in the pale smock who had been in front of him in the line. The man pointed out the gap in the mountain above his farm. He said that after climbing through the gap, the trail led a long way through the forest, went through similar gaps and across several other ridges until it came out "somewhere down in Greer County." The man had gone that way with two friends on a winter hunting expedition. He said the trace emerged from the mountains at a village with a mill, beside which stood "a mean sort of watering hole called the White Crow."

Your morning sun may set at noon,
And leave you ever in the dark

Chapter 28

———— ⋙⋘ ————

TRUE AND HER GRANDMOTHER COOKED MEALS AND BAKED BREAD.
True brushed the gelding Jack and braided his mane. She milked
the cow, which Gram Burns had never named, simply calling it "that
ugly cow" even though the cow was doe-eyed and sleek and a
pleasing shade of red. True suspected her gram did this to protect the
cow, recollecting her father saying that his mother had an evil eye so
little under her control that she dared not look at an animal she
owned and admire it overmuch lest it lay down and die.

True churned butter from the cow's milk and helped her gram
make cheese.

The two women picked corn, shucked the ears, and dried the
kernels. They hatcheled the husks. They shook last year's fusty cornhusks out of the mattress ticks. They washed the ticks, dried them in
the sun, sewed rips and tears, and refilled the ticks with the fresh,
sweet-smelling husks.

In the springhouse, True saw a salamander swimming sinuously in
the cold flow. It was orange as fire and freckled with black spots. Her
gram called it a lizard and said that seeing it would bring her good luck.

Gram Burns showed True how to find and cut down ash trees,
pound the wood, and pull and split the strips along the annual growth
rings; later they could plait the strips into baskets for carrying eggs
and vegetables and plants foraged in the brushlands and the woods.

Gram Burns introduced True to plants that they picked for
potions and remedies.

One day as the two of them made their way up the hollow, True
said, "I could live here forever."

"Not hardly you couldn't," Gram Burns replied. "You have your own home."

"I don't want to go back there."

"You'll go back. You have a life to lead. Gideon needs you, and you need him."

"I'm not sure I love him anymore."

"He loves you. Easy to see it from the way he treats you."

"I could stay here and take care of you for the rest of your days."

"No. You need to face life, not run away from it."

True looked at the ground solid beneath her feet. A sense of panic and claustrophobia began pressing in on her from all sides. She cast about for an excuse. "He won't let me into his heart. Not the whole way in."

Gram Burns scoffed. She left the path and hobbled up a shady slope. She pointed her stick at a fan of leaves like wan green tongues lolling below a wizened stem that held up a tan seedpod. "It don't look like much now," she said, "but in the spring the flower will stop you in your tracks. A big yellow flower shaped like a moccasin. That's its name: yellow moccasin. Use that hoe and grub out the roots; we'll dry them. The tea will make this dark world seem a bit brighter."

They went farther, came back into sunlight, stopped at a patch of plants where bees visited spiky, disheveled-looking pale lavender flowers. Gram Burns rubbed a leaf between her fingers, sniffed it, motioned for True to do the same. "Bee balm. A kind of mint. Pick a good many of the leaves. The tea will cure a sore throat. It brings the energy up, body and soul. Another plant to help chase the black wolf away."

Motherwort. "The tea eases childbirth. You need to know this one. Because you will bear another child someday."

True shook her head.

"You will," Gram Burns said. "Trust me."

True did trust her grandmother. She remembered as a child being afraid of the old woman, who had seemed ancient even then. Not the kind of gram to pick you up and cuddle you and baby-talk you.

Scared of her gram or not, True remembered how often she'd asked her parents if they could go to the cabin and visit. Having no horse or wagon, they walked. A whole day of walking each way, so they rarely went. A few times in summer her parents left her with Gram Burns for weeks on end.

Now she wanted to stay with the old woman and listen to her stories and find comfort in her understanding and strength. The old woman had never in her adult life been out of Colerain County, but to True, Arabella Burns seemed worldly and wise. Sometimes even otherworldly.

That evening both women sipped tea brewed from bee balm and rattleweed. True bathed again in water scented with sweetfern.

She went to sleep on a mattress cushioned with fragrant cornhusks.

She dreamed of Gideon. He was traveling. In search of someone. He rode Maude on a trail through the forest. The farther he went, the darker the woods became. In her dream, True's own vision seemed to shift into Gideon, so that she looked at things with his eyes: Boulders rubbling a ridgetop. Tall trees with thick vines coiling up their trunks. A stream to splash through. A carpet of hock-high ferns, the trail unspooling through them.

Then her sight pulled away and she saw him from above. Alone on Maude, a man and his horse by themselves in the wild.

He rode toward something that seemed to lie in wait. Something ghostly and pale. Out in front, a tall, rail-thin man sat on a small gray horse. The same man she had met on the road in Panther Valley. The one who called her a wildwood flower waiting to be plucked. The man watched as Gideon approached.

She cried out to Gideon, warning him not to go up to the man. But he didn't hear her. He kept riding, getting closer with Maude's every step.

The billows roll beneath your feet,
For death eternal waits for you

Chapter 29

⎯⎯∞⎯⎯

GIDEON RODE FROM SHADOW INTO LIGHT: FROM THE FORESTED convoluted mountains into the slanting afternoon sun in a narrow valley where weedy fields stood separated one from another by meandering rows of heaped-up rocks.

He stopped next to a blackened chimney above a pile of charred debris.

In front of the pile rose a crooked pole with a sign nailed to its top. On the sign, a crudely painted white crow gaped its bill skyward.

Across the road from the burnt tavern were a pond and a grist-mill whose wooden wheel slowly creaked as water sheeted from its tumbling blades.

Gideon dismounted and let Maude graze on the wiry grass beneath the sign.

He studied the charred wood and twisted metal and melted glass.

Expect the unexpected, his predecessor, Sheriff Payton, had told him. *And always go sufficiently armed.*

When preparing to leave Pastor Nolf's house that morning, Gideon had thought about riding to Walkersville, the Greer County seat, there to identify himself as the Colerain County sheriff and inquire with his Greer County counterpart about the settlement called McDonough, the White Crow Tavern, and a strong-appearing, cigar-smoking man who might dwell there. Walkersville was in the southern part of Greer County. To get there from Sinking Valley, Gideon would have had to backtrack over Mingo Mountain and ride west almost to Adamant to pick up the stage road south through the Seven Mountains. It would have added a day to his trip. Instead, he had chosen to leave Sinking Valley on the faint trail through the gap in Dark Mountain that he had learned about yesterday.

He had followed the trail through a succession of gaps in the wooded ridges.

Once Maude stopped short at a heap of bear dung so large and furred with mold that it looked more like a crouching animal than a pile of excrement.

They passed black fungi jutting up from the ground like the tips of dead men's fingers.

At another place in the forest, Maude stiffened, stared, and gave a low snort that ended in a hollow rattle. Gideon looked around. Had she heard or smelled something? A panther or a bear? A hidden varmint of the human type? He got the pistol out of his saddlebag. He sat for several minutes, holding the weapon against his breast. A strange glow played in a patch of laurel. It seemed to come from a sun shaft piercing the tight-knit tree canopy high overhead: an influx of light occasioned by the subtle revolving of the earth. The glow lingered for a while, then vanished. He touched his legs to Maude, and she went into a head-high amble, hurrying them down the path. He felt them pass through a pocket of cold air.

Now, in this tight valley, next to the burned-out tavern in the hamlet called McDonough, both Maude and Gideon startled.

A boy stepped out from behind the fire-scorched chimney. A negro boy. Young and thin, his color like fancy molasses. Apparently having hidden there while deciding whether or not this stranger was dangerous. In his hand the boy held several square-headed iron spikes. It was what you did after a building burned down: picked through the wreckage and recovered things of value, such as nails that could be used again.

"Hello," Gideon said. "I am looking for a man. I was told he may live here."

The boy wore threadbare clothes. Bony wrists stuck out beyond a stained homespun shirt. His knees looked like eyes peering through the holes in his trousers.

Gideon wondered if the boy was resident here or a slave run north from Maryland or Virginia. "Do you live in this place?"

The boy nodded, then angled his head toward the pile of debris. "Mister Craddock, I worked for him. But he's dead now. Had to go back inside and get his cash." The boy shook his head.

"I am looking for a stout, strong man with a bay horse," Gideon said. "He smokes little black cigars. My age or a bit older. I am told that he lives in this place."

"Thaddeus," the boy said. "What do you want with him?"

"I need to ask him about a woman who may have come here this spring."

"I'll take you to him." The boy stared at Maude, tilted his head to peer at the carbine's buttstock protruding from the saddle scabbard. "You the law?" Without waiting for an answer, the boy repeated, "I'll take you to him. Just a little ways from here."

Spikes clutched in his fist, the boy skipped away down the road.

Gideon followed, leading Maude.

The man was on his knees in front of a cabin, playing roughly with a small prick-eared dog, white with brown spots; he batted at the dog with his big hands while the dog growled and feinted and snapped. The man was hatless, his hair cropped close to his head. Pale scars hatched his scalp.

When the dog saw Gideon and Maude, it commenced a shrill barking. With every bark the dog's front feet lifted off the ground. From behind the cabin came the doleful baying of a hound.

The man said, "Settle, Mole," and the little dog whimpered and sat. The man hollered, "Luther, you shut up, too!" and the unseen hound fell silent. The man stood, and he looked like a bear coming up off all fours. He had blood on his hands. Casually he licked the blood off one hand, then the other. He was not tall but he was big and burly in all his other dimensions. He looked Gideon over; his eyes, like the boy's, lingered on the rifle in its scabbard.

The boy squatted down on his hams and clasped his hands in front of his knees as if preparing to watch a horse race or an athletic event.

The man smiled at the boy. "Hey, Otis," he said. "Who's your friend?"

"My name is Gideon Stoltz," Gideon said.

The man got a thin black cigar out of his vest pocket and stuck it in one corner of his mouth. He rolled it between his lips. "What do you want? The White Crow has been closed for some time."

"I am the sheriff of Colerain County. I heard that you came to our county this past spring. In April. You went to Sinking Valley and asked about a woman there."

"You sound like one of them Dutch yourself. You sound like all of them people who have went in and occupied that valley."

"Would you tell me your name, please?"

"Thaddeus Kirkwood. I'm the constable hereabouts."

Henry Harbison had said that the man had a fancy saddle with a *K* tooled into the leather beside a little pine tree.

Kirkwood.

"Why were you looking for that woman in Sinking Valley, Mr. Kirkwood?"

The man shifted the unlit cigar from one corner of his mouth to the other. "I am not sure I need to answer that question. First off, how do I know you're the sheriff up that way? I see that badge on your vest, but anybody can buy one of them pot-metal stars."

"I was appointed to fill the office of sheriff in Colerain County two years ago, after Sheriff Israel Payton died."

"Oh, Israel Payton, yes indeedy, I heard he fell over dead." Kirkwood grinned. "The sheriff here in Greer, that's Sam Cook, he told me about Payton. Said he was a stickler for following the rules. Now you tell me . . ." he paused, "well, I forgot your name already, I never been good at remembering names. Anyway, how the devil do you get things done up that way, you follow all them picky little rules?"

"Mr. Kirkwood, in April you talked to several people in Sinking Valley. You described the woman you were looking for as a Dutch woman, 'a pretty little thing.'"

Kirkwood nodded. "That's so." He looked at his hands, which had stopped bleeding. "I'm not sure I need to answer you, on account of we are in Greer County. Even if you are the law in Colerain, you are out of your jurisdiction here. But I will be polite and tell you that, yes, I went looking for that wench."

"Why were you looking for her?"

"You come down through Nomans Notch?"

Gideon nodded toward the gap through which he had entered the valley. "I came through there."

"Then you rode past the reason I went looking for her."

Gideon lifted his eyebrows.

"The fire, man. The fire that burned the White Crow."

"Go on."

"The tavern burned back in March. Caught fire in the middle of the night. There was five people in it. The proprietor, Noah Craddock. The woman who done the cooking; that's my ma, she's married to Craddock, though he ain't my pa, which she married him after my real father died. There was two paying guests, salesmen if I recall. And that Dutch woman. Small, dark-haired, a pretty face. The kind of wench makes your britches twitch, y'know what I mean?" Kirkwood leered. "She showed up that afternoon and helped out in the kitchen. Then she slept there that night."

"What about the fire?" Gideon said. "Did the people get out alive?"

"The two guests did. And my ma. Craddock got out, too, but then he had to run back inside and get some money out of his desk. He always was a fool that way, cared only for the almighty dollar. He didn't come back out again. Next morning we found him laying under a beam. We buried what was left of him on the hill. I kicked around in the ashes, looking for that Dutch woman's bones, but I didn't find her. So I think she got out. And I think she lit the fire that burned the place down."

"Why would she do that? Fires start for all sorts of reasons."

"Let me speculate," Kirkwood said. "I have no evidence for it, because everything got burned up. But I think she must have stoled the money out of Bill's desk and wanted to cover it up. So she started a fire and burned the place down." He looked at the boy, who was still squatting on his hams. Kirkwood's little dog had gone over to the boy, and the lad was petting it.

"Otis," Kirkwood said. "You seen that woman when she come here, walking in from the coach road. And you seen somebody looked like her walking north, didn't you, in the dark up the road into the notch after the fire broke out?"

The boy nodded.

"So there." Kirkwood turned toward Gideon. "I thought I'd go talk to that wench. I rode to Sinking Valley. I reckoned she was bound for that place, being as the Dutch are taking it over, coming in and buying up land. I tell you, they better not try that here."

"You talked to a blacksmith in Sinking Valley."

Kirkwood nodded. "He put a shoe on my horse. Said he didn't know of any such woman."

"Who else did you ask?"

"Some Dutch. Most of them just grunted like hogs, maybe they couldn't understand plain English, or maybe they was just dumb as rocks." He sniffed. "Felt like I got a door slammed in my face." He shrugged. "I turned around and rode back here."

"You say you are a constable, Mr. Kirkwood. If you meant to arrest that woman, why didn't you go to the sheriff of this county and get a warrant, or come and see me in Adamant?"

"I didn't say nothing about arresting her, did I?" Kirkwood grinned. "Thought I might teach her a lesson. Anyway, why follow all them picky rules? No, sir, I like to do things myself. That way I know they get done."

"Would it surprise you to learn that the woman you were look-ing for is dead?"

Kirkwood stared at Gideon, the grin fixed on his face. "I didn't know that. Like I said, I couldn't find her."

"Maybe not. But you were right, she went to Sinking Valley. Rebecca Kreidler was her name. She was alive until about a month ago, when her body turned up in a sinkhole. Let me ask you another question, Mr. Kirkwood. Where were you on the evening of Thursday, July the seventeenth?"

"How should I know?" Kirkwood jutted his lower jaw so that the cigar poked up toward his nose. "Must've been right here in McDonough. I'm always here. Ain't that so, Otis?"

The boy shrugged.

Kirkwood's eyes narrowed. "Well," he said, "you can't put much stock in what that one says or will not say. Why don't you ask my ma, she's inside the cabin. She come to live with me after the tavern burned down. Can't say I'm happy about it, but there you go."

Kirkwood clapped his hands together, and the little dog leaped up joyfully. "This here is Mole," Kirkwood said. "My hole dog. My hound runs a fox down a hole, I put Mole in after him. I put my Mole in the hole." Kirkwood laughed, restoring the grin on his face. "He muckles on to the fox, and he kills it and drags it out. Even if it takes him all day."

"I doubt that Rebecca Kreidler stole any money here," Gideon said. "As far as I could tell, she had no money with her when she got to Sinking Valley. She made brooms and sold them to pay for her keep on the farm where she was staying."

"That may be so, for all we know," Kirkwood said.

"But if she burned the tavern down, I suspect she had a reason."

The muscles in Kirkwood's neck tightened.

"She made your britches twitch," Gideon said. "What did you do to her here? And did you then return to Sinking Valley last month? To teach her a lesson?"

"You're talking hogwash. You're miles from home. You say you are a sheriff, but that don't mean a thing to me."

"Mr. Kirkwood . . ."

"I would like you to remember me," Kirkwood said. "I will give you something to remember me by every time you cough or sneeze."

He rushed in so fast Gideon barely got his fists up.

Kirkwood grabbed Gideon around the chest and drove him backward. The man locked his hands behind Gideon's back and squeezed. Gideon felt the air whoosh out of his lungs. He let go of Maude's reins. He heard a popping sound in the side of his chest. He tried to strike Kirkwood with his fist, but Kirkwood buried his face between Gideon's neck and shoulder and bit down hard. Gideon yelped at the pain. Felt himself lifted off the ground. He heard another pop in his chest and yelled again. He tried to gouge Kirkwood's eyes but couldn't get his thumbs near them. He drove a fist into Kirkwood's ear. To no effect. He heard the dog barking, felt it sink its teeth into his leg.

The cabin tipped and slewed past. He saw the boy squatted down watching. He saw Maude throw up her head and dance. The big man squeezed harder. Again the cabin, the boy, Maude. The club's butt sticking out of the saddlebag. Gideon grabbed at it. His hand got close but not close enough. He felt the dog yank his lower leg from side to side. Pinpoints of light cascaded at the edges of his vision.

Maude. The saddlebag. The club. He got his hand on it. As Kirkwood turned with him again, the club came sliding out of the bag. Two inches of its handle stuck out from the thumb side of Gideon's right fist. With all his might, he rammed the club's butt into Kirkwood's head.

Kirkwood let go. Gideon's feet hit the ground. He stumbled, caught his balance. Tried to pull air into his lungs. He switched the club around and brought it down hard on the dog worrying his leg. The dog let go and fell to the dirt, its hind legs kicking.

Kirkwood rushed him again. Gideon swung the club low and hard and hit Kirkwood on the side of his leg. A thud and a snap as the knee buckled inward.

Kirkwood screamed and fell.

Gideon stood with his sides heaving, pain shooting through his ribs. A hot pulsing where Kirkwood had bitten him on the muscle between his shoulder and neck. He felt blood running down his leg beneath his torn pants.

Kirkwood sat on the ground, legs out in front. His left leg bent oddly at the knee. He had lost his cigar. "You killed Mole," he gasped. "You broke my god-damn leg."

Gideon took a step forward and raised the club. Kirkwood cried out and shot a hand above his head. Gideon felt a pure hot rage fill his body. He saw his *memmi* lying on the kitchen floor. The victim of someone like this man, by God he would club him, he would beat his head to a pulp . . .

He pulled back, caught his breath. Then stepped forward and raised the club again.

"What did you do to Rebecca Kreidler?" he cried.

"Fucked her. That's all! Fucked her in the storeroom in the White Crow. She wanted it! I couldn't find her in April. I never went back to that valley again. I swear it!"

Gideon lowered the club. He shook all over.

He prayed to God he hadn't used Rebecca Kreidler as Thaddeus Kirkwood had done. As someone had used his own mother before stabbing her to death.

He looked for the boy, but he was nowhere to be seen. The dog lay unmoving in the dirt, its tongue lolling out.

"I'm sorry about your dog," Gideon said. "It looks like I gave you something that will remind you of what you did to that woman every time you take a step."

Life with trials hard may press me;
Heav'n will bring me sweeter rest

Chapter 30

❦

THAT MORNING, AFTER DREAMING ABOUT GIDEON AND THE MAN ON the pale horse, True had risen at dawn.

Her gram was not in the cabin. Probably out picking berries or looking for plants. Or watching the new day come on from some vantage point on the farm. Maybe she'd roused herself in the darkness hours ago. True couldn't see much structure in the old woman's days; she got up when she chose to, did whatever chores seemed to suggest themselves, lay back down again when the urge came.

True made herself coffee. She was still troubled by her dream of Gideon riding through the forest toward the rail-thin man waiting on his pale horse.

One end of the cabin attached to a smaller structure built of stone. True took her coffee there. She sat down on a creaky bench, her back against the cool rock wall, her bare feet on the dirt floor. This small musty space was a fort. Square, maybe four steps across. It was the first thing Thomas and Sarah McCracken, True's great-grandparents, had built when they came from downstate to settle on land bought sight unseen in Panther Valley. They laid up the stone fort before they even started clearing the land. True recalled a story about the two of them fighting off an Indian attack, Thomas shooting out through the slitted openings in the walls, Sarah reloading their two muskets while the children, including eight-year-old Arabella, crouched on the floor. Later, the couple and their growing brood fled with other settlers in the Big Runaway, during the War of Independence, when British officers led Indian raids against settlements along the frontier.

Another story had come down through the generations: After the war, after the McCrackens returned to their farm and continued to make improvements and clear the land, a wagon came trundling down Panther Valley. Six horses pulled the big Conestoga with its blue-painted box and arching canvas cover. Accompanying the wagon was a large family, most of them afoot. Somehow these travelers had heard of the cabin up the side hollow, and they came calling. The McCrackens fed their visitors, whose last name was Burns, found places for them to sleep that night, and provisioned them, as well as they were able, for their continued journey west. The Burnses were bound across the Alleghenies, headed for land the father had been granted for soldiering in the war. A boy in the Burns family spent much of the evening talking to Arabella McCracken. The boy's name was Ezekiel. Three days after his kin set off down the valley, Ezekiel Burns came walking back to the farm. All of sixteen years old, he asked Arabella, age fourteen, to marry him. Ezekiel would never see his parents and brothers and sisters again. Over time, he and Arabella would inherit the farm, and the narrow vale in which it lay would become known as Burns Hollow—although, True reflected, it really should have been called McCracken Hollow.

And now fourteen-year-old Arabella McCracken Burns was white-haired and wrinkled and old as poverty, still living in Burns Hollow, but not long for this world.

True looked through one of the rifle slits and saw her grandmother limp past. Gram Burns came in to the cabin. True got up and went to greet her.

★★★

They sat in the shade on a log, shaving ash splints. Gram Burns showed True how to hold a long pliant splint in one hand and use a knife to shave off whiskers and other irregularities on the splint's edge.

"This thick one is a riser," Gram Burns said. "That thin one is a weaver. We get done shaving them, we'll make a basket."

True told her grandmother how she had dreamed of Gideon riding through the dark woods toward the rail-thin man on the pale horse.

"It was the same man I saw when I rode here on Jack. You told me that everyone comes to know that old man sooner or later. I recognize him now."

Her gram's crooked fingers worked the knife and the splint. "Anything else in your dream?"

"No. That was all. Gideon getting closer and closer to the man, and not hearing me when I called out to warn him."

"Do you think he's dead?"

True shook her head. "If he was, I'd know it."

"I believe you would, too." Gram Burns set the finished splint aside and picked up another one.

"I had a dream like that about Zeke once," she said. "It was after he went to work at the furnace in Panther and we left this farm and moved down there. He had gone off with a pack train freighting iron to Pittsburgh. Back then, they poured the ingots so they were shaped like a U to fit over a horse's back. I was doing wash, stirring clothes in the kettle. I looked up at the smoke from the fire, and in it I seen Zeke. He fell off his horse. He lay there on the ground with the green hills all around him, the other horses in the pack train bucking and running this way and that.

"I seen it in all its particulars. Him laying there with blood pouring down his face. When he got back from that trip, he told me how something spooked their horses, and all hell broke loose." Gram Burns paused in her work. "When Zeke came to die, years and years later, we were back here in Burns Hollow. He died in our bed, an old man. Do you recall him?"

"Maybe a little bit."

"I don't think your Gideon is dead, either. But he's troubled. And he puts himself in danger, being a sheriff. Do you tell him of your dreams?"

"He doesn't believe in dreams, says they don't signify anything. He doesn't believe in the sight, either."

The old woman shrugged.

"You have it," True said.

"Yes. Sometimes I see bad things and good things. Mostly bad. Miseries abounding in this world."

"And you can see into the future."

"Usually I see things right when they happen. But I have seen a thing or two before it has come to pass."

"Did you see David's death? Did you know it was coming?"

The old woman drew the yellow-white splint toward her as her knife perfected its edge.

Tears filled True's eyes. She put down the splint she was holding and let the knife sit quiet in her hand. "I think you saw it. And knew it would happen, and knew there wasn't a thing could be done to prevent it.

"Before David died," True continued, "I had a dream. In it I saw a face with bloody teeth. The teeth were white, not yellow, so I knew it was a young person who would die and not someone old. I didn't know it would be my own son. I told Gideon, and he said it was just a dream."

Tears ran down True's face. Gram Burns put down her knife and took her granddaughter in her arms.

"I buried two little ones on this place," Gram Burns said. "I was up on the hill with them this morning watching the sun come up. They are there with my ma and pa, and two of my brothers and a sister who died young. And Zeke. I'll be with them soon. I am not afraid to die. My soul is untroubled. I've been on this earth long enough. But you have a while left."

Gram Burns pressed True's face against her breast and stroked her granddaughter's hair.

Waters swell and death and fear
Sets thy path no refuge near

Chapter 31

———⊷⊶———

G IDEON LEANED AGAINST MAUDE. HIS LEGS SHOOK, AND PAIN flared on both sides of his chest, more than a twinge, less than pure agony. Likely Kirkwood had cracked some ribs.

He led Maude to the stream whose waters fed the mill pond in the hamlet called McDonough. He let her drink and graze on the grassy bank. He eased himself out of his vest and shirt. Turning his head all the way to the side, he could just see the livid bruise where Kirkwood had bitten him between his shoulder and neck. With difficulty, wincing at the pain, he pulled off his boots and struggled out of his pants. The dog bites on his lower leg oozed blood.

Skinned the bark in a few places, Gideon imagined his deputy Alonzo saying.

He got a piece of soap out of his kit and stepped into the stream. The water cold as perdition. He found a deep spot and lowered himself onto slick rocks on the stream bottom. He gritted his teeth and scrubbed his wounds, gasping and cursing in *Deitsch*. He raised himself out of the water. Made sure all the cuts ran blood. Eased himself down in again and rinsed.

He ducked his head and stayed under as long as he could and came up sputtering and shivering. He took a deep breath. The pain chiseling his ribs made him hiss.

When he got out of the stream, the boy was sitting on a stump watching him.

"Thaddeus' mother gone to fetch his brothers," the boy said. "Two of them. They will be here soon."

"Oh, hell and damnation," Gideon said.

"You could hide somewhere and shoot them down with your gun."

Gideon shook his head.

"Then you best get on your horse and go."

"Do they have horses, those brothers?"

The boy nodded. "Knives and guns, too." The boy got up and came closer to Gideon. "You go back the way you came, up through the gap in the mountain. The same way that woman left the night the tavern burned down. I will tell the Kirkwoods you went the other way to get to the stage road."

"They'll look for my tracks. They won't see them on that road."

"Mr. Seth Gilliland rode his horse down the road an hour ago. Headed to Mackeytown to buy tobacco chaw. They'll see his tracks."

"All right. Thanks. Why are you helping me?"

The boy regarded Gideon with serious eyes. "I do you a favor, Sheriff Gideon Stoltz, maybe you will do one for me. I hear that Adamant is a place where some colored folk live. A place where jobs can be found. I can handle horses and oxen and cows. I can harness a team and drive a wagon. I can fix or repair just about anything you set in front of me. I ain't afraid to work. I get myself to your town, will you help me find a job?"

"I'll do the best I can."

★★★

The next morning Gideon woke at dawn, wrapped in his blankets near a spring in a small glade within the Seven Mountains. Mist crawled up the lichen-flecked trunks of surrounding trees. Maude stood sleeping, one back leg cocked under her.

His rifle and pistol tucked close at hand.

He lay there listening and heard nothing but a few wan birdcalls. He sat up, and the pain slammed into him. He was glad to be miles away from McDonough. Where fear and violence hung in the air like the stench from a burned-out tavern. Where he had been bitten by a dog and bitten by a man and had his ribs cracked, and where he had broken a man's leg, a man who would never walk easily again if he ever walked at all. Gideon wished he hadn't needed to kill the dog. He felt little remorse at crippling Thaddeus Kirkwood. The man had attacked him. He did not doubt that Kirkwood had raped Rebecca Kreidler this past spring in the White Crow Tavern. But he believed the man when he swore he had not gone back to Sinking Valley and taken her life.

He got up gingerly.

He rolled up his blankets inside the oilcloth, stifling a cry at the pain in his ribs. Holding his breath, he knotted a cord around the blankets and tied the bundle behind his saddle.

Near the spring was a small fire ring used by previous travelers. Gideon gathered some sticks. He found a mouse nest in a hollow log, pulled it apart, took his flint and steel, and struck a spark into the mass of fine rootlets and plant fluff. He blew gently, produced and nurtured a flame. He built up a small fire. He yearned for coffee but hadn't packed any grounds or a pot. He put a handful of dried apple slices in a mug of water from the spring. Over the fire he fried some bacon in a pan and ate it along with bread that Pastor Nolf had given him. He finished off his breakfast with the apples, still leathery but with a good tangy taste.

When he put away the pan, he got out Rebecca Kreidler's silver cross.

He took it out of its linen wrapping and held it in his hand. He strained to remember the night when he went to the bakehouse.

It came to him.

Even in his shame, he felt a surge of relief, some small degree of exoneration.

He had stood facing Rebecca. He reached out and gently took hold of her arm. That touch, that slightest physical contact, sent a jolt racing through his body fast as whipcrack.

"No!" She pulled her arm back, moved to put a chair between them. She shook her head. "No!" she said again. "*Ich will des net!* I don't want this! Go away. Please go away!"

He had stared at her, crestfallen, his face on fire. He felt deeply ashamed. And angry at himself. Not angry at her, whose earlier actions he had misinterpreted and upon whom he had intruded and wrongly, basely presumed.

He remembered saying "I'm sorry, I am truly sorry." He put his hat on and left the bakehouse. He remembered striding, almost running, to where he had left Maude tied to a bush. Fumbling the reins loose and mounting. Riding away, pushing Maude, kicking her, faster, faster. They galloped through the night, up the side of Mingo Mountain. Finally he let her walk. Across the mountain top, down the other side, into the valley where Adamant lay. He got a bottle out of the saddlebag. He drank the mule-kick whiskey. Furious with himself. Shocked and horrified at his behavior. A would-be adulterer, rightfully scorned. He knew it was wrong, so wrong, to have sought to betray True, the woman he loved, the woman he had married.

He was drunk by the time he finished the whiskey and threw the bottle in the brush. The bottle smashed, and some animal went crashing off. Maude scooted out from underneath him. He lost both stirrups and tumbled out of the saddle. He felt the impact as his body hit the ground, his head slamming onto the road. Then blackness.

He blinked, and he was back in the clearing in the Seven Mountains, his body throbbing with pain from the wounds he had received in the fight with Kirkwood and his dog. Which were as nothing compared to the wounds that life had inflicted on Rebecca Kreidler.

But she had fought back.

The woman had slain her husband. She had burned down a tavern with folks sleeping in it, causing the loss of another life. In plain fact, she was an arsonist and a killer. She hadn't seemed like someone who could do such things. A chill rippled down his back. Maybe it showed how close to the surface murderous rage lay. In anyone. He had come within a hairsbreadth of clubbing Thaddeus Kirkwood to death. Were the killings committed by Rebecca Kreidler justifiable? He didn't know.

What he did know was that he was filled with shame. Because of why he had gone to see Rebecca in the first place. He was guilty of betraying True. And of many other things, certainly. But not Rebecca Kreidler's death.

He closed his fingers around the cross. She would have worn it next to her heart, beneath her dress.

He had spent many days in Sinking Valley. Talking to people, studying the way they stood and how they breathed and where they cast their eyes—watching their faces as he probed with his questions. During some of the interviews he had stood holding Maude's reins. At other times he had left her and gone inside barns and houses.

Someone must have put the cross in his saddlebag when he was away from Maude.

Someone who knew he had visited the bakehouse. Someone who knew he had fallen off his horse and hit his head and suffered a lapse in his memory. Had that same someone murdered Rebecca Kreidler?

When beneath to their darkness the wicked are driv'n,
May our justified souls find a welcome in heav'n

Chapter 32

⊸⧓⊸

H E ARRIVED AT THE TRAUTMANNS' FARM MIDMORNING. THE *scheierhof* was not the peaceful place he had expected to find. Wagons parked haphazardly, horses tied at the fence switching their tails. Twenty or more *Neigeboren* men stood in a knot talking. Women clustered in a separate group. No children. The buzz of conversation ceased as Gideon rode up.

Pastor Nolf looked at him. Nolf's brow was creased, his eyes pinched. Beside him Jonas Trautmann stood stooped over, a hand pressed against the side of his head.

The farmer came up to Gideon. "*Mir kenne Maria net finne. Sie fehlt.*" We can't find Maria. She's missing.

"For how long?" Gideon asked in English.

"Since last evening. She was not feeling well. She went for a walk. I fell asleep, and when I woke this morning she was not in our bed."

"Have you searched for her?"

"Abe and I looked all over."

"We just went through the barn and the outbuildings again," Nolf said. He shook his head.

Gideon walked Maude to the edge of the hayfield and looked up toward the mountain where forest met field. He touched Maude with his calves and started her up through the grass.

He stopped at the sinkhole and dismounted, slowly, trying to protect his ribs. He heard footfalls and panting breath, and there was Abe Trautmann sprinting after him. The others were partway up through the field.

Gideon found the path. Before he started down it he yelled at Abe, "Stay back!"

But Abe followed him.

All the way down Gideon heard him saying, "Oh no, oh no, oh no."

When Gideon neared the bottom he turned and let Abe run into his arms. The sudden pain in his ribs took his breath away. "You stay here!" He turned and went the rest of the way down in.

He saw the dark blue dress. No cap or bonnet. Graying blonde hair tumbling down. The weight of the body bowed the sapling. Maria Trautmann's feet dangled inches above the ground.

Gideon heard an anguished cry, "*Memmi*!" He turned again and caught Abe in his arms.

"You don't want to look at this." He spun the young man around and shoved him. Abe went to his hands and knees.

Gideon heard words in *Deitsch*, saw hats bobbing toward them from above.

Nolf was the first to arrive. "Keep him here," Gideon said, pointing at Abe, who knelt sobbing. "Everyone else stay back."

Alone, he approached the body. Maria Trautmann's face was red, her eyes bloodshot and bulging beneath half-shut lids. Her long-fingered hands dangled. The body hung from a short length of rope tied to a branch in a tree.

A small maple with a trunk about six inches in diameter. The same tree beneath which Rebecca Kreidler's body had lain. The greasy spot marking her corpse's resting place still darkened the ground.

Near the base of the tree sat a rock. Frau Trautmann must have stood on the rock, tied the rope to a limb, put the noose around her neck, and stepped off.

He heard Jonas Trautmann cry out.

Gideon turned and held his arms apart to block the way. The farmer's face was almost as red as his wife's. "You must stay back." Gideon spoke firmly but with as much compassion as he could muster.

When he was certain Trautmann would heed his words, he returned his attention to the body. He touched one of Maria's hands. It was cold and stiff. He took the woman's hand in his own hands, looked at the back of it, examined the fingers and nails and palm. He did the same with her other hand. Big hands for a woman. Roughened by work. But otherwise unmarked. Gently, he turned the body on the rope. He looked at it, front and sides and back. He let it go and allowed the body to rotate back again, pivoting slowly as the rope untwisted.

He went to the men jammed together on the path. Jonas and Abe were both seated in the dirt, their shoulders touching; they stared up at him.

"I'm sorry," Gideon said.

He looked at the other men, pointed. "You and you. Go back to the farm. Get a plank or a door. Something to carry her on." He said to Pastor Nolf, "I want everyone else out of the *sinkloch*." They stood and looked at him like cattle. "Now!"

Gideon stayed with the body as the others vacated the sink. He said a prayer—feeling like an imposter, addressing God when he himself was such a vile sinner.

In the quiet of the sinkhole he continued to examine the body, its position, the condition of the clothing, taking it all in, trying to fix these observations in his mind, until the men finally returned carrying a door taken off its hinges.

He had chosen the men because they looked strong. Gideon directed one of them to climb into the tree, the other to hold the corpse and take the weight off the rope.

The man in the tree untied the knot.

"Don't let her touch the ground," Gideon said.

"Put her on the door. There." He removed the rope from Frau Trautmann's neck. "Now carry her out of here. Carefully. The body must not fall off."

Carry me home, when my life is o'er;
Then carry me to my long-sought home

Chapter 33

ᴊᴏɴᴀs Tʀᴀᴜᴛᴍᴀɴɴ ᴡᴀʟᴋᴇᴅ ᴏɴ ᴏɴᴇ sɪᴅᴇ ᴏꜰ ᴛʜᴇ ᴅᴏᴏʀ, ʜɪs ʜᴀɴᴅ on Maria's shoulder. Abe stumbled along on the other side. Both men appeared scarcely aware of the people around them. No one spoke.

Gideon followed, leading Maude. He thought of how the lives of these two men had now changed. How the life of an entire family would be painfully different from this day hence. Different, and defined by a great evil.

Maria Trautmann, wife and mother, had taken her own life. Or so it appeared. Taken her life in the same spot where Rebecca Kreidler's corpse had been found. How could one not assume that the two events were connected?

The women in the farmyard came forth to meet them. Many wept openly. Two sturdy *hausfrauen* held up Elisabeth Trautmann between them. Elisabeth's face was white and her eyes were round as she stared at her mother's corpse.

When they reached the house, the strong men maneuvered their burden inside, then into a separate room. Jonas and Abraham accompanied them, as did several older women. Gideon followed, his hat in his hands.

Jonas lifted Maria's corpse off the door and placed it gently on the bed.

Pastor Nolf entered. In his calm, quiet voice he asked everyone to link hands. He said a prayer in *Deitsch*, a simple prayer asking forgiveness for all sinners and imploring God to take Maria's soul unto him. He embraced Jonas, then Abraham, and left.

Jonas stood weeping quietly. Abe just stared. Jonas reached out and gripped his son by the arm, and the two of them left.

The women looked at Gideon. He knew they expected him to leave, too, so they could proceed with undressing the corpse. Washing the body. Tying the mouth shut with a band of cloth. Prettifying the face to the extent possible, so that people could lay eyes one last time on their departed sister.

"I will watch," he said in English.

The women looked shocked.

"I am the sheriff. You will not argue with me about this. I will view the body as it is disrobed."

When Gideon left the room a half hour later, he found Jonas seated in a chair, holding a young daughter in his lap, while another child, a boy, clung to his arm.

"Please do not take her away," Trautmann said.

Gideon thought he probably should carry the body to the coroner in Adamant. Failing to do so might risk the wrath of Alvin Fish, the state's attorney, even though it seemed clear what had happened: Maria Trautmann had hanged herself. "All right," he said, "I will not take the body. I'll leave you now. We can talk later."

★★★

As darkness fell, he stood at Nolf's fence watching the slow-shuffling shadows that were his two horses and Nolf's cow.

The air was hot. A body would not keep long in this weather. They would bury Maria Trautmann tomorrow.

In the morning, women would arrive at the Trautmanns' house and wrap the body in a *dodegleed*, a funeral shroud. Others would bring or prepare food. Ham and potatoes. Squash and carrots. Cakes and pies. Loaves of bread. Someone would bake a big flat cake made of flour and sugar and butter and pearl ash salt and caraway seed, and scratch on it the initials *MT*. The cake made not to be eaten but to be kept as a memento. As had been done after Gideon's own *memmi* died.

Light winked for a moment from the door to the house. Nolf came up and held something out. Gideon took it. A glass. He raised the glass and sipped. The pastor's *shumack* drink, with an added bite.

"I put in it some whiskey," Nolf said. "I think we need it tonight."

Katydids began calling from the trees around the pasture and house. A few scattered calls at first, then more and more of the unseen host joining in. The chorus swelled, became almost deafening. Its volume waned, then strengthened again, a pulsing dome of sound. Gideon had never forgotten the katydids' strident calling: part of the nightmare he carried with him from the time of his mother's death.

Deitsch folk called those insects *shrackack*. An observant description of their noise, to be sure; but Gideon, thinking of Gram Burns's story, decided he preferred the term katydid, with its implication of guilt.

Katy-did, she didn't. She did.

"Such a day." Nolf's voice was weary. "With all this trouble and grief, I never asked if you found that man—the one from south of the mountains who came here in the spring looking for Frau Kreidler."

Gideon told Nolf about his encounter with Thaddeus Kirkwood: how the man had attacked him, and how he had fought him off. "I think he spoke the truth when he told me he had not been able to find Rebecca here last April. I don't think he came back after that."

"What a hard and dangerous job you have," Nolf said. "Maybe now you can go back to Adamant and take your rest."

"Did you have any idea that Frau Trautmann might kill herself?"

Nolf shook his head. "None whatsoever. As you know, Maria invited her sister-in-law to come here after Rebecca got out of prison. Before she did that, Maria asked me whether I thought it was a good thing. I told her that it was a generous thing to do—to give the woman a chance to be reborn in Christ, to start a new life in a new place. Maria asked me to write the letter inviting Rebecca here."

"Frau Trautmann could not write?"

"No, she couldn't read or write." The pastor swirled the liquid in his glass. "After Frau Kreidler arrived, Maria tried to help her. To make Rebecca feel she was welcome, that she could become a part of this community and this congregation. But Rebecca held herself apart. And the two women never came to love each other. I know this, because Maria talked with me. She wanted me to help her find in her heart the Christian compassion to forgive Rebecca for causing her brother's death."

"That must have been hard for her."

"Yes. Maria and her brother were close. I don't think she overcame her grief at his death. Or her anger at the one who killed him."

Nolf continued, "Maria told me that when she was young, their family lived on a small farm. One of those places that never amounts to much. Not enough acres, the soil poor and played out. Too many mouths to feed—nine or ten *kinner*. Their parents decided they couldn't keep all of their children. So they sent Maria and John to live on the farm of Maria's mother's sister, a woman named Ada Bauer. Maria told me that Ada's husband had a terrible temper. He beat John severely many times. For small disobediences and mistakes. It's not surprising that John Kreidler became a hard, cruel man himself.

"In the end, I believe Maria's anger and hatred drove her to kill Rebecca—perhaps she poisoned her, or killed her in some other way. Then, still filled with rage, she pounded those nails into Rebecca's body. Maybe it was some sort of perverted *hex* charm. She must have carried Rebecca's corpse to the sinkhole; she was a strong woman, capable of doing that. She hid the body in the brush. In the end, overcome with guilt and despair from having killed another human being, and with the law closing in"—he turned his face toward Gideon—"she took her life." Nolf shook his head. "I was so blind. I should have realized that something like this could happen—I should have kept it from taking place. Dear God, how the Trautmann family must be suffering."

Gideon understood how murder could mark a family. How people instinctively withdrew from those who had lost a loved one to murder. How some seemed to conclude that if a person had been murdered, they must have done something immoral, something that caused them to deserve a cruel and unnatural death. That they had flirted with evil, maybe even embraced it.

It would be worse for the Trautmanns since the one who had committed the murder was herself a family member. A woman who then displayed her guilt for all to see by hanging herself above the spot where she had hidden her victim's body.

"Soon you will go back to Adamant," the pastor said. "I will stay here. I failed both of those women. I failed this congregation. Now I must try to help the Trautmanns back to a place of light. Help them and the rest of our people survive."

Thou art gone to the grave, we no longer behold thee,
Nor tread the rough paths of the world by thy side

Chapter 34

⸺◈⸺

THE NEXT MORNING A WOMAN WORKING IN THE KITCHEN TOLD
Gideon where to find Jonas Trautmann. Gideon climbed the
hill slowly, the pain in his ribs elbowing him as he went.

The farmer was waist-deep in his wife's grave. He stared up at
Gideon, then continued digging.

Green and blue swallows zipped past on bladed wings. Orange-
and-black butterflies flapped and drifted on the breeze.

After a while Trautmann straightened up from his work and
climbed out of the grave.

"I am very sorry for what happened to your wife," Gideon said.

The farmer, soaked in sweat, said nothing.

Gideon looked around. Sinking Valley stretched from west to east,
the land largely wooded, although that would change as more acres were
cleared for farming. He could see Pastor Nolf's small white house down
near the stream, the Rankins' impressive stone house and mill farther to
the east, other farms and their fields checkerboarding down the valley.
The place where Trautmann was digging reminded Gideon of the hilltop cemetery on his own family's farm, where three generations of
Stoltzes had been buried and where his *memmi* lay beneath the sod.

"This is a good place for a cemetery," he said.

"I'll build a wall around it, keep the cows out." Trautmann
twisted his hands on the shovel's handle. His mouth a taut line.
"People are saying that Maria poisoned Rebecca and then killed
herself. Is that what you think?"

Gideon waited. Then said, "What do you think?"

No answer.

"I need to ask you a few questions," Gideon said.

"Go on."

"Did you have any idea that your wife might take her own life?"

"No."

"Had she been acting strange lately?"

Trautmann gave a slight nod. "She had not been herself ever since Rebecca died. Worried. Afraid of something."

"Did she say why she was afraid?"

"She wouldn't talk about it."

"Did she leave behind a note or a letter?"

"She could not write. The life she led as a young person, there was no time for schooling."

"The rope she was hanging from . . ."

"From our barn."

Gideon nodded. "Your wife told me that she grew some herbs in the garden—*raude*, *grodebalsem*, *kamille*, and the like. For medicine. Did she also know anything about poisonous plants?"

"Then you do think it." His face was contorted. "I can't believe Maria poisoned Rebecca. And those nails."

"The evening before last, the last time you saw her. What do you remember about that evening? Anything she may have said?"

Trautmann sighed. "Just that she was feeling unwell. She wanted to go out and get some fresh air." He stared off down the valley. "If only she hadn't asked Rebecca to come live with us. I told her nothing good would come of it."

"Why did you think that?"

"Just something I felt. *Lieber Gott*, I wish I had put my foot down." Tears tracked down Trautmann's cheeks. "The woman was a criminal. If Rebecca hadn't come here, my Maria would still be alive. My children would still have a mother. I would not be digging this hole. You would not be asking me these questions." Trautmann swiped at his tears with a grimy hand. "You would not believe that my Maria killed Rebecca."

"The evidence points to her having done so."

Trautmann stabbed the shovel into the dirt. He looked down at the half-dug grave. "I must finish this. Please leave me alone."

★★★

Gideon returned that afternoon for the burying.

The people on the hilltop were all *Neigeboren* except one: James Rankin, who stood at the edge of the group. He was wearing a good suit; it contrasted with the plain clothes of the *Neigeboren*. Rankin directed a stare at Gideon, his eyes showing anger, pain. Elisabeth stood well away from her former suitor, between her father and her brother; the other folk also kept their distance. Gideon wondered why Rankin had come. Just paying his respects? Neighbors did that, of course.

The people also held back from Gideon. No one greeted him. Both men and women looked aside when he caught them glancing his way. Perhaps they regarded his investigation as the goad that had caused this further loss of life.

Pastor Nolf spoke. So did several others. All of them men, all in *Pennsylfawnisch Deitsch*.

No one used the word *selbstmord*, suicide, or referred to Rebecca Kreidler or her murder. It was all just platitudes, faith, and love, and a belief in God and life after death. Although a murderer and a suicide could expect nothing better than damnation.

After hymns were sung, after the coffin was roped down into the grave, after the hole was filled with dirt, after Nolf said a last blessing, the people made their way down the hill. Gideon didn't see James Rankin; he supposed the man had gone off in a different direction.

As they walked, the *Neigeboren* continued to avoid the sheriff of Colerain County. The one who no longer was seen as *Deitsch* by these Dutch people. The one who was mocked as "the Dutch Sheriff" by the English residents of this place.

In his otherness, he pondered.

Frau Trautmann, illiterate, had not left a letter explaining why she had ended her life. Nor, it seemed, had she admitted to anyone that she had killed her sister-in-law; at least no one had told Gideon of any such confession.

Maria Trautmann knew that Gideon had suffered a loss of memory. She knew that he had visited Rebecca Kreidler in the bakehouse around the time of her death. She must have put Rebecca's cross in his saddlebag. To make him think he had murdered her. To scare him away.

It all tied together neatly. Horrifically but neatly. He could end his investigation before his week was up—the week the Cold Fish had given him to solve the crime, before the state's attorney would recommend that the county commissioners dismiss Gideon Stoltz as an incompetent sheriff.

He slowed as he entered the farmyard, where tables had been set up for the funeral meal.

He wasn't wanted here. He would go back to Nolf's place. Gather his things and get his horses and head back over Mingo Mountain.

He hoped he would find True in their house in Adamant, although he doubted it. He hated the distance that separated him from the one person in the world whom he loved, the one person who seemed to understand him. The person he had wronged. Somehow he would make it up to her.

He waited for the others to get ahead of him. Glancing up, he saw a bird high in the air. It went flapping and shifting across the sky on long narrow wings, its dark streamlined shape standing out against the clouds. The bird looked to Gideon like a *nachteil*. The sort of bird True called a nighthawk. But it must be some other kind; one never saw a *nachteil* flying by itself.

He looked away, kept walking down the Trautmanns' lane. He had not gone a hundred paces when he heard someone call out "Sheriff!"

He turned to see Abraham Trautmann jogging up.

"You think my *memmi* killed herself." The young man's face wore a fierce frown. "Everyone thinks she killed herself. I tell you, she would never have done that. My mother was strong. She was tough."

"Do you think your mother killed Rebecca?"

Abe broke eye contact. "I . . . I'm not sure." He swallowed. "I knew my mother. She was like her brother John. She could be cruel. Hateful, even. At times she was cruel to me. Cruel to all of us.

"I don't know if she poisoned my *aendi* or not. But I do know that she would not have killed herself. Never. If she murdered Rebecca, she would have made you catch her. She would have forced you to put her on trial. She would have held her head high and walked up the gallows steps. She would have made you hang her before she put a noose around her own neck."

When, freed from earth, my soul shall tow'r
Beyond the reach of Satan's pow'r

Chapter 35

⸙

"You're still here." Nolf paused in the doorway of his house. Gideon stood studying the framed piece of *fraktur* art on the pastor's sitting-room wall, the pen-and-ink and watercolor eagle with its wings spread, its talons gripping a banner proclaiming GOTT SIEHT ALLES in a flowing script. The fanciful, primitively rendered bird surrounded by red and yellow flowers and green leaves and intertwining vines.

"Do you believe that God sees all?" Gideon asked. "That he watches when we do good, and that he sees when we commit evil?" He glanced at Nolf, a half-smile on his face. "I have a friend in Adamant, the headmaster of the school there. He doesn't believe in God. He told me once that if God exists, he's probably a cross-grained old codger who pays no attention to us here on earth and instead sits around complaining about his hernia or his ingrown toenail."

"Your friend is a most irreverent soul," Nolf said. He entered the room. "Why did you leave before the funeral meal?"

"They didn't want me there." Gideon turned away from the *fraktur* art and looked at the *schrank*, the elegant wardrobe that dominated the room. What he had thought was highly figured grain in rich brown walnut proved, on closer inspection, to be painted graining hand-swirled over wood that was probably poplar or pine stained dark. Despite this craftsman's subterfuge, the *schrank* was still a beautiful piece of furniture.

"Did the *fraktur* and the *schrank* come from your family?" Gideon asked.

"Yes. They are all that I have left from my parents' home." Nolf laid his hand gently on the *schrank*. "When I didn't see you after the funeral, I assumed you had left to get your horses, and that by now you'd be on your way to Adamant."

"Abraham stopped me as I was leaving the farm," Gideon said. "He told me his mother would never have killed herself. That she was tough, too tough to do something like that. Cruel, even. He seemed very sure of what he said."

A white-faced hornet flew in to the sitting room and went tap-tap-tapping along the wall, hunting for flies.

"I have known Frau Trautmann for many years, and I never saw her being cruel," Nolf said. "Tough? Yes, I imagine she could have been tough. Of course Abe does not want to believe that his mother killed herself. That she further damned her soul in that way. I feel very sad for Maria; the guilt and anguish that she felt for murdering her sister-in-law finally destroyed her. She saw no way out other than ending her life."

"Jonas identified the rope as coming from their barn. Certainly it appears that she used it to hang herself."

"Are you planning to stay another night?" Nolf asked. "You're welcome to do so."

"Thank you. I will do that. There's something else." Gideon reached into his vest pocket and brought out the silver cross. He put it on the table.

"I found this in my saddlebag. It belonged to Frau Kreidler; Elisabeth Trautmann mentioned it to me a while ago. Someone put it in my bag earlier this week. I suppose to make me think I killed Rebecca."

Nolf regarded the cross.

"It must have been put there by someone who knew I'd gone to see her in the bakehouse," Gideon said. "Someone who also knew I had fallen off my horse and suffered a loss of memory."

"I believe Frau Trautmann knew those things."

"Many people did. I'm glad to say that I have mostly recovered from my fall. My memory of that evening has come back. I now know what happened between us in the bakehouse."

He went on: "The first time I saw Rebecca was when I came to the Trautmann farm this past spring to settle that land dispute with the Rankins. Then, around the middle of July, I saw her again on the street in Adamant. I spoke with her; I bought one of her brooms. I felt deeply attracted to her. I thought she felt the same toward me. Things weren't going so well between me and my wife. I rode to Sinking Valley intending to . . ." He looked at the floor, then said it: "To commit adultery. To lie with Rebecca.

"She let me in to the bakehouse. But she didn't welcome me. I can still see the fear in her eyes. She was terribly afraid. Afraid of me as a sheriff, afraid of me as a man. And no wonder. She had been used by men like me. Abused by men. By her husband, who beat her and caused her to lose her unborn child. By that constable in McDonough, Thaddeus Kirkwood. He raped her in a tavern there. Who knows what other men might have done to her as well."

Nolf remained silent.

"I was in the bakehouse with her for only a few minutes," Gideon said. "Then I left and rode back to Adamant. I had a bottle. I got drunk and fell off my horse. The next night, Rebecca was killed."

Gideon didn't see condemnation in the pastor's eyes: perhaps a weary acceptance of human frailty.

"And you now believe that Maria Trautmann didn't kill herself?" Nolf said.

"When I found her hanging in the tree, I looked at her closely. I should have noticed it then. Today, after Abe swore to me that his mother would never have killed herself, I went back in their house and found the dress she'd been wearing.

"On the back were several stains. Green stains. I didn't see them at first against the blue cloth. Stains like what you'd get from lying on your back in the weeds or grass. Why would Frau Trautmann have been lying on her back? She wouldn't have been. Not if she'd gotten up on a rock and tied a rope to a tree limb and put a noose around her neck and jumped off.

"I was present when the women disrobed Frau Trautmann to prepare her corpse for burial," Gideon continued. "The only marks on her neck were from the rope. No bruises from fingers gripping her throat. I don't think anyone strangled her. So I am puzzled. I guess I still have some questions about her death."

Nolf nodded. "It is clear that you must think about this more." He raised his hands. "I am a poor host. Let me get you some food."

"I'm not hungry."

"Something simple, then."

Nolf set bread, ham, and cheese on the kitchen table. He sat down across from Gideon and offered a short blessing. Then, saying little, both of the men picked at the food.

Later they took chairs outside into the darkness. Nolf brought a ewer and two glasses.

The clouds had cleared off. The constellations assumed their identities in the star-filled sky.

"Have you noticed the shooting stars these last nights?" Nolf said. "So many of them. And so bright."

As if on cue, a meteor flashed across the sky, a white streak that glowed for a moment before fading. A few seconds later another came shooting out of the Big Dipper, brighter yet and with a red glow to its tail.

Nolf poured from the ewer into the glasses, handed one to Gideon. Gideon took a sip: the pastor's *shumack* cordial, strengthened with the generous addition of the local rye whiskey. He tipped the glass, downed a long draught.

The katydids sounded their calls.

Gideon found himself wondering if the katydids' ceaseless ratcheting was the sound made by the constellations as they wheeled across the night sky.

In the pasture the pale heads of wild carrots shimmered and thrummed like stars brought down to earth.

"I fear that Satan has found our community," Nolf said. "The devil was once an angel named Lucifer. It means 'light bringer' in Latin. The Bible says that Lucifer fell from heaven as a star, into an abyss both narrow and dark. I suppose your headmaster friend doesn't believe in Satan, either. But I tell you, he is real. And his greatest achievement comes when he convinces us that he does not exist."

Gideon had no head for theological discussions, especially not this evening. He lifted his glass again. The drink's taste, both biting and sweet, agreed with him. The beverage seemed to dull the pain in his ribs. He finished off the glass.

He noticed that his hands were trembling. He tried to remark on this strange phenomenon. He heard himself mumbling. His mouth felt dry, clogged with cobwebs.

"Have some more," Nolf said. The pastor lifted the ewer and refilled Gideon's glass.

He put his hand on Gideon's arm. "Drink."

The cordial went down smoothly. Gideon leaned back in his chair. He giggled.

A meteor streaked overhead. He shot up his hand and caught it as if it were a slow fly. His fist closed around it, he brought it down to his breast. Kept it prisoned in his palm, where it buzzed dully. It didn't burn him. He laughed at the absurdity of catching a falling star in his hand. His laughter mingled with the katydids' ratcheting.

Katy-did, she didn't, she did.

Suddenly his ears couldn't stand the racket. The noise so loud and piercing. He pressed his hands over his ears. He felt his limbs quivering, his whole body shaking.

Then he was up and walking, one foot in front of the other, one awkward step at a time. The sound of the katydids pulsed all around him. It lifted him, carried him through the darkness. Down the road, up the lane. On up the slope in the Trautmanns' hayfield. He seemed to float above the field. Headed toward the dark funnel of the sinkhole.

He held on to the end of a rope. He gripped it with all his strength. If he let go, he would fall upward through the stars.

All feeling sense seems to be gone,
Which makes me think that I am wrong

Chapter 36

———— ∞∞∞ ————

TRUE CAME SUDDENLY AWAKE. SHE HEARD WINGS FLUTTERING IN the darkness. A bird trapped inside the cabin, frantically beating its wings to get out.

She rose from her bed and searched. She found nothing. All she could hear was her gram snoring.

Maybe that was what had wakened her.

As she stood in the darkness, the cabin's walls seemed to press inward, and a powerful choking sensation overcame her.

She saw Gideon.

He lay on his back in a closed-in place. A dark place, one without any light, yet she could see him. He was bound hand and foot. His eyes open and staring. She feared he might be dead; then he blinked. He thrashed about, struggled against the ropes binding him. Then he seemed to give up. He lay back down and heaved a sigh, his shoulders sagging, his head coming to rest in the dirt. The dirt floor of a cave.

The vision vanished like smoke from a dying fire.

She could breathe again.

She stood there panting, blood pounding in her temples. A dream? A waking dream? No, it was real. She had seen him, she had seen Gideon. It was the second sight, like the time her grandmother had seen her husband Ezekiel fall off his horse and lie bleeding on the ground with the packhorses running all around him, had viewed the thing in great clarity over many intervening miles.

True hurried to her gram's bed and shook the old woman awake.

"I saw Gideon! He's in a cave. He could die!"

The old woman coughed and sat up.

"I have to help him!"

"If you think so," Gram Burns said.

True tugged on her grandmother's bony arm. "Get up, Gram. You have to come with me."

The old woman gently freed herself from True's hand. "What time of night is it?"

Gram Burns did not own a clock.

The inside of the cabin was almost black. True found her way to the door and went out. The only light she could see came from a sinking sliver of moon and a thousand thousand stars.

She hurried back inside. Went to her gram, still in bed. "We need to get ready!"

"Settle yourself, child," the old woman said. "Tell me what you saw."

True described her vision of Gideon lying bound on the floor of a cave. Panic rose in her breast. "Come with me, Gram! Help him."

"This is for you to do."

"We'll hitch Jack to your wagon."

"That wagon ain't been off the farm in years. The harness is mouse-chewed and worthless. Where do you think that cave is?"

"In Sinking Valley. He must be there. The place where he was trying to solve that crime."

"You rode here on that Jack horse," Gram Burns said. "Put a saddle on him and go."

"I've never been to that place!"

"Nor have I."

"Come with me, please!"

"I'd be of no use. I'd just slow you down." The old woman eased out of bed. Straightened and rubbed her lower back. "Let me round up some clothes for you. Go saddle Jack. I'll put together some things for you to take along." She hobbled in her nightdress to the small window and peered out. "Get moving. You can be ready by daybreak."

As the sky brightened in the east, Gram Burns tied to the back of True's saddle a drawstring poke containing bread, jerked venison, cheese, a tinderbox, some tow, a candle, a small lantern, a knife in a leather sheath. She had given True a dented broad-brimmed hat and made her put on a pair of her grandfather Ezekiel's musty old trousers, blue stripes on white ticking cloth. "They might look odd and scarcely proper, but those pants will help you ride. And get off and on Jack when the need arises." Gram Burns had True tighten the saddle's girth and set the bit in the horse's mouth. "Jack is a good horse," she said, stroking his nose. "But he's lazy. I'll cut you a switch."

True mounted, and Gram Burns handed her a sassafras switch. The black gelding showed white around his eyes and took a big leap forward. True grabbed his mane and held on tight with her legs. "Slow down, Jack, slow down!" Jack seized the bit and tossed his head from side to side. It scared True, and she almost threw herself off the horse's back. But she thought about Gideon in his plight. She had to reach him. Not knowing what else to do, she brought the switch down smartly on the gelding's shoulder. Was surprised when he did not buck her off or explode into a headlong gallop but instead made a big circle, then took off down the road in a jouncing trot.

True didn't dare turn around and call goodbye to her gram. At the bottom of the hollow she turned up Panther Valley.

★★★

True rode into Adamant, her rump sore and inner thighs aching.

The sun stood at the top of the sky. Another hot day. Jack had varied his pace between an energetic walk and a slightly faster trot as she rode him up the valley, across the bridge near the ironworks, and on to Adamant. Jack's hide ran with sweat. He tried to steer them toward the livery, but she brandished the switch on that side and cropped him lightly with it, pushing the gelding along the road toward the center of town.

She passed promenaders who stared at her, families with squalling children, churchgoers dressed in their Sunday best. She had not remembered that it was Sunday; all the days seemed to run together at her gram's cabin. True worried that Alonzo might not be at the jail. She had counted on enlisting his help. She would tell him what she'd seen—she prayed she could find the words to persuade him of the truth of her vision of Gideon lying trussed up in a cave.

She dismounted at the jail. The door was locked. She pounded on it and called out, but no one answered. She felt panic rising. She almost wept in frustration. She couldn't do this by herself.

She unwound Jack's reins from the hitching rail. She tried to recall exactly what she had seen of Gideon in his predicament, but the vision was now just a memory, lacking in sharpness and immediacy. She let out a choked cry. How could she find him? How could she save him?

She got back up on Jack and prepared to ride on. To Sinking Valley, wherever that was.

A man came out of a nearby shop. It was Gaither Brown, the leatherworker, who watched over the jail when Gideon and Alonzo were out. True had never liked Gaither Brown. The man was free with his eyes and always talked down to her.

"Where is Alonzo?" she asked.

"He's over to Earlystown serving a summons." Brown chuckled. "Figured he'd catch the fellow coming out of church."

True knew that Gaither Brown would not believe what she had envisioned about Gideon. He would roll his eyes at such female hysteria and treat her like a child.

She tried anyway. "Gideon is in trouble. In Sinking Valley." Brown stood and stared. She went on. "I saw him in my mind's eye, in a vision. The sight, it was the second sight. He was tied up. In a cave." How stupid it sounded when spoken aloud.

Brown smiled. He looked at the striped trousers she was wearing. "Why don't you get down off that horse, Mrs. Stoltz," he said. "I know you ain't been well. Everyone knows it. We are all worried about you." He came near and reached out to catch Jack's bridle.

True brought the sassafras switch down hard and cut him across the face. He yelped and leaped back. "Damn you to hell!"

She kicked Jack and rode him straight at Gaither Brown so that he had to jump aside or get knocked down.

What is this absorbs me quite—
Steals my senses, shuts my sight?

Chapter 37

⊗⊗⊗

IN THE FADING LIGHT GIDEON STAGGERED ACROSS A FOGGY PLAIN. HE had to reach some far-off destination. But he did not know where he was going. Only that he had to get there soon or someone he loved would die.

Shadowy wraiths lingered at the edge of his vision. One of them drifted toward him. He tried to shrink back but found that he could no longer move his legs. The wraith drew near, its face blurred and featureless. Then it lost its gray pallor and took on the pink hues of the living, and he saw that it was his *memmi* come to greet him. She smiled at him. He tried to reach out to her, but he could not lift his arms. Slowly her countenance faded, and he was confronted again with a pallid featureless face. A creature of the grave.

He jerked awake. Tried to swallow. His throat scratchy and parched. He felt groggy. But he was awake, he knew he was awake. Awake and returned to his own mind.

He blinked, but all was dark around him. He tried to get to his feet but was incapable of rising. He gave his body a wrench, lurched from his back onto his side, felt a searing pain. His ribs. His cheek pressed against something cold and gritty. He smelled the dank odor of dirt, the faintly sulfurous scent of limestone rock.

He blinked again, opened his eyes wide. He couldn't see a thing. Was he blind?

He fought down a rising panic. Tried to remember where he'd been. Last evening he had sat in Nolf's dooryard looking up at the night sky. Drinking the pastor's *shumack* cordial fortified with whiskey. How much had he drunk? He remembered being giddy enough to think that he could reach up and catch a falling star.

He tried to get to his feet again and was thwarted. His feet and hands felt heavy and cold. The front of his trousers were wet. He smelled urine.

His heart beat rapidly, each thump audible and distinct. He could hear something else, slow and repetitive: *Drip, drip, drip.*

He racked his memory. He recalled holding on to a rope while following someone across a field in the darkness. Pastor Nolf. They approached the sinkhole. Nolf removed a covering from a lantern, letting its yellow light shine out. Gideon followed, still holding the rope. He went skidding down the steep trail through the brush. Past the tree where Rebecca Kriedler's corpse had lain. The tree from which Maria Trautmann had hanged herself.

In the bottom of the sinkhole Nolf set down the lantern and the rope. He bent and moved some rocks, exposing an opening in the slope. He motioned for Gideon to let go of the rope and crawl through the portal. For some reason, Gideon had dumbly obeyed.

He was in a cave. Of course. Some sinkholes connected to them. Cold, clammy places where light was absent. It wasn't like being outdoors at night, where if you waited long enough your pupils would open wide and you could always see something, even if it was only dark shapes.

No. He was trapped in a cave. Where the darkness was total and unrelenting. Where smells of earth and stone surrounded him. Where silence, save for the relentless dripping of water, was absolute.

Frantically he twisted his hands. A rope dug into his wrists. His hands were bound together and secured to a second rope cinched around his waist. He tried to pull his hands free, but the rope had no give to it. His legs were bound as well, at the knees and at the ankles.

He heaved himself onto his back. Pain lanced through his ribs. He looked up into darkness that was blacker than black.

Nolf had bound him and left him here. Left him to die alone in darkness. No one would ever find him. True would never know what had happened to him.

Nolf. He had grown fond of the pastor, trusted the man enough to tell him about his *memmi*'s murder, his lusting after Rebecca. He had felt some suspicion toward Nolf, but when you investigated a murder, you felt suspicious toward almost everyone.

And now this.

He cursed his stupidity.

He felt himself shivering.

How long before the cold drained away his life?

To fight down his fear, he clenched his eyes shut, concentrated on the colors that bloomed and faded behind his eyelids. Starbursts of gold and green. Waves of purplish red. Blue cascades.

But there were walls around him. He sensed them even if he couldn't see them. Stone walls that closed in on him, threatened to suffocate him.

A spasm of shivering shook him. His teeth chattered. His lips felt numb. Desperation kicked his heart into a gallop. He had to free himself, he had to get out of this hellish place. He fought against the ropes. A scream issued from his mouth. The cry vanished into nothingness.

Though our enemies are strong, we'll go on,
Though our hearts dissolve with fear

Chapter 38

———— ⦁⦁⦁ ————

ON THE ROAD TRUE MET A BEARDED MAN TRAMPING TOWARD town. He wore a blouse check shirt and fustian pants and carried a knapsack on his back and held a walking staff that was higher than he was tall. He told True he was returning after "an exceedingly pleasant day spent peregrinating." She cut short his description of his ramble by asking him how to get to Sinking Valley. Without hesitation the man told her where the road branched left at a big beech tree blazed with an ax mark; after a mile, the track forded a stream, then rose to climb up Mingo Mountain and drop down into Sinking Valley on the other side. The man did not remark on her odd trousers or her hat or call her a flower ready to be plucked. He offered her half a loaf of bread. She declined and thanked him, then tapped Jack with her calves and rode on.

Vultures circled in a rising draft of air. The heat swelled up from the land. The sun behind her threw her shadow long upon the road. Deerflies and horseflies pestered Jack, causing him to switch his tail and sling his head back to bite at them when they gadded his flanks.

True could tell that Jack was worn out from how sloppy his walk had become. They had traveled a long way since dawn. She rode him into a stream and let him drink and stand in the cooling flow. She watched out that he didn't try to roll with her on his back, a vice of some horses that Gideon had warned about. In the stream's limpid water, gray-green shadows of trout flickered like thoughts past Jack's legs. A halcyon came flying down the stream with little bursts of its blue wings. It lit in a bankside tree and raised its spiky crest and cursed her with piercing stuttering cries.

The road up Mingo Mountain was steep, and she wondered that people drove wagons up and down it. But she knew they did. She hated to do it, but she cropped Jack hard, driving him up the grade.

They crossed the top of the mountain. On the far side, when they started down, Jack seemed as if he would fall over from weariness, so True got off and led him by the reins. She took long strides and jogged down the slope in places even though her heart pounded and her lungs felt ready to burst.

She wondered if she would be in time to help Gideon or if she would be too late. She hadn't seen him in her mind's eye after that one vivid glimpse, even though she'd tried to unfocus her thoughts and open her awareness to receive another vision, whether hopeful or steeped in misery. She began to doubt herself, to ask whether this long trip was needed or foolish or if it would end in frustration or grief.

How could she find the cave where he lay?

It must be on the Trautmann farm. Gideon had told her and Gram about the body of the woman found in a sinkhole there. Sinkholes often had caves at their bottoms.

Should she ask the Trautmanns for help? She didn't know them. And someone had already been killed on their farm. What if they had slain the woman, what if Gideon had gotten close to finding it out and they overpowered him and bound him and put him in the cave to die? No, she would find the sinkhole and the cave by herself. She would go into the cave and rescue her husband. Even though the thought of entering a hole in the ground scared her half to death.

She hurried down the switchback road. The branches of trees knit high above her. Fragments of sky beyond the trees' crowns, a strange gold-red light that gradually became livid. Thunder rumbled.

The slope leveled off. She clambered up on Jack's back. She took up the reins and used the crop to set him off at a trot, painful though that was to her seat. In a while the road emerged from forest into open land. Above the valley the heavens looked like folded purple cloth. The road intersected with another road. She stopped. Turn right or left? Gideon had said the Trautmanns' farm was close to where the two roads met, but she couldn't remember which way he had said to turn. She looked all around, hoping to spy another traveler, even though she hadn't seen anyone since the bearded man directed her to Sinking Valley.

A bolt of lightning leaped upward from the ridge, flickered dazzlingly before dying out. A clap of thunder carried across the vale.

A dark shape, little more than a shadow, went flitting overhead. Against the roiled sky she recognized the sideslipping flight of a nighthawk. She heard its high-pitched buzzy cry, like someone calling out *beer*. The nighthawk called again and again, its cries becoming fainter as the bird flew east.

She turned left on the valley road and went east. A minute later she saw the bird again. It flew up high in the darkening sky on its fluttering white-banded wings. It paused against the firmament, tucked its wings against its body, and plunged downward. It picked up speed in its headlong descent. When it seemed the bird must strike the ground and be killed, it checked its dive and swooped gracefully upward, its wings making a hollow *boom*. True felt the sound behind her breastbone.

The nighthawk's calling and booming led her up a lane. Thunder muttered from a sky that was purple and yellow and leaden in different sectors. Lightning winked inside a cloud, then forked out sideways like a snake's tongue. She saw a window lit gold in a house. A stone farmhouse, with a stone bakehouse near it. A big barn, outbuildings clustered around. This was how Gideon had described the Trautmann place. A dog started barking. She turned Jack onto another lane that led away from the farmstead into a hayfield. The nighthawk's booming sounded somewhere up the field's long slant.

Dear God, let me find the sinkhole.

Dear God, don't let the storm break till I get the lantern lit.

Jack walked up through the field. He stopped at the edge of a depression that she knew must be the sinkhole. The hole black and broad and formless, a navel into an unknown world.

True slid stiffly off of Jack. The gelding blew, thrust his head downward, and began grazing. She untied the poke that Gram Burns had fastened to the saddle.

Let the high heav'ns your songs invite,
These spacious fields of brilliant light

Chapter 39

———— ∞∞∞ ————

IN THE LOW GOLDEN LIGHT HE WALKED THROUGH A FIELD OF GRASS. The grass waved in the breeze. Maude was waiting for him. She whickered as he made his way up to her. He stopped and used his knuckles to rub her forehead the way she liked it. He came around to her side. He placed his hands on her back, felt her brown hide warm from the sun. She turned her head toward him, and he saw the horizontal bars of the pupils in her dark sideward-seeing eyes. Long black lashes fringed her eyes below and above.

Her eyes held a depth of acceptance and wisdom that touched his soul.

He took a hank of mane in his left hand. He hopped up lightly from the ground, balanced for a moment with his belly touching her back, then swung his right leg over to her far side and lowered his weight.

His legs dangled down on both sides.

Maude stood quietly beneath him. Her ears pointed back. One ear perfectly formed, with a graceful inward curve at the tip; the other ear clipped short where, years ago, a screaming pistol ball had removed the last inch. While she carried him to safety, carried him on into life.

He bent forward and wrapped his arms around her neck. Lowered his head and breathed in her sweet exhalations. Breathed her acceptance and wisdom inside him.

He straightened. Beneath him, Maude turned so that they might go onward.

He looked across the field toward the far-off trees. Beyond the trees a river lay sparkling in the sun. They would cross the river. Maude would carry him.

He touched her with his calves.

Together they walked through the gently waving grass toward the river beyond the trees.

The storm of justice falls,
And death is nigh

Chapter 40

———⊗⊗⊗———

I T WAS ALMOST DARK.

True opened the sack and got out the lantern, candle, tinder-box, and tow.

She opened the glass door of the lantern and set it aside.

She had to move fast. Because of the approaching storm and because Gideon needed her.

Lightning briefly illuminated her work. She teased the tow apart and placed it on the ground. As thunder rolled, she opened the tinder-box and got out a jagged piece of flint and a horseshoe-shaped steel.

She held the flint in her right hand and the steel in her left hand poised over the tinderbox. As Gram Burns had taught her, she raised the flint and brought it down sharply, raking a glancing blow against the steel. The blow spawned sparks that died out immediately. She raised the flint and struck again. And again. A few small sparks scattered, none of them large or long-lived and none of them landing on the char inside the box.

She felt tension building in her back.

Raindrops spattered. If it started pouring, she wouldn't be able to make a light.

Bending to her work, she struck with the flint again. And again.

She got a good spark that landed on the charred linen in the box. Quickly she held the tow against the char and blew on it gently. Smoke rose and bit her nose. Blinking against the smoke, she continued to blow.

The rain came down harder. She arched her back and raised her shoulders, huddled over the tow. She kept blowing. The tow gave off clouds of smoke. Fighting against panic, she forced herself to keep blowing out gentle streams of air.

With a *puff* the tow blossomed into flame.

True grabbed the candle and held its wick to the small conflagration. The wick took flame. Still hunched over, she turned to the lantern, fitted the candle in its circular housing, and closed the glass door.

Lightning pulsed inside a towering flat-bottomed cloud: the crack of thunder almost instantaneous, followed by a low rumbling that went on and on.

True stood up, holding the lantern by the bail.

She searched around at the lip of the sinkhole until she found what seemed to be a path. She started down it. Then stopped. She went back and got the sack with the knife inside it. *Keep your wits about you.* The rain fell harder. She followed the trace downward, taking careful steps so she would not stumble and fall, her progress lit by flashes of lightning and the lantern's glow.

The bottom of the sink was a leaf-strewn pocket a dozen feet across. She stood and listened. She heard nothing except lightning sizzling high overhead and thunder ramifying down the valley. Big drops of rain thudded against her hat brim.

Holding out the lantern, she peered about. A ledge of limestone stuck out from one side of the sink. The leaves at its base appeared to have been disturbed, with dirt showing dark in places. A few dead branches looked as if they'd been laid against the rock wall.

She set the lantern and the sack down. She removed the branches, then knelt and held her face near the rocks. She wet her lips with her tongue. Against her lips she felt cool air issuing from between the rocks. She took hold of a rock in both hands and tugged at it. It came loose with a grating sound, and she drew it toward herself and set it aside. The rain stepped up. She dislodged another rock and placed it in the leaves. She worked quickly, continuing to remove the rocks, some of them big and heavy, making her gasp at the effort. The rocks came out readily, as if they'd been laid in place.

When the opening was large enough she put the lantern inside it, out of the rain. She grabbed the sack. Before she could dwell on her fears, she took off her hat, knelt down, picked up the lantern, and crawled into the cave.

The yellow light revealed a narrow passage angling downward. She saw what she thought were stars glinting overhead: crystals embedded in the gray limestone.

She called out "Gideon!" Her voice dulled by dirt and rock.

She crawled ahead. Daddy longlegs skittered in the light. Colorless tapering things fingered down from the ceiling; she thought they must be rootlets of shrubs and trees. Glossy toothed formations like wolf jaws stood out from the passageway's walls.

She stopped and called again. Heard only the echo of her own voice and the muted sound of thunder outside the cave. She shivered, at the dank air working its way inside her sleeves and pantlegs and collar, and at the idea of being underground beneath tons of stone and dirt. *Dear God, don't let this candle go out.*

She hated closed-in places. Once she'd gone into a cave with some friends, and two minutes later she was back outside, gulping fresh air, vowing never to put herself in such a cramped, threatening place again. Her brother Jesse, who was always deviling her, once told her that if you stayed in the dark inside a cave for a week, your hair would turn white and you'd go blind.

She gritted her teeth and continued crawling, preceded by the lantern's light. The passageway was slightly wider than her shoulders and hips. Two, maybe three feet high, so she couldn't lift her head. The passage sloped down for a ways, then leveled off. Smooth sections of wall beaded with moisture like sweat. Her breath clouded in front of her. The roof sank lower yet. Water trickled across the floor of the passage. She stifled a cry of panic. She took a deep deliberate breath and made herself crawl on her elbows through the water and mud, the front of her pants and shirt soaking.

She came to a place where the passage narrowed even further and bent to the right. She hesitated, then pushed the lantern through the choke point, followed by the sack, and then she turned her shoulders sideways and squeezed through the opening herself.

On the other side was a large room, its ceiling high enough for her to stand up. She heard a steady dripping sound. The lantern's light revealed angular boulders fallen from the roof; it threw their shadows against the wall. She looked around and saw a bundle of dirty clothes.

Gideon.

She rushed to him. He lay on his back with his eyes closed and his mouth open. She placed the backs of her fingers against his cheek. His skin felt cold. She took his head in her hands and raised it.

His head jerked a little between her hands. She laid his head back down, grabbed his shoulders, and shook him.

He mumbled.

She shook him harder. She saw the ropes binding him. She needed to get him moving, get his blood flowing. Get him out of this cold cave. She opened the sack and got out the knife, slid it from its sheath.

She slipped the blade beneath the rope around Gideon's ankles and sawed upward. The rope parted and fell slack.

She cut the rope at his knees. She severed the rope around his waist. The rope binding his wrists was tight, cutting into his flesh. She worked carefully to avoid slicing him with the blade.

He groaned. Opened his eyes and stared up at her.

She thought for a moment of the way David had looked at her when the midwife laid her firstborn in her arms.

She couldn't waste time thinking about that.

She worked at cutting the rope.

Gideon struggled.

"Hold still!"

She had almost cut through the rope when she heard a sound behind her.

Thou art a God before whose sight
The wicked shall not stand

Chapter 41

━━◦◦◦◦◦━━

A HAND ON HER SHOULDER JERKED HER BACKWARD.
True caught her balance before sprawling in the dirt. She
looked up and saw a man holding a pistol in one hand. The man used
the heel of his other hand to cock the hammer back. The *click* so loud
it filled the room.

The man pointed the gun at her face.

The light was strengthened by the man's own lantern, sitting on
the ground near his feet. Mud smeared his trousers and shirt, a pale
shirt with a single suspender across his chest. The man had a neatly
trimmed gray beard and hair. Despite the weapon in his hand, his
expression seemed to be neutral, perhaps even genial.

Maybe this is all a mistake, True thought. *Maybe I can talk with him,
reason with him.*

The man backed up a few steps, still pointing the pistol at her. He
beckoned with the index finger of his other hand. "Toward me. On
your hands and knees. Put the knife on the ground. Push it along in
front of you."

Behind her, Gideon struggled to sit up.

"Toward me!" The man's voice cut through the chill air.

True did as she was told.

"Now back to where you were."

True crawled backward until her foot bumped into Gideon.

The man booted the knife into the shadows. "You are his wife?"

She nodded.

"Did anyone else come with you?"

She stayed silent.

"Of course not," the man said. "There is only one horse in the field."

Gideon got up to a sitting position, his hands still bound in front of him. His shoulders trembled. He tried to speak, but only a harsh croak came out.

"People know I'm here," True said, her voice quavering. "Lots of people know it."

"Is that so?" The man waved the pistol to one side. The gun's curved wooden handle extended forward almost to the end of the barrel. The flint was padded with a piece of red felt cloth where it was clamped in the hammer. "Move over," the man said. "So I can see both of you."

True shifted sideways.

The man aimed his pistol at her again. The end of its barrel shaped like an octagon. At its center, a round hole that looked big enough for her to stick her finger into.

"How did you know I was here?" she said.

The man smiled. "I was sitting outside watching the storm come on. There's a place near my house—from it, you can see up into the Trautmanns' hayfield. I happened to be looking that way, and I saw your light."

Gideon's voice was weak. "How did you . . . what did you put in . . .?"

"In your drink? Jimsonweed. Also known as the devil's trumpet. A most interesting plant. An extract from the seeds, combined with some alcohol and gentle persuasion, can let one control a person's behavior. You need to be careful, though. Too concentrated of a dose, and convulsions, coma, and death can result."

"Why didn't you just . . ."

"You're too big for me to carry or drag. Much more convenient to get you to walk here on your own and then crawl into this cave. I found it a few days ago. I knew that if I could get you inside, you would never be found."

"You need to let us go," True said. Her mind was whirling. Her hands shook. "The deputy sheriff in Adamant knows I came here." Gaither Brown would tell Alonzo what she'd said to him; at least she hoped so. "He will come looking for us."

The man stared at True. "Perhaps he will. But your husband's horses will no longer be in my pasture. Later tonight I will take them, and your horse, too, deep into the woods. They will die there. The bears and wolves and ravens will clean up the remains." The man shifted his gaze to Gideon. "I will tell your deputy that Mrs. Stoltz came to my house looking for her husband. But she was too late; Sheriff Stoltz, in carrying out his duty, had already gone back through the Seven Mountains to arrest a man in a town south of here. A town whose name he never mentioned. Despite my advice, his headstrong wife decided to follow him. Who knows what might have happened to them? There's a lot of wild territory in those mountains, a lot of complicated terrain. Easy to get lost in. And many dangers to face. I'm sure you will not be the first souls to have vanished there."

"You remind me of a man I once knew," True said. "A man who thought he was above the law. A man who didn't care if he hurt people or ruined their lives. My husband finally killed him."

The gray-haired man continued to stare at Gideon. "Your wife is bold. And she talks too much. Especially since we have not been properly introduced." He looked back at True, holding the pistol so that one of his calm eyes regarded her down its barrel. "I am Peter Nolf. The pastor for the *Neigeboren* community here. A position I expect to hold for many years to come. Long after you and your meddlesome husband are dead and forgotten."

"A preacher," True said. "Today is Sunday. I bet you led a church service this morning. You probably talked about God and forgiveness and Christian thoughts and deeds. When you had just put my husband in a cave to die. To die alone in the cold and the dark. What a god-damned hypocrite you are."

"You killed Rebecca Kreidler," Gideon said to Nolf. "How?"

Nolf shrugged. "Well, it's raining hard outside. I may as well tell you. In fact, I did not kill Rebecca. Frau Trautmann did that. I simply supplied the agent of death."

"You poisoned her with cowbane," True said.

Nolf's eyebrows rose. "Yes. A common enough plant. Fast and deadly. I gave Frau Trautmann some of the root, and she cooked it in a stew for Rebecca's dinner."

"Only a truly evil person can be a poisoner—can cause such a painful death," True said. "You think you'll get away with it. But you'll be found out."

"'*Gott sieht alles*.'" Nolf laughed. "'God sees all.' Don't be so sure of it. He doesn't see you now."

"Why did you help Frau Trautmann kill Rebecca?" Gideon said.

"Maria thought that three years in the penitentiary was not enough punishment for Rebecca taking her brother's life."

"But you—why did you help her?"

A look that seemed both chagrined and sardonic came to the pastor's face. "You were not the only man who was attracted to Frau Kreidler, Sheriff Stoltz." He shot a glance at True, then looked back at Gideon. He appeared to relish the consternation on both their faces.

"When Rebecca came here this spring, I wanted her from the moment I laid eyes on her," Nolf said. "As I told you, my wife Grace had been in poor health for many years—she never gave me children, never fulfilled her duty as a wife.

"If Grace died, I would be free to marry Rebecca. I let our cow graze in a patch of white snakeroot." His eyes found True's. "Maybe you know of that plant, too. Its toxins come through in cows' milk. The milk sickness, it's called. I gave the milk to Grace; she always liked to drink milk. She became weaker and weaker, and then she died—no one recognized the symptoms, they just thought her time had come. It wasn't a bad death. She just faded away."

"She didn't just fade away," True said. "You poisoned her. You murdered your own wife. What a terrible guilt you must feel."

"Guilt?" Nolf smirked. "Ask your husband about guilt."

"Why did you help Frau Trautmann kill Rebecca?" Gideon asked again.

"Because Rebecca spurned me. She refused to marry me. I would have been a good husband to her. I am respected by this congregation, this community. We could have had a fine life, raised a family together." He gave a short mirthless laugh. "By killing Grace, I had damned my soul for Rebecca's sake. Why should I not help Maria kill her? In fact, I planted in Maria's head the idea that Rebecca deserved to die. That she was an evil witch who needed to be removed from our community."

"The nails," Gideon said. "Why did you drive nails into her?"

"Maria's doing." Nolf shook his head. "Some *hexerei* charm. To make a thief return that which has been stolen. In this case, I suppose, Maria's brother John's life. Of course, that was impossible; the dead do not rise again. No, Maria hammered in those nails out of bitterness. A desire for revenge."

"Was Rebecca dead when the nails were driven in?"

"I can't tell you that. I wasn't there. I had no idea that Maria had done it until you told me what the coroner found."

"And you dumped Rebecca's body in the sinkhole. Where you thought no one would find her."

"She was a Jezebel. A whore. She aroused impure feelings in men. You know all about that, don't you, Sheriff?"

True looked at Gideon. She saw shame clinging to her husband's face.

Nolf narrowed his eyes. "We would not be here now if that dog had not found Rebecca's hand. If Jonas Trautmann hadn't been so stupid as to send word to the sheriff. If the sheriff of Colerain County hadn't been so dogged in trying to uncover the truth."

Nolf aimed the pistol at True. "I will kill your wife first. Shoot her in the head. She won't feel a thing. Just a sudden vanishing of the light. Then I'll deal with you."

"Please," Gideon said. "Spare her. She'll say that I went into the Seven Mountains and never came back. She will go home to Adamant and never speak a word about you or what happened in this valley. You'll do that, won't you, True?"

True kept her mouth shut. Saw agony rive her husband's face.

Nolf pointed the gun at Gideon again. "Do you want to hear the whole story, Sheriff? The truth that you will give up everything to find out? Aren't you curious about why Frau Trautmann ended up hanging from a rope just a few feet above where we are now?"

Nolf didn't wait for Gideon to answer. "You kept coming back," he said. "Asking your questions. Asking them again and again, each time in slightly different ways. Maria was tough, but I knew she couldn't stand up to that kind of probing. And when she broke down, she would tell you everything, and you would know that I helped kill her sister-in-law."

True wondered why the Dutch preacher didn't just kill them. He was a fool to go on like this. Maybe he had to show off his power over them.

She looked at the pistol in his hand. She looked for the knife but couldn't spot it in the shadows where the preacher had kicked it. She looked at the two lanterns. She might knock one of them over before he shot her, but not both.

Her heart beat fast. She tried to calm it by breathing slowly, steadily.

She didn't know much about guns. But she did know that the hammer with its flint had to fall, strike a spark, and ignite powder in the pan, which would set off the charge inside the gun and send the ball flying down the barrel.

"I suggested to Maria," Nolf continued, "that she meet me here at the *sinkloch*. I told her I would tell her what she could say to satisfy your curiosity. To make you finally go away."

"Did you poison her, too?" Gideon asked.

"I doubt she'd have drunk or eaten anything I gave her. No, I pushed her backward into the *sinkloch*. The fall stunned her. I was fortunate. She was a strong woman. I was able to smother her. I used a wadded-up shirt."

"The cross," Gideon said. "Rebecca's cross."

"I found the cross when I put Rebecca's body in the *sinkloch*. I kept it, which was a foolish thing to do. And then I got scared. At the way you wouldn't give up, the way you kept trying to find out what had happened. I put the cross in your saddlebag hoping you would believe that you had killed her." Smiling faintly, Nolf looked down and, as if reproaching himself, shook his head.

True made up her mind.

Though our enemies are strong, we'll go on,
Though our hearts dissolve with fear

Chapter 42

———— ⚬⚬⚬ ————

I MAY DIE DOING THIS.
I will surely die if I let him shoot me.

She launched herself from the floor. She grabbed for the pistol with both hands and thrust one hand between the hammer and the pan as Nolf wrenched the gun's muzzle toward her, held it against her breast, and pulled the trigger. The hammer fell and caught in the webbing between her thumb and forefinger. No spark from the flint. The gun did not go off.

She kicked over the preacher's lantern.

Nolf swept the pistol sideways, tearing the skin on True's hand. She managed to keep hold of the gun, gripped it hard. Hot blood poured down her hand.

The preacher was wiry and lithe. She went with his greater strength, letting him jerk her sideways. Their shadows flared on the cave wall. She kept her feet. She tried to reach the other lamp. She didn't know what would happen if she killed that light, and feared the terrible darkness that would result, but at least the preacher wouldn't be able to see her or Gideon.

He flung her in the other direction.

She felt herself lose her grip on the pistol. She kicked the preacher as hard as she could. Kicked him again.

Then the preacher threw up his hands and let go of the pistol and fell over backward.

Gideon. He had managed to get up off the ground, break the rope around his wrists, and find a knife.

Not the knife True had brought, the one Nolf had kicked away.

The knife Gideon kept hidden in his boot.

It stuck out of the preacher's throat. Nolf lay on his back on the cave floor. Blood spurted from the wound. Nolf's body writhed. With a choking cry he pulled the knife out.

From caves of darkness and of doubt,
He gently speaks and calls us out

Chapter 43

⸻⸎⸻

THEY LAY OUTSIDE THE CAVE, SPRAWLED ON TOP OF NOLF'S COAT, which they had found just inside the entrance. The lantern cast a feeble light. Cool air ponded in the sinkhole. A chink in the clouds let a star wink through. In the forest, the katydids called slowly and sporadically in the storm's wake.

Katy-did.

She didn't.

She did.

"You saved me," Gideon said. "You saved us."

"We saved each other," True said.

"I'm sorry for what I have done."

True didn't answer.

"Nothing happened between Rebecca Kreidler and me. But I went to her." He couldn't make himself say why he had sought the woman out, but True would know that. "She told me no. She was a better person than I am."

"You have some guilt to bear. I do, too."

"No."

"I went away from you. You tried to help me, but I wouldn't let you. Maybe I couldn't let you. I'm just glad I made it to my gram's."

"I'm glad you went there, too. And that she could help you where I couldn't." Gideon stared up into the sky. "How in God's name did you find me?"

"I saw you lying in a cave."

"And you believed in that vision, and rode here from your gram's?"

"I stopped in Adamant to get Alonzo, but he wasn't there."

"How did you find this farm, the sinkhole, the cave?"

"You told me about the farm and the sinkhole. And there were . . . There were portents shown to me. They led me here." True was quiet for a moment. "When I figure it out for myself, I'll tell you more. But I want you to know that what I saw in my mind's eye was real. You, lying bound in darkness. It was the real thing happening. It was the sight, the second sight. I have it, just like my gram. For better or for worse."

Gideon had cut a strip of cloth off his shirt and wrapped it around True's hand to stanch the bleeding where the lock of Nolf's pistol had torn the flesh. Now he found True's other, unwounded hand. He squeezed it gently. He turned to her and put his arm across her. He had begun shivering again, and he knew that he reeked, soaked in urine and smeared with mud, and he hoped she wouldn't care.

He thought about killing Nolf. He had to do it. He had been so terrified when the man said he would shoot True. If Nolf had killed her, Gideon thought he would have given up, let the man kill him any way he wanted. Life wouldn't have been worth living.

He felt cold. He started shivering harder. He knew he had to move.

They got up, climbed out of the sinkhole, and collected the gelding Jack. Good old Jack. With Gideon holding the lantern and True leading the horse, they made their way down through the rain-soaked field. They passed the Trautmann farm, where the dog still barked.

They followed the road to Nolf's house. Gideon unsaddled Jack and turned him in to the lot with Maude and the chestnut gelding and Nolf's cow. He threw the animals some hay. Inside the house, True built up the fire and heated water; they stripped down and cleaned themselves as best they could. True saw the bite mark between Gideon's neck and shoulder, and the jagged scabs on his leg, but she didn't ask. Was too tired to ask. They lay down between blankets on the floor in Nolf's front room beneath the piece of *fraktur* art on the wall proclaiming in German that God sees all. True blew out the candle in the lantern. They slept the sleep of the weary and the spent.

★★★

In the morning they went to the Trautmanns' house, where they were met with stiff politeness and an air of mistrust. Gideon asked Jonas Trautmann and his son Abe and daughter Elisabeth to gather up as many of their neighbors as they could. "Men and women," he said, "*Deitsch* and English. I have something important to say to you. Don't bother asking Peter Nolf to come."

"Why not?" Jonas said.

"You'll find out soon enough."

At noon in the farmyard, Gideon explained to more than thirty residents of Sinking Valley that Pastor Nolf had drugged him and led him into a cave at the bottom of the big sinkhole here on the Trautmann farm, with the intention of leaving him there to die. The same sinkhole that had held the corpses of Rebecca Kreidler and Maria Trautmann. He told the people that Nolf admitted to having poisoned his wife Grace this past spring. That he had coerced Maria Trautmann into poisoning her sister-in-law, when Rebecca had refused to marry him, and then disposed of the body in the sinkhole. Fearing that she might reveal his role in helping to kill Frau Kreidler, Nolf suffocated Maria Trautmann and hung her from the tree beneath which he had placed Rebecca's body. The preacher now lay dead in the sinkhole cave.

"How did he die?" Jonas Trautmann asked.

"I killed him. In defense of myself and my wife. With help from my wife." That comment elicited a murmur from the gathering. "I will be going back to Adamant," Gideon said. "I will report all of this to the state's attorney. I suspect there will be an inquiry, and some of you will be called to the courthouse to testify." Gideon looked at faces that wore guarded and puzzled and frightened and sad expressions. True stood in the back of the gathering. He caught her eye and felt a rush of love. He wondered how he would explain to the Cold Fish that he had survived this strange and dangerous episode because his wife, True Burns Stoltz, had somehow divined that he was in trouble and had come to Sinking Valley and rescued him. Had come far and bravely on her own.

He told the people in the farmyard that they could go to the cave and fetch Nolf's body and bury it if they so desired. Though he wondered to himself who would want to undertake such a task. He thought it more likely that they would leave the corpse there. Seal the entrance to the cave and walk away. It didn't matter to him what they did.

"I hope the Trautmann family can go on from this tragedy," he said. "And that all of you will help them. Show them the sympathy and understanding that they deserve and need." He studied the faces of the English folk: Henry and Sadie Harbison and their son Matthew, Andrew and James Rankin, a dozen others. "The *Neigeboren* are in a difficult situation," he said. "They have come from a faraway place. They are here to work hard and raise their families and be good neighbors. I know they are concerned with how the rest of you see them. Peter Nolf does not represent who these people are or what they believe in. He was an evil man who knew well how to hide his wicked deeds. He is gone now. Please show your neighbors courtesy and respect. That's all I have to say."

Let gentle patience smile on pain,
Till dying hope revives again

Chapter 44

⸺∞⸺

GIDEON AND TRUE LAY IN THEIR BLANKETS BENEATH A SKY FULL of stars.

They had stopped in the glade on the side of Mingo Mountain where Gideon and Alonzo had camped more than a fortnight ago while conveying Rebecca Kreidler's remains to Adamant. Tomorrow they would ride the rest of the way to town.

Maude, Jack, and the chestnut gelding, hobbled and grazing, were comforting presences in the glade.

The katydids in their unfathomable numbers sounded their calls from the surrounding forest.

Katy-did, she didn't, she did.

Sometimes the calls rang out in perfect unison. Sometimes the imagined syllables clashed in a cacophony of sound.

The katydids sent their harsh unknowing din into the sky from all over Mingo Mountain. From the woods scattered through Adamant's broad valley. From Sinking Valley. From the great rugged sprawl of the Seven Mountains.

Gideon turned toward True and she to him.

Acknowledgments

———◦≫≪◦———

I thank my wife, the writer Nancy Marie Brown, for her encouragement, plot suggestions, and editing. I also thank my agent, Natalia Aponte, and Skyhorse's Lilly Golden, both of whom helped make *Nighthawk's Wing* a better story.

Doug Madenford advised me on the *Pennsylfawnisch Deitsch* dialect.

Jennifer Anne Tucker is an herbalist who lives on a farm in central Pennsylvania. Jenny took me on plant walks, taught me about the medicinal (and nefarious) uses of plants, and loaned me books. She and her husband, Jerry Lang, are talented photographers of plants, landscapes, animals, and people. They made me welcome in their home many times when I traveled to Pennsylvania.

Others who generously hosted me include Randy Hudson and Cynthia Nixon-Hudson, Peter and Elaine Jurs, Jim and Gretl Collins, and Richard Fortmann and Anne Crowley. A special thanks to my friend Alice Ryan, who gives me a way station on the road between northern Vermont and Pennsylvania.

Thanks to the staff at Cobleigh Public Library in Lyndonville, Vermont, for helping me obtain research materials.

Claire Van Vliet created the map depicting Colerain County.

Both Colerain County and the town of Adamant are fictional places modeled loosely on the part of central Pennsylvania where I grew up and lived for many years.

The short epigraphs that begin each chapter are drawn from the lyrics of shape-note hymns widely sung in America in the 1800s.

Charles Fergus is the author of twenty books, including the first Gideon Stoltz mystery, *A Stranger Here Below*. A native of Pennsylvania, Fergus now lives in Vermont's remote Northeast Kingdom with his wife, the writer Nancy Marie Brown, and four horses.

Dear reader: If you enjoyed this book, please tell your friends about it and post an online review. Such recommendations really do help an author succeed. Thanks in advance for your support.

www.charlesfergus.com